ATLANTA LIVE

Vivian E. Carter
5/05

ATLANTA LIVE

Carmen Green

sepia

★BET BOOKS

BET Publications, LLC
http://www.bet.com

ATLANTA LIVE is a work of fiction. Any similarity of names, places and events depicted in this book to actual ones is purely coincidental.

SEPIA BOOKS are published by

BET Publications, LLC
c/o BET BOOKS
One BET Plaza
1900 W Place NE
Washington, DC 20018-1211

All Kensington Titles, Imprints, and Distributed Lines are available at special quantity discounts for bulk purchases for sales promotions, premiums, fund-raising, and educational or institutional use. Special book excerpts or customized printings can also be created to fit specific needs. For details, write or phone the office of the Kensington special sales manager: Kensington Publishing Corp., 850 Third Avenue, New York, NY 10022, attn: Special Sales Department, Phone: 1-800-221-2647.

BET Books is a trademark of Black Entertainment Television, Inc. SEPIA and the SEPIA logo are trademarks of BET Books and the BET BOOKS logo is a registered trademark.

ISBN: 1-58314-293-2

First Printing: February 2003
10 9 8 7 6 5 4 3 2 1

Printed in the United States of America

ACKNOWLEDGMENTS

Thank you, God, for blessing me with this story years ago and for showing me the way to finish it.

I owe a hug and a huge thank you to Glenda Howard for being a great editor with equal talents of vision, compassion, and patience. Thank you to Jeremy, Dane, and Steven for comic relief. Thank you to Terra Thomas, Wanda Smith, and Mike Roberts of Atlanta's V-103 radio station for allowing me into the studio to get a real-life perspective of how radio works. Thank you Egypt Sherrod and Mike for making it possible for me to tour 97.5 radio station.

To Shirley, Reverend Lisa Tait, Marge, Karen H., Haywood, Carla, Stephanie, Rita, Jacquelin, Mom, and Whitney, thank you for giving me support and encouragement when I needed it most.

ATLANTA LIVE

One

Jasmine Winbury maneuvered her silver Mercedes Benz through Blacktown: the armpit of Atlanta, Georgia, where the poor lived to die. She hadn't lived there for nearly ten years, but that didn't stop bitter childhood memories from reaching back and slapping her like the stench that permeated from the streets.

Jasmine blamed a lot of people, but mostly Adelia. Mothers were supposed to protect their daughters.

The five hundred dollars Jasmine had tucked in her mother's panty drawer was an intentional bribe to keep the woman, and the rest of their beggin' relatives, out of Jasmine's life.

As she sped away from the black hell, her anxiety lessened. Jasmine didn't stop taking sharp breaths until she hit the radio station parking lot and pulled into the space that everyone knew was hers.

One hour later, Jasmine had settled comfortably into her role as radio personality Dr. Jasmine. But the caller, Nancy, was causing her to lose patience and she had to restrain herself from disconnecting the call.

"I want a committed relationship," Nancy said. "But I'm always

1

attracted to married men. I just can't seem to get excited about the single men I meet."

"Know why?" Jasmine offered.

"Why?"

"Because you're a ho."

Malone laughed and Evelyn gave Jasmine a disgusted stare.

Evelyn's hair spilled over her shoulder in a wavy black curtain as she leaned into her microphone. "No, she's not. Nancy's seeking forgiveness, Jasmine. She doesn't *want* to want another woman's man. She wants to know how to get single men interested in her."

"I'm so glad you understand me, Evelyn," Nancy added.

"You're such a Dorothy." Jasmine eyed her best friend, a real bleeding heart. "Sometimes I wonder how you made it out of Oz."

"Ha!" Malone laughed again. "That's for damn sure. How did you get all that out of her admitting she likes sleeping with married men?"

"I, unlike you two, see that Nancy is searching for alternatives."

"How about a man that's not married! Since love ain't got nothin' to do with it," Jasmine challenged, "why not give that a try?"

Evelyn's twenty-nine platinum charms, one for every birthday, tinkled on her wrist when she pointed at Jasmine.

"You don't believe in love, so I don't expect you to agree."

"I do believe in love," Jasmine refuted. "But not in this case. Back me up, Malone."

"Evelyn?" he said.

"Yes, dear?" she answered just as sweetly.

"She's a ho."

"And a bad one at that," Jasmine added.

"How can you say that?" Despite herself, Evelyn laughed.

"Wake up, Atlanta," Jasmine yelled. "Nancy doesn't want the drama of marriage, kids, bills, and trying to figure out whose turn it is to change the kitty litter. She wants to do what she wants to do when she wants to do it. When her lover gets flaky, she cuts him loose and finds a quick replacement. All I'm saying is if she's gettin' it like that, be happy and get more."

"I'm not going there." Malone dismissed Jasmine and folded his arms on the console.

"You've been married and divorced, so I don't blame you."

"How the hell did this turn into something about me?"

"It didn't, Malone." Evelyn bared her teeth at Jasmine and received a wink for her effort.

"Sweetie, I'm sorry I mentioned your divorce."

"Yeah, I can see how sorry you are." He addressed the listeners. "Y'all, she's got this slick grin on her face, and all these braids hanging down, looking like a flea market rattlesnake."

The trio burst out laughing. "You're always preaching about women gettin' theirs. Women are queens of the universe. Get your orgasm, sista, and all that crap. How is she a ho if she's doing what you preach every day of the week?"

"Nancy isn't sorry. My motto is 'If you want to play the game, don't cry about the rules.' If she can't handle sleeping with a man that wasn't hers from the beginning, get him the hell out of her bed. But don't call here looking for sympathy.

"This is Dr. Jasmine, Evelyn, and Malone, hosts of *Atlanta Live*, baby, and we tell it like it is! We're sitting in for J.P. on this early Friday morning. He's got a cold so we offer him our get-well wishes. This is WKKY 104.9."

The commercial cued into the silence and Jasmine stretched.

"I like this audience much better than the afternoon crowd."

Evelyn sipped her coffee, not yet awake. "These early hours would kill me. How are we doing, Lee?"

The producer of the show, Lee Fitzgerald, stood on the other side of the soundproof glass, controlling calls and handling fifteen other things at once. His bald head shined, his glasses on the end of his nose.

He gave them a thumbs-up. "Good. Quit preaching so much and give some advice, Jasmine."

"Screw you, Lee."

"Promise?" he said, bored.

"What the hell is wrong with you two?" The red in Malone's Atlanta Falcon tattoo matched the tint in his eyes.

"Nothing." Jasmine turned away from the booth and situated her headphones over her microbraids. "Good radio isn't always about spouting advice, and good producers don't get in the way of real talent."

Lee pressed his third finger to the glass, leaving a lasting imprint. Otherwise, he ignored her. "Lindsey on two wants to talk about a mistake. Control from inside the booth, the system is heating up in here. This thing is as old as me. Damn. You're back on, three, two—" He pointed.

"Welcome back to *Atlanta Live*. It's seven forty-five and I'm Dr. Jasmine along with Evelyn and Malone, and we're here to set you straight! We have Lindsey on the phone, and she wants to talk about a mistake. Go ahead, Lindsey. What did you do?" Jasmine fired at her.

"Thank you for taking my call." The young woman sucked in an emotional breath.

"You're welcome. What's the mistake you called about?"

"Dr. Jasmine, it's hard to say aloud."

Jasmine waited.

"I'm pregnant."

"Now we're getting somewhere. So, is the problem with you having the baby, keeping the baby, or what?"

Lindsey sighed. "I can't do this. Maybe it'd be better if I wasn't here."

The room grew hot as if the thermostat had just been turned to one hundred. Malone swore softly.

Jasmine mouthed "Did you get that?" and Lee nodded, waving his hand for her to continue. "Clarify what you mean, Lindsey."

"You know what I mean," came back the watery reply.

"I'm not putting words in your mouth. How old are you?"

"Seventeen."

"Certainly old enough to tell me what you're talking about."

"She didn't mean anything. She's looking for help." Evelyn's usually soft voice resonated with firmness.

"Don't," Jasmine barked at her sharply. "Let her tell us. What did you mean, Lindsey?"

"I want to kill myself."

Evelyn rushed to her feet and moved as far from the console as she could as Lindsey began to sob. "No, you don't."

"Evelyn, you don't know my life. I can't do this to my family."

"You can't do this to *you*," Malone said finally, his gruff voice hoarse. "This situation can be dealt with. You know what I'm saying?"

"I can't have a baby. If I'm not here, they'll at least forgive me, one day."

"Is that what this is all about?" Jasmine pushed. "Is this just a cry for everyone to feel sorry for you?"

"No, Dr. Jasmine. My boyfriend and I were just experimenting. We didn't mean for it to happen."

"But you knew it was a possibility."

"It was one time! I swear," she cried in broken sobs. "I'll be labeled a slut. My parents will hate me."

Persistent rapping shook the glass between their booth and Lee. "Shut your mouth!" he told Jasmine.

She sat back, pissed. Who did he think he was talking to? She was doing her job.

Lee gave the lead to Malone and Jasmine's blood began to boil. "I have a son," Malone said. "I was just a few years older than you when he was born. He's everything to me."

"He is?" Lindsey sounded hopeful.

"Yes. Even if you can't think about keeping the baby, why not adoption?"

"My life," she whispered, "isn't conducive to having a child out of wedlock."

She's rich, Jasmine thought. "Why did you call, Lindsey?" Jasmine asked. "What do you want from us?"

"Absolution," the girl said, hope winging on the end of the whispered word.

"I'm not the most religious person, but I know you'll have to live with the consequences of your actions. Are you prepared for that?"

"Jasmine, you're pushing her too hard," Malone snapped.

"She wants to finally hear the truth, right, Lindsey?"

"Just because I need to hear what you're saying," she admitted, "doesn't make it easier."

Jasmine lifted her head, victorious. "That's one of the roads you learn to navigate as you grow up. You're rich, aren't you?"

"My parents are."

"Do you have brothers, sisters?" Jasmine said.

"Two brothers, one sister. All older than me."

"You didn't go to any of them, did you?"

"I can't." Lindsey broke down again.

"Why? They'd beat you?"

"No."

"Turn you in?"

"No."

"Then why not turn to a family member instead of calling a live-broadcast radio show?" Jasmine demanded. "What did you hope to accomplish?"

"I don't want them to know what kind of person I am."

An animalistic tug of war took place in Jasmine's chest. "What kind of person are you?" she demanded softly. "Are you good? Or are you bad?"

"Jasmine, stop it right now." Evelyn yanked on the cord of Jasmine's headset. "Help is on the way, Lindsey."

Jasmine held on to her microphone for dear life. "I think I know, Lindsey."

"I don't like you, Dr. Jasmine." The young woman sounded so immature and young, Jasmine smiled.

"Linds, let us help you," Evelyn coaxed gently. "I'll help you. Please, can I?"

"Thank you, Evelyn, but I know what kind of person I am."

There was a moment of silence, then a gunshot.

Two

Evelyn heard herself screaming.

Her mouth went dry as her throat was stripped of its humble southern charm. She took the Lord's name in vain in rapid succession, until her brain directed her to calm down.

Even then, Evelyn felt herself winding up again.

Lindsey had shot herself. *We're in trouble, we're in trouble* rattled around in Evelyn's head until she could do no more than mumble the young girl's name. "Lindsey? Please, God. Lindsey." No response. "Lee, somebody, help her."

Inside the booth, the control panel smoked. Lee was gone.

They were all alone with an injured girl on the other end of the phone. Evelyn didn't even know if they were still on the air.

Rigid, Jasmine stumbled out the studio door, her face a mask. Evelyn prayed for her sake she didn't come back.

Malone had taken over the telephone lines and stabbed the flashing buttons repeatedly. "Listen up," he told the callers. "Clear the lines. We have an emergency, and we need to keep these lines clear."

Malone prompted Evelyn with a wild gesture, then covered his microphone with his hand. "Say something. You've got to keep talking."

Evelyn swallowed convulsively and coughed. She wanted to cry as she had so many times in her life, but she couldn't, wouldn't. She grasped at the only will her body understood.

"This is Evelyn Smith Howard of the *Atlanta Live* talk show, and we had Lindsey on the phone. There's a possibility that there's been an accident." To her own ears she sounded calm and reassuring. "We're trying desperately to get help to Lindsey and I'm confident we can, but we need your help. We're experiencing much technical difficulty, so we need you to hold your calls."

Malone nodded and encouraged her on.

"Lindsey? Lindsey?" Evelyn repeated. "Can you hear me? Malone, are we still connected to her?"

"I don't know. The whole system could go down at any moment. Hold your calls," he barked, but with each call he disconnected, the buttons flashed again. Except for line one. It stayed brightly lit. Malone protected it like a mother bear.

"I'm Evelyn Smith Howard," she repeated, "and this is WKKY. We're in a state of emergency, because we believe one of our callers has injured herself. Lindsey, if you can hear me, say something."

Two seconds of unbearable silence passed.

Suddenly Lee's bald head appeared in the booth, a dark angel emerging through the fog, the chief engineer at his side.

Evelyn could hear snatches of their conversation, but wasn't picking up everything through her headset. Obviously her line to Lee was affected by whatever was overheating.

Malone continued to reassure listeners as Lee scrawled on a piece of paper and slapped it on the window.

"We have an update," Evelyn told everyone. "They've traced the call, and police and EMTs are due to arrive within five minutes."

Time seemed more precious than gold. Even as relief flooded

Evelyn's body, her heart raced anew. What if they were too late? What if Lindsey was already dead? And what about her unborn baby?

Malone tilted his head in a way that told Evelyn he could hear Lee. "We have confirmation that we're still live with Lindsey's number."

Evelyn reached for that one grain of hope. "The EMTs are minutes away from a caller who felt there was no way out of her situation besides taking her own life. Let me tell you something. There's *always* another way. If we have the chance, we want to prove to Lindsey, and anyone that may be struggling with consequences that seem overwhelming, that there is a way out of no way.

"Lindsey? Can you hear me? Help is on the way. You're important to us. We've all made mistakes." Evelyn conversed as if they were sitting beside each other. "There are decisions we all wish we could take back, but nothing is worth taking your life over. I like to think that although tomorrow seems like forever, the next minute is a chance to start new."

"She'll come through this, Evelyn." Malone's eyes were as serious as she'd ever seen them. No cocky grin covered his face and no flippant words raced out of his mouth.

"I'm praying." Evelyn shook her head. "We won't give up, will we?"

"Never."

"Good, because we're not mad at her and we're not going to judge her. The professionals are almost there. Lindsey, just hang on, honey."

Evelyn kept looking from Lee to Malone, waiting for word that help had arrived. She denied fear access to her mind because she knew if she didn't have hope, she'd break down completely.

"Please, honey, talk to me."

Seconds of silence passed, and nothing.

Evelyn pushed on. "I have the power to help people and so does this precious child on the phone. Your life is so much more valuable than the one mistake you made."

"ETA, one minute," Malone said.

"Thank you, Lord," Evelyn said into her microphone. "Almost there," she told everyone. "The community has people that are skilled to deal with crises. Reach out. Tell someone your problems. Help is a phone call away—"

Jasmine stalked into the studio, talking on her cell phone.

Malone yanked off his headset and rushed around the console.

Jasmine's bold stare reminded Evelyn of a crocodile. They sized each other up. Malone had the advantage because of height and size. But Evelyn was more afraid of the danger he exuded.

"What you gone say now, Jasmine?" he taunted her. "Have a machete with your damned gun?"

"Get out my face, Malone, now isn't the time."

Malone's hands flexed, and it was clear to Evelyn that life was like fragile crystal. These two were blood cousins and with this level of anger, words were as powerful as the rippled muscles in his arms.

Malone crushed his microphone in his fist. "You're fucking nuts," he spat at Jasmine.

"I didn't create the call, or the caller. So why are you blaming me?" She issued the statement the same way she debated a charge on her credit card.

Evelyn had been quiet too long. "Lindsey? Honey, can you hear me?"

"Evelyn." Lindsey's voice scared Evelyn. Chills skated over Evelyn's skin and stars danced in her eyes. She dropped her head to meet her hand, but felt her body hit something hard. A bitter taste flooded her mouth, and banging rammed her head.

She nearly passed out.

Evelyn took a couple of deep breaths. Malone's leg was wedged against hers as he balanced to keep her upright. He finally gave up and forcefully sat her in her chair. Evelyn's teeth clicked, and the jolt was enough to get her past the light-headedness.

"Talk to her, Evelyn."

She looked for Jasmine, but she was gone. "Lindsey. I'm so glad to hear your voice."

"I shot myself," the girl uttered in disbelief.

"Where does it hurt?"

"My chest. Arm," she said slowly.

Malone's head jerked toward Lee in the booth. "The EMTs are outside the door, Linds. Where's the gun?"

"I dropped it. Please, let me die."

"Honey, it would tear me up if I let that happen. I sincerely understand your situation. I can't let you go."

"My father'll be so angry."

"I know, I know," Evelyn murmured. Malone squeezed Evelyn's hand until she smacked his arm. What was he doing?

She looked into his eyes and saw the warning. "Watch your step," he murmured and she knew.

Evelyn sucked in her lips and focused. "Lindsey, when you get better, I'd like you to help me start a foundation that would help women such as yourself find responsible answers to their problems."

"I don't know."

"Please say yes. I really would." Evelyn let her heart speak where polished words failed. Malone finally moved away. "But you have to let help come in. We're on your side."

Lindsey didn't speak for several seconds, and the tension mounted. "Okay. They can come in."

Suddenly the room was awash with sound. The professional-speak of paramedics and police officers filled the airwaves.

Jasmine stepped up to her microphone, humble and professional. "This is Dr. Jasmine of the *Atlanta Live* talk show, and for the last thirty minutes cohosts Evelyn and Malone have been talking to seventeen-year-old Lindsey, who attempted suicide."

"Lee," a strong female voice said from Lindsey's end.

"Who are we talking to?" Jasmine asked.

"Evelyn, Malone," the woman said pointedly, ignoring Jasmine. "I'm Sergeant Robin Boyd of the Atlanta Police Department, and I've been in constant contact with Lee. Is he there?"

"Officer Boyd," Jasmine said, "what can you tell us about Lindsey's injuries?"

"Nothing."

"Can you confirm how seriously she's hurt?"

"The victim has what appears to be a bullet wound to her left side."

"So the wound isn't life threatening?"

"I don't have any information to support that statement."

"Was the baby harmed?"

"I don't have any further information."

The background chaos prevented anyone from speaking for several seconds.

Evelyn covered her microphone. "Why don't you just go?"

"Don't tell me how to do my job." She moved her microphone back into place. "Sergeant Boyd, can we assume the wounds are superficial?"

"Why would you assume that?"

"Because she was able to talk coherently to our hosts for a couple minutes."

"It's inappropriate to speak on a subject of which I have no expertise, but that doesn't seem to be your problem."

Jasmine reeled back from the criticism looking as if she'd been hit by a stun gun.

"Let's stick to the facts, shall we, Sergeant Boyd? What is the victim's last name?"

"No comment."

Malone threw down his headset, like he was walking out. Evelyn grabbed him and held on. He wasn't abandoning her.

"How many people are on the response team?" Jasmine fired.

"Once we got the information from Lee, he was instructed to keep the lines of communication open, and units of police, fire, and paramedics responded immediately."

A buzz of excitement spread through the room. "Sergeant Boyd, can you tell us what's going on?"

"The parents have arrived and are in quiet counsel with their daughter and medical personnel."

Evelyn stopped herself from walking out the studio door. She couldn't believe what had happened and she couldn't believe Jasmine's gall.

"Malone, Evelyn," Sergeant Boyd said loudly. "The parents have requested a word with you."

"*Shit.*"

Malone said what Evelyn felt.

She pulled her headset back on. "This is Evelyn Smith Howard, reporting from WKKY. Sir, ma'am, we'd like to extend our deepest sympathies and our apologies. We tried in every way to help your daughter."

Malone jumped in. "I want you to know we did everything we could to help Lindsey. I have a son, and I hope if he were in the same position, somebody would help him."

"Malone, hold on," the man said, his voice smooth yet weary. "You did more than that."

Evelyn whispered an urgent prayer.

"I'm Senator Larry Kane. Today, my daughter Lindsey tried to kill herself. I hold the station personally responsible for everything that's happened."

Three

"Evelyn, Malone, my wife and I want to express our appreciation for how you stepped in and saved Lindsey's life."

The senator broke down. "Thank you," he said, his voice heavy with tears. "You don't know how much your efforts mean to us."

Malone sank into his chair and Evelyn rested her elbows on the console, her face on her closed hands.

The praise rang in Jasmine's ears. She walked out, and everywhere she turned, accusing eyes glared back at her. She pushed into the stairwell and went down three flights.

The door above opened and Lee called out. "Damn it! Where is she? Keep looking."

The door closed and Jasmine exhaled.

While she battled with pure unadulterated envy for the cheap accolades heaped upon Malone and Evelyn, adrenaline rippled through her body like a narcotic. She was pumped, no longer able to hide her most misunderstood trait—ambition.

Why had Lindsey shot herself?

I just wanted to push her so far and then bring her back.

Lindsey had outsmarted her. Called her bluff. A door several floors below opened.

Holding her chest, Jasmine darted up another staircase, then stopped. She was a shark now. Occasionally, she'd get bitten.

She had to face her accusers and let them know they weren't dealing with a scared woman who couldn't handle the consequences. Jasmine left the stairwell on the sixth floor and walked into the studio, but Lee wasn't there.

Satchell Bolton, the sound engineer, lay on his back on the floor.

"Where are Missy and Kym?" she asked.

"Remote, from the parking lot."

"What about Malone and Evelyn?"

"Getting ready for the press conference in an hour." He regarded her through bulging eyes. "Lee said if you turned up to tell you to get to his office, immediately."

Fear raced up her spine. "Mmmm." Jasmine hesitated, even as Satchell's knowing smile crept under her skin. "I've got an interview in ten minutes."

"If you say so."

She bit her tongue and walked out.

"Hey, Jasmine?"

"What?" She turned back.

"Who's your interview with?"

"CBS," she lied.

He grinned again. "If you say so."

Jasmine wanted to knock the shit-eating grin off his face, but started through the long office. Satchell didn't matter. But she couldn't say the same for Lee. He was in charge of the tiny empire that was Sharpe Enterprises.

Splitting her time as his sometime girlfriend, sometime sounding board, sometime cheerleader was wearing thin. Lee wasn't ambitious enough for her taste. And, she wasn't about to waste time with a man who was trying to hitch his horse to her cart. She was going places. But today he had power. Today he could end her career.

As she turned toward the private offices, Jasmine heard her name on his secretary's small television and stopped short.

"Is this a ready-made lawsuit?" the announcer asked a visiting attorney.

"Ham and cheese couldn't go together better. Here you have an irresponsible adult and a mentally stressed teenager with a gun. The combination is already unevenly balanced; then add a reckless comment from the authority figure, and you have a malpractice settlement that will line this young woman's padded cell or her coffin comfortably forever."

"That's extreme, Duke. Give me evidence to substantiate your statement."

"And I quote, 'What kind of person are you?' There's an implied assumption here by Dr. Jasmine. She's inciting the young woman—judging her, when all she's ever been is judged—and probably by her biggest adversaries. Her parents."

"I'll give you that much, but there's no incitement. The question is reasonable."

"I'm reading out of context, but, 'Why don't you just do it?' And then, 'I know what type of person you are.' Inflammatory. Any third-year law student could make a case for reckless endangerment of a minor."

"In Georgia, teens are considered adults at seventeen."

"Only in certain circumstances. They're not old enough to drink, but they can join the military. A double standard if I ever saw one."

"Your bottom line is—"

"If I were Will Sharpe, I'd already have Dr. Jasmine's butt on the curb."

"Fair enough," the announcer said. "Thank you, Duke Marino, for joining us. This is *CNN News*."

Jasmine stepped back into the shadows and ducked into the ladies' room. She wiped her mouth, anxious and afraid. Were they going to fire her? More people had listened to the show than ever before. Where would she be if Will, the president of the station, had the same feelings?

Her side had to be heard.

Pulling out her cell phone, she dialed a reporter from CNN and got her voice mail. "Ellen, this is Jasmine Winbury. In light of some of the things I've heard being said about me on TV, I wanted to share my position. This morning, I came to work as I've done every day for two years and tried to give listeners an entertaining show. When Lindsey Kane called and threatened her own life, we had no idea that she was serious. We get these types of calls all the time, but I don't believe anything that was said on my part, or that of my cohosts, would have swayed Lindsey Kane from her intentions. I'm glad she'll get the help she needs. Our prayers are with her and her family. Thank you."

She flipped her cell phone closed and walked back into the hallway when she heard Senator Kane's voice from the TV.

Still giving interviews? Her mouth twisted. He didn't truly care for his daughter. If he did, he'd own up to being a terrible father. All Lindsey could talk about was how her father would be angry, and how she'd disappoint him. Some caring father he was! No wonder she'd tried to kill herself.

"I understand the tough-love position Ms. Winbury took," the senator said. "I've used it myself when it comes to gangs in our streets, and at home with my own children." The senator went on. "Had Lindsey not called the station, we might have lost her. The goal of the family is to help Lindsey get better."

Finally! Jasmine took back her earlier thoughts. She'd been redeemed by the girl's own father.

Head raised, she stalked out of the shadows and up to Lee's door.

"Have a seat, Ms. Winbury. I'll tell him you're here."

Coretta Hammond was an old embittered woman who, at one time, had been the station owner's mistress. Over the years she'd been demoted from Will's bedroom, and then, the executive office. Last year, Lee had inherited the sour-faced witch. For some bizarre reason, they got along well.

"I can tell him myself."

"You trying to speed up the dismissal process?"

Jasmine's blood ran cold. "You can't fire me, so what are you talking about?"

"I'm typing your walk-out papers next."

"You're lying. I've been exonerated."

"Senator Kane don't pay the bills around here. Sponsors have been canceling advertising all morning. So why don't you sit down, before you get tossed out, and get no severance?"

Jasmine sat.

Anxiety, thick and rich, dragged down her mood until her confidence had disintegrated.

Ten more minutes passed. "Go in now."

Fuming, Jasmine threw open Lee's door. The old feeling of being in trouble snuck through her body, loosened her bladder enough for a trickle of pee to wet her panties.

Jasmine clenched hard. She might get fired, but she would *not* piss all over herself.

Lee sat behind his desk, as she walked over as if she had no cares in the world. "Would it help if I said I was sorry?"

"What the hell were you thinking?"

She threw her braids over her shoulder in a motion of bravado. "Of the show. This tragedy is our ticket, Lee, look at all the publicity. We're going to be on the map."

"At what cost?" he snarled. "Did you even think before you recklessly invited a teenager to kill herself?"

"I thought confronting her would make her think, not send her over the edge."

"This time you were wrong." His hands flattened on the desk. "Give me one good reason why I shouldn't fire you."

Her muscles quivered in an effort to contain her urine.

"Tell me, what's so special about you that you deserve another chance?"

She dropped her hands on her hips. She wasn't some hood rat

that didn't have the sense of a doorknob. She was an intelligent woman, who very soon would be calling her own shots. "You pay me to be controversial!" she threw at him. "I was doing my job."

"She shot herself, you idiot. If someone in Senator Kane's camp convinces him that you were reckless, we could be sued until there's nothing left of this building but the foundation. Stupid," he exclaimed, glaring at her. "Stupid."

Lee slumped into his chair, his hands to his mouth.

Who did this motherfucka think he was? Just because she'd let him go south of the border didn't mean he could treat her as if she were scum.

They were going to be famous because of this. Lee was riding on *her* coattail. "You let the call through, where's your piece of the responsibility? You talked to her enough to find out she'd made a mistake. You could have said no. So how much of this do I assign to you?" He lowered his head. "What, Lee? I don't hear you."

"I didn't tell her to kill herself."

"What about her parents? Her father is using his daughter's attempted suicide as a platform to get his issues in front of the public. Want to bet he doesn't pay an ounce of attention to those children except when it's time for reelection?"

"Senator Kane doesn't work for me, you do."

"Well then, how much of this is Lindsey's fault? I didn't lay her down and spread her legs. Where's the baby's daddy, huh? No answer, I didn't think so."

"The whole time you were on the air, I was trying to figure out why you went after the kid. Just now . . ." He leaned back. "I see it. You're jealous."

"Of what? A suicidal teenager?" Jasmine straightened her suit. "Please."

"You're going down."

"Lee, the phones were ringing off the hook. I put *Atlanta Live* on the map. Can't you see that?"

"That's it for you, isn't it?" A humorless smile wrapped his mouth. "I see tomorrow's headlines. 'Talk host urges teen suicide.' I can smell a lawsuit, a settlement, and unemployment for everyone associated with you and the *Atlanta Live* show. And *that's* more important than anything you've said in the past fifteen minutes."

Panic struck. Coretta was right. Jasmine would be let go and no one would care.

How would she pay her bills? Her credit cards alone were in the thousands. The mortgage, the car note, and her lifestyle were all in jeopardy.

A cramp snaked through her thigh and Jasmine released her contracted muscles. The tart smell of urine wafted up to her nose and she recoiled. This couldn't be happening.

She had to save herself.

"What can I do to make this better?" she asked.

"Don't know."

"Then why didn't you fire me as soon as I walked through the door?"

Lee's gaze was unapologetic. "Will wants to see the ratings and hear public opinion. If the response is unfavorable, your termination will be retroactive to this moment, and you'll be advised to seek legal counsel."

Jasmine's chin almost hit the desk. "The station wouldn't represent me?"

"You set your ship on fire. Nobody wants to go down with you." He paused as dispassionate eyes looked back at her. "The station would also pursue litigation."

"Lee, you could help me, if you wanted to."

He shrugged. "If by some miracle I can bail you out, you'll owe me big time."

"Your markers are always good with me." She'd been leading him around by his nose for months. A few more times in bed with him wouldn't kill her.

Lee gripped her wrist across the desk. "Whenever, however."

His eyes gleamed. Men were all alike. "Whatever you say," she ground out.

Unceremoniously, Lee pushed her aside and retrieved papers from the printer. He read each page twice, then pushed them across his desk. "Read every word before you sign."

"What are those?"

"Sit down," he said coldly.

He'd just made it clear the price she'd have to pay to keep her job, but now he couldn't even be civil? It took all her strength not to tell Lee where he could go.

She sat and pulled the pages into view. *Letter of Termination.*

"What the hell is this? You just said Will was waiting for the ratings and public opinion."

Lee dialed his secretary. "Coretta, come in here, please."

Lee didn't even bother to acknowledge that Jasmine had spoken.

The door opened. "Coretta, you're here as a witness and notary to the documents Ms. Winbury is signing. This letter will be placed in her personnel file until further notice."

"Yes, sir." The older black woman stared at Jasmine as if she were a grub. These people were insane if they thought she was going to take this lying down. She'd get each and every one of them back.

She scrawled her name in a zigzagged line and with each letter gained a new lease on life. From now on, it was all about her.

"My pen," Lee said. He signed his name, gave Coretta the papers, which she signed and stamped. She dropped additional papers on Lee's desk and he reviewed them quickly.

Jasmine walked to the door, ready to face the dozens of reporters that had been milling in the cafeteria. She could put a positive spin on this. She could plead with troubled youths to talk to their parents. The *Atlanta Live* staff had saved Lindsey's life.

Lee called her name.

"What now?" she demanded.

"You're suspended without pay for one week. And, smart-ass,

you just signed away your right to discuss this matter for ninety days. We're going to the press conference where you'll read this statement, then be escorted out of the building."

Jasmine felt as if a huge vacuum were dragging her skin to the floor. "You're going to regret this," she promised.

Lee's eyes changed. "You're probably right."

Four

Jasmine boldly faced the reporters, each word of the prepared statement tasting like dried-up processed food. Fake, plastic, and untrue.

"Are you sorry?"

She looked for a hard moment at Lee, then at the masses. "I've been told to make no comments beyond this statement." Jasmine shifted left, then right. Cameras recorded her movements as reporters shouted questions.

"Has any disciplinary action been taken against you?"

Again, she looked at Lee. If she was going to fry, she was going to drag Lee to hell with her. "Sorry, guys, no comment."

"Isn't the objective of the show to be controversial?" Tiana Shabazz was an up-and-coming news reporter who'd graduated from Spelman a year ago and was blazing a trail in the media with her neatly kept locks and her African style of clothing.

"Yes, but—" Lee stood.

"Then why is Dr. Jasmine under a gag order? You called the press conference, Lee. What was the point if she can't answer questions?"

Lee consulted the attorneys, then came to the podium. "We're concerned that statements made might be misconstrued. We don't want to have any further misunderstandings."

"Ms. Kane sought *your show* as her venue. Don't you have some opinion about that?" Tiana asked with just enough disbelief in her voice that cameras were now trained on her.

"Of course. Uh, we only know some of what the young lady was going through, so we can't speculate beyond that. We do know that life is precious and we want our listeners to know that we do care about them."

Lee hurried to his seat, leaving Jasmine standing at the microphone alone.

"Have you been fired, Dr. Jasmine?" Tiana asked.

"No."

"Suspended?"

She turned back to the persistent reporter. "I'm scheduled to report to work next Monday."

"Suspended with pay?"

"No," she and Lee said together.

"Comment," Jasmine said alone.

Tiana's frustration raced up to her brazen brown hair. "Again, does WKKY hold Dr. Jasmine responsible for what happened to Lindsey Kane?"

"No comment," Lee said, as Jasmine looked at him from beneath hooded eyes.

"Obviously the station is worried about a lawsuit. Will charges be pressed against Ms. Winbury?"

Lee looked to their recently hired legal counsel and watched the two men confer. "No comment," they said together.

Murmurs of disapproval rebounded off the walls and Jasmine wanted to howl. They'd bought bottom-basement lawyers that might as well have been bus drivers for all they helped.

Jasmine stepped to the microphones, and the attention shifted back to her. "I firmly believed Lindsey Kane when she said 'The truth is sometimes hard to hear.' It was never my intention to hurt her, and I'm truly sorry that as a last resort, this young girl injured herself."

"What's your degree in, Jasmine?" a blond man with a hairstyle that worked only for Ted Koppel asked her.

"I have several degrees."

"Are you a doctor of psychiatry?"

"No."

"Really? And you're not worried about a lawsuit?"

"No." She stopped herself from saying something nasty. "We give free advice for entertainment purposes only. This was an unfortunate onetime incident."

"Yeah, I guess telling someone to kill themselves wouldn't come up every day."

Malone tapped his microphone and the receivers shrieked.

"In black families, we have a 'shit or get off the pot' mentality. Ninety-nine point nine percent of the time it's BS to make a person back down. Every one in this room has challenged someone before, if only to show them their behavior is stupid."

"Were Lindsey's Kane's actions stupid?"

"Are your questions stupid?" Malone shot back.

Several members of the press laughed.

"I'm using your words, sir," the Koppel look-alike said, before wiping his hair over his forehead.

Malone grinned for the cameras, but his eyes dripped acid.

"No, you're twisting my words. Our kids don't usually kill themselves. That behavior has been more predominant in youth of non-African descent."

"So you're blaming white America for Lindsey Kane's attempted suicide, even though she was goaded by a black talk show host, at a station owned by a black man. Isn't that, to borrow your word, stupid?"

"What's negligent is a society where children are so afraid to admit to a mistake, they think taking their life is better than seeking a solution to their troubles. None of us knows what goes on behind somebody else's closed doors, so placing blame on us is stupid."

"So it's fine for the Lindsey Kanes of America to have children that society will have to take care of?" the reporter asked.

"I guess you're saying suicide is the better option, rather than talking to a parent or seeking professional advice? Glad you didn't run for president. Folks," he said, above the roaring response, "we have time for only three more questions. Let's not make these stupid."

"Dr. Jasmine, how do you defend your actions?" asked Ellen Connor from CNN.

"Lots of people use tough love as a form of discipline. Senator Kane admitted to this method also. As the show's hosts, we were thrust into an extraordinary situation. We're just thankful Ms. Kane is on the road to recovery."

"In your own words, what kind of person is Lindsey Kane?"

"Someone to be taken seriously."

"Malone, after your witty repartee, I'm wondering if you have the energy to play professional football again. Jordan made a comeback."

"Who asked that?" Malone charmed the cameras with his smile. Josh Cavallaro, former tight end of the Tennessee State Titans and an old teammate, emerged.

"Josh, I should have known you would be here asking the wrong questions at the wrong time. Your timing always sucked."

Several reporters laughed.

"Care to answer?" Josh asked.

Malone shook his hand. "Why you asking me this in front of my boss? Trying to get me fired?"

"Yeah, man. You belong on the field."

"Let's talk football later. Since you got football advice, I've got a few commentating tips."

Josh took the ribbing in stride as other reporters enjoyed their friendly exchange.

"You wish, buddy. Let me ask you this. How should parents explain this to their children? Your son and mine are about the same age and I know they'll have questions."

Malone's face transformed and in the blink of an eye, he became a father. "Explain only what they need to know. Kids are strong, but we overwhelm them with too much information; then we wonder why they're acting so grown-up. My son knows more about arterial knee injuries than most first-year med students. Give them the information in small doses and be there for questions."

Josh nodded. "Thanks, man."

Malone pulled his beeper off his waist. "Last question, folks."

A crescendo rose, but Ellen Connor approached, her camera crew close behind. Jasmine stepped forward, glad to see her colleague. Now the tide would turn, she thought.

"Evelyn?" Ellen said after a brief look at Jasmine. "How has your father reacted to the news of your involvement in this situation?"

Jasmine stammered as Lee guided her firmly to the side, blocking her from the action, and the cameras.

"I've not spoken to my father, Ms. Connor, but in any situation where a tragedy such as this has occurred, my entire family unites to express our support."

Evelyn stood and the men around her shot to their feet like the water display at Centennial Olympic Park. Jasmine could hardly see.

"Is it true your father has condemned your job here at WKKY?"

Hot white lights shined down on Evelyn. Malone bent to hear her and then stepped back.

Evelyn crowded Ellen and the taller woman had an up-close and personal look at Evelyn's perfect white teeth.

"Ms. Connor, Lindsey Kane called the *Atlanta Live* show this morning and tried to kill herself. It's terribly sad that she didn't have someone other than us, but I'm honored we were able to help her."

"Come on, now. This has boosted your ratings and your audience tremendously. Didn't this fall right in line with what you do?"

"We faced a near tragedy today, so no, this isn't what we're here for. We don't do crisis intervention. But since we were called upon to help her . . . I don't know what everyone else would do, but I won't be folding my hands pointing at others."

"Why not? Weren't you at least partially—"

"I'll keep my hands folded in prayer that she recovers and can move on with her life. I'm thankful we were there to help her. I just ask that parents, grandparents, whoever, reach out and talk to your children."

Jasmine watched the surge of reporters from over her bodyguard's shoulder. Evelyn extended an elegant hand and Lee took it, pulling her through the crowd. Damn. She'd stolen the glory like a smash-and-grab thief in a jewelry store.

The entire lunchroom emptied.

Jasmine hit the kitchen doors and didn't break stride until she was behind the wheel of her car. She started the engine and gave it a little gas, eyeing her rearview mirror.

Maybe Ellen was waiting and they could speak off the record. She could be the "unidentified source."

Jasmine backed a couple of feet out of her space.

No one was behind her, not even her rent-a-cop.

Pissed, she gunned the engine and headed for Stonecrest Mall. There would be plenty of people who'd have something to say about today.

Five

Malone broke away from the crowd, and headed for Lee's office and a private phone. School dismissal wasn't for another hour and a half, but his pager reflected an urgent message.

He prayed Lonzo wasn't hurt. Sick, he could deal with, but nothing had better be broken.

The secretary to the principal answered.

"Principal MacNamara, please."

"He's in a conference. Would you like to hold for a moment?"

"No. I want to know why I received an urgent page from him. This is Alonzo Malone's father."

"Yes, sir. Just a moment."

Malone felt anything but easy as he listened to the commercial music. Right about now, all he felt like was soothing his pounding head.

He banged the phone on the desk, irritated. How long did it take one little fat woman to walk ten feet to the principal's door? The tinkling cymbals in the music were driving him crazy.

"Somebody better get on this phone before I—"

"Mr. Malone?"

"Principal MacNamara, what's the problem?"

"Mr. Malone, Alonzo isn't prepared for class again today."

"What are you talking about? He has every school supply known to man."

"Yes, you did purchase the supplies on the list, but Alonzo was also supposed to have his supplies for the precollege prep geology course. The rock specimens are essential. He's a week behind because he hasn't had them. This class was optional and there was an extensive list of students considered. Alonzo didn't have to sign up for this, but now that he has, he must fulfill his obligation and be prepared."

Malone thumbed his forehead, stabbing his headache. "You talked to his mother?"

"She's been downright hostile and—and . . ." The principal searched for the words.

"She cursed you out." Malone filled in the words the educator couldn't find.

"Exactly. I don't have to take that, Mr. Malone. I told you before I wouldn't deal with the former Mrs. Malone, and you assured me we'd only be dealing with you."

"You're right, Mr. MacNamara. I apologize." Malone stood, his body aching. "Where do I need to get these rocks?" he asked, and wrote down the address. "He'll have them today."

"We will make an allowance, this time. But this can't happen again. Young Mr. Malone is the one who suffers when he falls behind the rest of his class."

Malone knew exactly what the man was saying. People whose money reached back generations had their kids in St. Timothy's Preparatory Academy. They were among the city's richest, and brightest. His son wouldn't be held to different standards just because his father was an ex-pro football player.

"Are you on your way to pick him up, sir?"

"School isn't over until three-fifteen."

31

"No, sir. Today is a half day. Parent-teacher conference." Principal McNamara had no idea how much the reprimand in his voice urked Malone. He felt ten again.

"Mrs. Malone signed up for a conference for yesterday, but didn't show up."

Malone's stomach started burning. "How did Alonzo get home if his mother didn't come get him?"

St. Timothy's didn't do yellow buses. All the children were chauffeured or driven by their parents.

"Your former neighbor Mrs. Chow returned for him. We tried to reach you, but you were unavailable."

Mohala was supposed to get him from school every day. Unless she was dead, there was no damned excuse.

"Where's my son?" Malone asked.

"Helping the children of some of the teachers change bulletin boards."

Malone couldn't stand the sympathy that oozed from the man's voice. He could take care of his family. If only his ex would act like she had some sense. He'd deal with her later. "I'm on my way."

Malone lowered the phone and saw Lee out the corner of his eye. "How long you been standing there?"

"Long enough to say three words. Call your lawyer."

Malone wiped his tired face. "We were trying to work things out on our own."

"So who's it working for when Lil' Lonzo doesn't get picked up?"

"I'm going now." He walked toward the door, his knees aching. "Any news on Lindsey?"

"She's in recovery."

"The baby?"

"Doing fine."

Malone sighed. "We barely got out of that."

"Our asses might still get fired. Stay available. There're bound to be more interviews."

32

"I hope to have my boy all weekend."

"Bring him along."

"Cool. Hit my pager or cell."

Malone was nearly out the door when he heard Lee's parting words, "Call your lawyer."

Six

Lenox Palisades Condominiums were a stone's throw away from Peachtree and Piedmont, the luxurious multimillion-dollar homes attracting the trendiest of the rich.

The hippest and wealthiest twenty- and thirty-somethings got pleasure from the elite Buckhead address and the many other amenities. They enjoyed equal access to downtown Atlanta and Hartsfield International Airport, as well as the sexually charged nightlife. Those who chose to indulge also found benefit of the surreptitious cocaine dealers off Buford Highway.

The newly retired dot-commers hobnobbed with sons of sheiks. They stayed tuned to CNN in the fully equipped workout room, watching their money grow by the hour.

Evelyn lived on the sixteenth floor of the luxurious condominiums, and fit right in. There was, after all, always one black person who was able to infiltrate the majority and become accepted.

She exited her car and left it for the valet, who greeted her with a friendly "Good afternoon, Ms. Smith Howard."

"Hello." Evelyn tried to clear the weakness from her throat as she approached the gleaming gold-trimmed glass doors.

"Afternoon, Ms. Smith Howard."

She smiled up at the friendly doorman. "Good afternoon, Hosea." His attractive, tall, lean figure reminded her of the actor Ben Bratt.

"Shall I have your dry cleaning sent up?"

She patted his arm. "Tomorrow morning at nine, please."

"Good day, ma'am."

"Good day, Hosea."

Black and gray marble covered four thousand square feet of the lobby floor. An elaborate waterfall dominated the center, while twisted stalks of pristine white and yellow art deco reached for the ceiling.

Imported Persian rugs held angular handcrafted coffee tables, and baby-soft leather love seats had been added for the residents' comfort.

Every visitor was greeted and announced by the guest services staff, public and cell phone use strictly prohibited in the common areas of the building.

This ban had passed unanimously at the last tenants meeting. The rich didn't mind sharing, but they didn't want "the help" to buy low and sell high.

Sixty-four nannies, maids, and maintenance men—all of Latin descent—had quit after striking it rich in the last stock market surge, leaving the building's tenants temporarily paralyzed.

Now, money-talk was reserved for the second-floor men's club, where it was rumored that the Swedish women gave deep-tissue massages and the best blow jobs in town.

The women's club on the fourth floor was far more casual. The ladies met for exercise, facials, and pampering by twenty-something men who knew how to meet their needs.

In turn, they were handsomely rewarded and remained loyal to the clientele that was making it possible for them to retire by the time they were forty.

Evelyn rode the elevator up and headed home. Her father had purchased the property in the early eighties, when Buckhead, while exclusive, wasn't as expensive.

He'd been asked to sell many times, but Raynard Howard knew a good investment when he saw one. The condominium was worth over four million dollars and the mortgage was paid in full.

Evelyn paid the taxes and association fees and her father had given her the condo two years ago for her twenty-seventh birthday.

She used her card key and walked inside.

Smooth jazz programmed to start when her key deactivated the security lock offered the strains of Boney James to comfort her heavy heart.

Here was where she could let down her guard. Away from the judgmental eyes of her parents. Away from Jasmine and her bitch-slapping tongue. Away from the surprisingly observant eyes of Malone.

Evelyn slipped out of her high heels. The white-on-white pile hugged her feet and she had to fight the urge to just lie down on the floor.

Maybe if she was still, she could finally cry. Maybe if she pried the lid off her pain, she could mourn for Lindsey and for herself.

For the child she was when she'd had her baby boy. He'd been such a sweet thing. Precious and soft. Beautiful like his father who'd died too young. He'd been seconds old when she'd held him. A minute old when she'd given him away.

Jasmine had been there. So had Malone. But she'd felt as alone then as she did now.

Evelyn's knees bent, but wouldn't let her fall.

She was the daughter of a preacher.

Walking up the winding staircase, Evelyn drew her shirt from her waistband and released the buttons down the center.

The air-conditioning chilled her already cool skin. A sigh escaped.

No tears. Just a soft breath that confirmed that she was still alive. This hadn't been a nightmare, but a reality check.

Lindsey could have killed her baby.

One foot followed the other as she trudged up the steps.

How many times had Evelyn thought of ending her own life years ago? She would have eaten a bullet before telling her parents the truth. Had she come home pregnant and unwed, they'd have withdrawn their love permanently.

Evelyn climbed onto her four-poster bed, caught in the memory. At twelve, she'd been a little girl with neatly pressed hair, and a dress too mature for her slight frame.

Her mother's mother had come to visit and brought rays of sunshine to Evelyn's listless life. So starved for affection, she'd talked her ear off and when her grandmother had tucked her in one night, she'd confided concern for her mother who'd cry when Evelyn's father didn't come home until the wee hours.

Evelyn hadn't known of her grandmother's intense dislike for her father. Her grandmother had gone to the church elders and he'd been brought before the board.

Evelyn closed her arms around her stomach and rocked.

Her father had been so angry, she was sure he'd whip her straight into hell where she belonged. She'd violated the code of silence that ministers' children lived by in order to keep families and congregations together.

Enraged, he dared her to tell another iota of family business. Dared her to jeopardize what he'd built.

And after he paddled her, he promised if there was another hint of trouble from her, he'd take her where bad little girls went. She didn't dare ask where.

To the congregation, they looked like the perfect family. But Evelyn knew right away, she'd not been forgiven.

At first, she thought her parents hadn't heard questions she'd ask or heard her calling their names, but slowly reality sank in.

They'd excommunicated her.

The nanny had arrived that following Monday.

Evelyn was no longer their beloved child, but the enemy, the spy who'd blemished their impeccable image.

Desperate, Evelyn had cleaned her room spotless, brought home straight As, and said her prayers loud enough for them to hear her plea of repentance.

But they didn't forget. They passed orders to the nanny for Evelyn, like a stranger passed money to a cashier.

Eight months later when her thirteenth birthday had passed and nobody said a word, Evelyn decided to end it all.

"Help me, Jesus," she'd said aloud, but couldn't stop the memory from continuing.

In her mother's vanity she'd found her stash of Valium. Thirty-four white pills that would end her suffering.

She'd hidden them in her jumper pocket and gone back to her bedroom unnoticed. In the closet, she'd fingered the pills and selected the white chiffon Easter dress, white patent leather shoes, white and yellow purse, and white ankle socks.

Even as a teenager, she hadn't been allowed to wear tights.

She'd dressed for dinner, hoping to be invited back to the family table. But her parents never called her name, and the nanny went to get her evening meal.

Evelyn had stood before the mirror in her bathroom looking into the vacant eyes of the girl she used to know.

She hadn't been a person. Only a breathing entity.

They wouldn't miss her when she was gone.

Lifting her hand, she'd prepared to swallow, when her mother had called her name.

The girl in the mirror had blinked. Her mind was playing tricks on her. Then her mother called her name again.

"Evelyn."

Evelyn flushed the pills and smeared the remnants of the chalky white residue on her dress.

Her mother came into the bathroom holding the empty bottle, the nanny crying behind her.

"Evelyn, did you take these pills? Marcie says she didn't do it. You're the only other person here."

Two hundred forty days had passed since her mother had said a word directly to her.

Now she was looking into Evelyn's eyes for the truth.

Evelyn's heart lifted and she said the words that would be the cornerstone of change in their relationship. "No, Mother. I didn't do it."

Marcie was fired and Evelyn was again a part of the family.

Today she'd been a step away from shame when she'd almost said to Lindsey, *I'll take your baby.*

How could she risk years of work with four little words? Especially since she'd given her own child away? A tide of guilt crashed into her. "Oh, God, forgive me," she whispered. "Forgive me."

What would Carvel think? Would he damn her, too? Evelyn lost the desire to call him and she just lay there.

She had to make the foundation happen for all the women who were like her and like Lindsey.

Sleep beat tears to Evelyn's eyes.

Seven

Alonzo Malone Jr. spotted his father's brand-new Escalade, but didn't run to it like he wanted to.

He was nine. Not a baby, and definitely not a wuss.

He was glad, though, that the kids that had surrounded him minutes ago had seen his father, too.

As soon as the grill of the big black truck appeared at the top of the hill, one by one, their menacing faces transformed into those of scared, openmouthed sissies.

His dad tapped the gas and Lonzo wanted to laugh, because he knew his father wasn't the monster he acted like on TV. But the stupid kids didn't know that.

Corey Wright stood there longer than the others, a smirk on his face. His family could be traced back to the Pilgrims, or so Corey said, and had been one of the families to start St. Timothy's.

Corey felt that gave him special permission to lie and act as if he were better than everybody else, but Lonzo knew different.

His father had told him that none of the first Pilgrims survived the harsh winters, and that if Corey's family had come on a later boat, they were criminals that had gotten kicked out of England.

Why else, Lonzo wondered, would a person cross the sea to a land he didn't know if the government wasn't about to chop his head off?

The truck rolled to a stop. Tense anticipation captured the boys. There was only one way for Corey to get to the car-riders line, and that was to pass in front of Big Black, Lonzo's father's affectionately named truck.

Corey tried to act big and bad, walking with his white-boy "I wanna be a pimp" step. He got to the curb and turned back and, keeping his hand low, flipped Lonzo the bird.

Lonzo's father didn't see the exchange, but when Corey turned back, the SUV had been raised on hydraulics two feet off the ground.

Corey's mouth fell open as Lonzo's father decompressed. When the truck slammed home, he gunned the engine.

Corey Wright wet his pants, and ran screaming across the WATCH FOR CHILDREN lane, past the campus administration building, where he disappeared from sight.

Lonzo didn't see anyone else, so he started toward the parked truck. He liked that his father had that affect on people. He wasn't known to football fans across the country as Maniac Malone for nothing. The kids didn't know he wasn't really crazy. Today, that mattered.

Lonzo opened the door and climbed in, dumping his book bag on the backseat. He looked at his dad. "If you value my life, you won't kiss me."

"You think I give a damn about those kids I saw you about to fight?"

"Wasn't no fight." God, why was his dad already mad at him?

"Then what was it?"

"Nothing." Lonzo snapped his seat belt in place and stared out the window wishing it would rain. Then at least the weather would match his mood.

"Why didn't you tell me you didn't have the supplies for your science class?"

"Because Mom said she'd get them."

"Well, what the hell happened!" he yelled.

"How do I know? Why are you cursing at me?"

His father shot him a venomous look and Lonzo decided to shut his mouth. His father drove with his wrist over the steering wheel, a scowl buried deep on his forehead.

Mrs. Rutherford, Lonzo's science teacher, called it stress lines, but to him it looked like plain old mad.

He stared out the corner of his eye at the wing of the falcon on his father's arm. *His one arm probably weighs as much as my whole body.*

Lonzo flexed his muscles and didn't see his uniform shirt move. He was puny. Got it from his mother's side. Sick to death of being small, he pressed his back into the seat and prayed for all green lights. That way his father couldn't put him under the visual microscope.

The light at Peachtree Industrial Boulevard caught them.

When his dad fixed Lonzo with the "I'm going to get the truth out of you one way or another," look, Lonzo reconsidered his options. "I could have called, but Mom said she'd get the specimens and meet me at school yesterday, but she didn't show."

"Could she have dropped them off and you didn't receive them?"

"She was supposed to bring them when she came for the conference."

"When she didn't show, why didn't you call me?"

"Why am I in trouble? She said she was coming!"

"Boy, who you raising your voice at? You'd better check yourself."

A red light. Dang. Lonzo stared out the passenger window until his father's glare drilled a hot hole in the back of his head. "I thought she was coming. After a couple hours, I called Mrs. Chow, and she came and got me."

"My question remains the same."

"I knew you two would fight, and I didn't feel like hearing it. I had a headache."

"You had a what?"

His father gave him the most incredible, incredulous stare, Lonzo felt like a wart. He couldn't back away now. "My head was hurting."

Boys don't get headaches, his mother had said two weeks ago when she'd gotten him out of bed at one in the morning to clean the kitchen. He'd wanted to call her a liar and tell her to clean it herself, but his head hurt too much, and he didn't want to get his butt kicked. "That's right, sir." He didn't feel like a wart. He felt like an oozing wart.

"You must be out of yo—" His father banged the steering wheel and jammed his foot on the accelerator. The truck shot forward. "I'll deal with your mother."

Not only did Lonzo's head pound, his stomach started to ache.

Now he was really in trouble. His mother fully enforced her "What goes on in this house is none of your father's business" rule, even though his father still owned the house.

Lonzo mentally kissed his Dreamcast good-bye.

His mother's temper was diluted by her half-Hawaiian, half-African-American blood, but when she got worked up, Lonzo usually found something quiet to do in his room.

They pulled up on the driveway of his house, and his father said one curse word after another under his breath.

Old newspapers lay haphazardly on the driveway, and the once-nice flower bed was overrun with weeds. "She can't keep the place up, so why did she want it? Get those newspapers. Every day when you walk up this driveway, you don't see them?"

Lonzo didn't say a word. Just shouldered his backpack and stacked the papers in his arms.

He hated being wrong. Lonzo thought if his father saw his face and the hurt he felt deep in his heart, his father would do the right thing. Instead, everything was going wrong, and Lonzo didn't like it. As he walked up the steep driveway, he slipped.

His father sighed loudly, casting Lonzo into a pit of despair. "I'm okay," he told his dad.

Malone shook his head.

Lonzo walked to the first of three garage doors and pressed buttons on the security pad. The door rose and when it was halfway up, he walked in and dropped the papers into the recycle bin.

His father came around the thick bushes, his mouth open.

"Where'd this come from?"

Lonzo reached for two white kitchen garbage bags, and took them to the large blue can.

"Does she even live here anymore?" Malone mumbled. Her 2000 hunter-green Lexus was gone. "Don't tell me you come home and nobody is here."

Lonzo walked inside the house and closed the garage door.

"Sometimes." He unloaded his backpack in the corner, his jacket on top. Dishes and ashtrays were all over the island and kitchen counters, the little color TV blaring. Lonzo turned to *Dragon Ball Z*, nudged the sound down, and started emptying the sink. He was like his father in one way. He hated a filthy house.

"I can't believe this," his father kept saying. "I can't believe this . . ."

Shit. I'm old enough to fill in the blanks, Alonzo wanted to say. But his father was a "Do as I say not as I do" father, and he didn't take no mess when it came to cursing. *But he can't read my mind, so I can cuss whenever I think about it.*

"I'm washing," he told his father, who made the water too hot. Lonzo looked up, glad to see his dad even though he was mad.

Two of his spelling words this week were *ferocious* and *despair*. He had to use them in sentences and give the definitions. *My father looked around our house, his face covered in despair. In the car, he looked ferocious.*

"I'll dry," his dad finally said.

By seven o'clock they'd cleaned the kitchen, Lonzo's bedroom, and his bathroom. Then they walked into the laundry room and that was when his father didn't bother leaving out cuss words while he scrubbed out the washer. Something had died in it, Lonzo thought at the eye-watering smell.

His father said, "Fuck it," threw the rag against the wall, and slammed the door.

"Dad, do you want hamburgers and french fries?"

Alonzo Malone dressed in black stood out against the white cabinets and fruit-covered wallpaper. "Yeah, that's cool."

"After we eat, do you want to play Dreamcast?"

Lonzo hoped against hope his father would tell him to get some clothes together so he could spend the night at his house. But his parents had worked out a detailed visitation schedule, and technically, this was his mother's weekend.

His parents never asked what he wanted to do or anything. He just followed the schedule, but just this once, he wanted his father to take control and break the stupid rule.

"Sure," his father said, "let's eat and play Dreamcast."

Lonzo hid his disappointment behind stiff shoulders as he pulled ground beef patties out of the refrigerator and dropped them into the frying pan. "Will you watch the meat?" he asked his father as he dug two premade kid-size Baggies of fries from the freezer, and dumped the contents onto a cookie sheet.

"Yeah," his father said as he watched him closely. "I got the meat."

They worked in silence, then ate in his room.

"What do you want to play?"

"I don't know."

His father looked bored. Maybe they should talk about what happened on the radio today. Kids talked about dying all the time. But Lonzo wondered how it'd feel to shoot himself. Probably not worse than having a nurse beat on your back to move fluid from the bottom of your lungs. Nothing was worse than that.

"Daddy, do you think the girl that shot herself is going to be okay?"

His father's head jerked up. "How'd you hear about that?"

He couldn't believe his father wasn't better informed. "They played it on CNN while I was in the media center at school."

"Damn."

Lonzo shrugged at his father's anger. His dad paid for the best education in the state, and now he was mad they got CNN at school.

"Last I heard, she and the baby will be fine."

His dad studied him as if he couldn't make the right decision.

"What is it?" Lonzo finally asked.

"Nothing." His father turned off his pager.

When his father didn't pick up his controller, Lonzo waited for the inevitable rejection. They used to do stuff together all the time. His father had an intense workout routine, and as soon as Lonzo was old enough, he went to the gym every day with his dad. They used to wear matching sneakers and jerseys. They used to have fun.

Now they sat quietly eating overdone burgers and undercooked french fries.

Lonzo pried the plate from his dad's hand and grabbed the controller. "We'll play Zelda, okay?"

"Yeah, boy, hop up."

A thrill rushed through Lonzo. His father had stopped letting him sit on his lap when he'd turned nine. He'd told him it was time he started acting like a man. But today he must have forgotten.

Lonzo tried not to compare his scrawny arms to his dad's as they played for over an hour; then the garage door started up.

His father wrapped the cord around the controller, signaling the end of the game. "Get your shower and take your inhaler. I need to talk to your mom."

"Don't cuss at her. She won't let you come back if you do."

This was the first time since his mom and dad had split that his father had hung out in his room for more than five minutes. Now his mother banned him to the foyer and if he cussed, the porch.

His father's eyes had squiggly red lines in them like raw shrimp. "Let me be the grown-up, okay?"

Before his dad could fully stand, Lonzo launched himself at his chest. His dad caught him in a bear hug and pressed a hard kiss to his head. Lonzo held on for a long time, even after his father tried to remove him. His father might get mad and even cuss, but here Lonzo felt safe.

Finally his dad's hands slowed and he stopped trying to disengage his son. His chest drew in and he whispered, "I'm sorry."

The words restored Lonzo, and filled him with hope that his father did indeed love him.

Malone lowered his son to the floor and the boy resisted begging for his father to be nice to his mother. "Everything's cool. Get in the shower. Take your radio in the bathroom, but use the plug—"

"In the hallway, I know." This was going to be a long fight.

Eight

Lee rolled off Jasmine, a smile stretched wide across his face. "That was good."

She kept her eyes closed, her chest rising and falling. "Yep." Maybe he'd leave now that he'd gotten what he came for.

But Lee was under the misguided notion that she was having a good time too. The whole *lick her all over and screw her quick* wasn't working for Jasmine. He sat up on the side of the bed and she finally turned over on her stomach.

Lee caressed her ass. "You're the best I've ever had."

A silent sigh escaped. What did he want? Applause?

Jasmine slid from the bed on the other side. "I've got to get some groceries. Want to come shopping?"

As expected, Lee's facial expression crumpled into distaste. "Nah. I'd better get back. Got lots of stuff going on."

Jasmine had her hand on the bathroom knob in a heartbeat. "Go ahead and let yourself out. I've got to go real quick."

She hurried and locked the door, then started the bathroom fan. She could hear Lee on the squeaky floorboards outside the bathroom. "I'll call you later," she said, not meaning it, but wanting him to go with as little fuss as possible.

She heard him waiting, shuffling his feet, could feel him lurking, but it didn't take long for Lee to give up, get in his car, and drive away.

She came out and poured herself some wine and flipped the channels between *Inside Atlanta Sports* with Malone as the guest, and the evening news on channel five with Evelyn.

Jasmine's finger stammered over the PREV CHAN button, and she wondered why she was torturing herself.

This was the tenth interview. The tenth time she'd heard her so-called friends describe the call of the century as "an unfortunate incident." The tenth interview where they'd never once mentioned her name.

Jasmine's hand throbbed as the sports announcer Bill Quick questioned her credentials, and her ability to give advice.

"Malone, your cohost told a troubled teenager to kill herself. How can you sit here and not say something to the public about where you stand, bro?"

"He's *my* cohost!" Jasmine screamed. "I created that show, you moron."

"Why you tryin' to sound black?" Malone asked him. "Be yourself, man. Just be you," Malone said, imitating a white man's voice.

Offstage, the crew howled with laughter.

She couldn't listen anymore, and before she could stop herself, flicked back to channel five and caught up to the conversation with Reggie Marrow and Evelyn.

"Obviously listeners of your show have opinions about whether Dr. Jasmine should have prompted Lindsey Kane to kill herself. It's been four days since the incident and you haven't taken sides. Tell the viewers where you stand."

"On the side of the victim."

"Have you spoken to Dr. Jasmine, and what have you said?"

"We haven't spoken," Evelyn pushed on despite his attempt to interrupt. "Lindsey was hurting when she called the show and sought our help. In a situation like this, as talk show hosts, we encounter the unexpected. This was just an unfortunate incident and we want her to get the help she needs and anyone else out there who's feeling defeated by something in their lives."

"It sounds to me like you agree with Dr. Jasmine's tactics. Care to comment on that?" he said, clearly annoyed that Evelyn was being evasive.

Evelyn looked directly into the camera. "It was a bluff tactic that backfired. Anyone who heard that terrifying call knows I wanted to help Lindsey. My intentions were always clear. I can't comment on anyone besides myself."

No, she didn't leave me hangin' like that! Jasmine's elbows dug into her thighs like knives. *After all we've been through, she kicked the chair from under me.*

"Isn't that a cop-out?" he scolded gently.

"No."

"A person can't be pushed to the limit?"

"Yes," Jasmine yelled.

Against Jasmine's echoing voice, Evelyn sounded confident. "The problem didn't start with that phone call or end with a gunshot. Lindsey wanted to kill herself before she called the show, before we answered, and before we tried to talk her out of it."

"So how do you justify such reckless behavior?"

Evelyn looked down her nose at Reggie. "*Atlanta Live* has always been about helping people, and that will continue. We love Atlanta. We love the grassroots following we've developed and we want more listeners to tune in for our show. We're not reckless, we're honest. We cater to a group of people that society has forgotten. Why else would people call with such serious matters? They don't feel they can turn anywhere else."

Jasmine had to give it to Evelyn. She'd pissed Reggie off with her unflappable demeanor.

Reggie despised black women like Evelyn that only had enough black in them to fill a thimble, and who acted as if the rest of the world should kiss their high-yellow behinds.

"Don't you think an immediate apology to Lindsey and her family is necessary?" The question would hurt Evelyn if she didn't answer the right way. Jasmine leaned in.

"No."

"What?" Reggie snapped.

"At this point in her recovery, I don't think anyone who isn't skilled to deal with her particular issues should have contact with her. My apology isn't going to help if her focus isn't directed at her recovery."

She'd made him look like a fool. His mouth moved but nothing came out. "Come on—"

"While I'm here," Evelyn pressed on, "I want to take the opportunity to thank all the listeners and viewers for their support, and for the many women across the country who've come forward with similar stories of tragedy and loss. Fortunately, this young woman was saved. My foundation called Safe Haven has been formed. The e-mail address and Web site are listed on your screen. Thank you for inviting me, Reggie. It's been a pleasure."

Jasmine watched as Evelyn unclipped her microphone, barely touched Reggie's hand, and waved to the camera, before exiting.

The show had no choice but go to a commercial.

Lonely tears slid down Jasmine's cheeks. She'd been locked up for days, banished with no chance of being free. How was she supposed to face Evelyn and Malone on Monday?

Even after the pain of listening to them, Jasmine felt a pang of regret when she turned off the TV.

She pulled her hot sweatshirt over her head and rummaged through the pile of laundry at the foot of the couch and found a raggedy T-shirt from the Blues and Jazz Festival.

She wasn't usually this way. She was so put-together. So classy. And now she was the pariah.

This was their big break. The one moment in a million that could launch *Atlanta Live* into a galaxy all its own.

But she'd always imagined herself at the helm of their meteoric rise. And she had been, until Friday.

Everything that had happened for the show over the past two years had been under her careful planning. But now she was no better than the exiled ruler of a country.

Not a phone call. Not a visit.

Just Lee coming over to make good on their agreement.

Instead, Malone and Evelyn traveled from interview to interview, gaining favor amongst the listeners, gathering their own personal fan base.

Women sixteen to sixty called the show cooing and giggling over Malone's brash manner, all believing they had the power to tame him. And when he flexed his maleness, they ate it up like food at a banquet.

What surprised Jasmine were the men. They treated his word as if it were gospel, elevating him to hero status, even though he no longer carried the pigskin every Sunday.

Evelyn's effect was romantic, garnering marriage proposals like a wool sweater gathered lint. Her sweet nature attracted men and women who'd never felt real honest sympathy.

Jasmine looked at the scorecard where she'd tracked people's reactions to her regarding this situation. So far the wind was blowing both ways.

Every other interview, she was fired.

And from the rubble of her career emerged a demographic she wasn't sure she liked.

Women thirty-five to seventy had become her champions.

They filled phone lines with stories of how they'd been hoodwinked by men and by life. They'd preached that when the FOR WHITES ONLY signs came down, the scales were supposed to tip in their favor, but the okeydoke had gotten them again. They were still victimized, single, mothers, and poor. To them, Jasmine's approach was pragmatic.

They wanted to tell their sons to shove the needle deep in their arms and to die so they wouldn't have to put up with their stealing and lying.

They wanted to tell their daughters to go ahead and catch AIDS. Maybe that would keep them alive long enough to see the youngest of their children through preschool.

They wanted to tell their husbands to drive drunk and this time, don't miss the damned tree. A car with a crushed fender was no good, but a totaled car would at least be paid off by the insurance company.

These women were vilified, treated like big-hipped women on a crowded bus. But they kept calling, jamming the phone lines, and preaching. And for the moment, they kept Jasmine employed.

Funk wafted by her nose and she realized she smelled. Her bare feet pushed at damp tissues, empty cans of soda, and Snickers bar wrappers. She looked at her baggy sweatpants and stomped to the pantry for a garbage bag. "I'm not wasting another minute waiting for them to do anything for me. I'm my own best damned friend."

Sniffling, she cleaned the house until not a speck of dust touched any surface. Tired, she trudged to the kitchen for cold water. It was still light outside. The show started at three, but because of the controversy, Malone and Evelyn would be on until midnight.

"Got to get out of here before I go crazy."

She thought about turning on the TV, but was saved by the phone. "Hello?"

"Hey, saw you cleaning. Want some company?"

Jasmine turned to the kitchen window and half waved to her neighbor Cecilie. "I'm tired of you spying on me. I'm getting blinds next week."

"You been saying that for six months, so you must want me to keep an eye on you. I'm going out. Wanna come?"

The gray cracks in Jasmine hands reminded her of her mother's. Chills raced up her spine. "Yeah, I need to get the hell out of here."

"Do what you got to do, but be ready by seven."

"You're driving," Jasmine told her. She needed about four Long Island iced teas to dull the sting of this mess.

"Next time, you're driving. I'm not your damned chauffeur." Cec sounded annoyed.

"Look, you called me."

"Because I thought you might like a change of pace instead of being cooped up in the house all day again."

Jasmine wanted to snap about Cec's funky attitude, but she was the only person who'd bothered to call. "I'll see you in a bit."

Jasmine walked out of her bedroom at seven-thirty in camel-colored leather from the corset to the jeans. She pulled the soft waist-length coat from the closet and went downstairs and found Cec staring up at the ceiling in the dining room. "What are you looking at?"

"You got a leak."

There was a small bubble in the stippled plaster that could have been there since she'd bought the house. But Jasmine didn't see signs of a leak. Cec was annoying, but she had connections and Jasmine didn't want to stay home another night.

"I don't see anything. Can we go?"

Cec took in Jasmine's outfit. "Your nightmare, not mine. I've been ready. Remember, I said seven?" She flashed two tickets under Jasmine's nose.

"What are those?"

"Skybox tickets to tonight's exhibition game."

"Whose box?"

"One hundred single men of Atlanta."

"One hundred single men?" Jasmine burst out laughing. "They're all gay. I'm not wasting my leather. Most of them will be dressed better than me, anyway."

"They're not gay," Cec protested. "I got these tickets from Jason at work."

"That's 'cause he's gay."

"He's getting married next month."

"To a girl?"

"You know what—" Cec started out. "I ain't got to put up with you."

"Hold on, dag. Everybody is so touchy lately. Let me see the tickets."

Cec handed one over, her foot impatiently tapping on the floor.

Jasmine wasn't moved by her nerves. Cec needed her. She was three hundred pounds of woman, and while some men liked it that way, Cec didn't have the confidence to go on the prowl alone.

Jasmine held the ticket up to the light. It looked legit.

Just maybe she would find a distraction worthy of dumping Cec for. She cut off the inside lights.

"Let's go meet some single nongay men."

The skybox at the Georgia Dome was crawling with Atlanta's finest. Men in mocha, Hershey's, caramel, and white chocolate mixed and mingled in the glass-enclosed room that made getting to know someone an inevitability.

The black sea parted when Jasmine hit the door, and stepped one, then two feet into the room. She checked, but didn't contact a single man, using her personal flowchart to sort the possibilities from the "really boy, please."

"Hey, Jas. What's up, girl?" She started to get annoyed but realized the voice belonged to hustler E.J. from Blacktown. He ran numbers, bounced at the club, did favors for the right people, and had gotten out of the neighborhood by buying one check-cashing business before the Arabs moved in.

He'd expanded years ago from one to nine, and now laundered whatever money he earned under the table through his legitimate businesses. Jasmine had always respected E.J., and though he was on the other side of right, he was still cool people.

"What's up?" she said, letting him bear-hug her. "You wreckin' my game."

E.J. laughed. "I see where your eyes are at, didn't mean to cut in. Just wanted to ask, you all right? You need anything?"

She smiled at the man she'd known since high school. "I'm straight. But I'll let you know, okay?"

He flipped a card into her palm and flowed into the crowd. "You look good, girl. Call me."

Jasmine continued on her journey and let each step take her deeper. Tonight would be memorable as Jasmine spotted the man she'd speak to. No gold or platinum on his finger or in his mouth. Suit, definitely designer—and not from K&G. The shirt classic Kenneth Cole. Cuff links. Real ones. A definite plus. The shoes, shined like a brand-new penny. He stood up, and she measured six feet three and three-quarters, and he sealed the deal with the gold money clip around plenty of bills.

Women flowed by like the Nile, all vying for his attention, but he reached his hand out and Jasmine took it, glad to meet him, the feeling reciprocated in his touch.

"Zeke."

"Jasmine."

"You lookin' for a friend or an encounter?"

Her kind of man. Direct, and he smelled good. "The latter, baby. But first I want two Long Island iced teas, and then we'll see how good you are at giving me what I need."

Nine

Although the sun had long set, it illuminated the moon and cast a silhouette around the idiot peering into Jasmine's house. It went black outside, and she hoped Zeke would take the hint and go to his own home and leave hers alone.

God sure had a weird sense of priorities to waste energy on him. Jasmine almost included herself in that group, as she was connected if only by an inconsequential liaison, but she didn't.

God wasn't bothering her and she wasn't wasting the "big call" on this. One day she might need God's attention for real, and she didn't want her call list to be jammed full of unimportant contact.

She longed for a hot bath followed by a good night's sleep—in the guest room. Her bed needed to be changed and she didn't feel up to wrestling with it tonight.

"Jasmine, I'm separated," Zeke pleaded from the other side of her locked front door. "Let me stay here a couple days. I can make you feel so good."

She shook her head.

No matter how much she loved sex, Jasmine hated the cleanup. Hated that men wanted to stay and stake a claim on her time. Once they found out that she was in radio, they somehow thought she could pull tickets out of thin air, or would be a broker for their future relationships with celebrities.

A long time ago, the using was mutual. She'd get an introduction to whoever she wanted, and they'd get a couple of hours of her time. She wasn't Dr. Jasmine because she'd followed the rules, and raised her hand before asking questions.

The only way she'd made it was to keep her booted foot firmly on any door that had what she wanted on the other side.

Sex was sex. Everything else was bullshit.

With every plea, Zeke's fuckability quotient plummeted.

She couldn't believe she'd chosen so badly. But he'd talked about his credentials as if they were DNA. He put out that he was such a good guy. He wanted to take her to breakfast to get to know her better. He could do things for her. Take her places. The sky's the limit . . . Yeah, right.

If he'd been so concerned about her well-being, why had he beat a path out of the front door, only to come back an hour later sounding frantic, claiming he'd lost something? When she'd hooked up with him, he hadn't been wearing a ring.

And now if she let him in, she'd be forced to witness his one-man act called *I ain't shit, but I'm tryin' to be*. The monologue would consist of language to which she'd built an immunity so tough, Ebola couldn't touch it.

"Me and my wife are estranged . . . living together but separate lives . . . doin' it for the kids . . ." Blah, blah, blah. Whateva, whateva, whateva.

He shouldn't have been perpetrating a single man's life. Now his ass was on the other side of nothing. No wife, nowhere to sleep, and no ring.

She exhaled a happy sigh and darted into the dining room, making a mental note to buy some curtains for the window panels beside the front door.

"Jasmine!" He was yelling now.

He's straight-up crazy. And he definitely wasn't getting in.

Finally, a car door slammed and a motor roared to life. Tires peeled against the asphalt and then he was gone.

Jasmine cleared the top step and pushed open her bedroom door. The covers hung off the bed, the sheets tangled and moist with their smell. She smirked as she looked around. He'd been all right, nothing memorable.

Swinging the belt to her robe, Jasmine picked up the remote from the floor, flicked on the TV, and heard Malone's voice.

"This is Malone coming to you live from WKKY 104.9, in the heart of the A T L. Holding it down with me is the lovely Ms. Evelyn, who uses her natural-born romantic skills to offer a softer perspective.

"Thank you to Channel Five for visiting with us tonight, so now everybody can see how busted up we look. Thanks," he said in his usual half-sarcastic half-joking way.

Jasmine couldn't believe Malone and Evelyn were wearing matching black *Atlanta Live* T-shirts, and had mugs with the show's name on them.

Evelyn even wore a black and white bandana around her neck with ATLANTA LIVE printed in white letters.

Shocked, Jasmine just stared.

"After last week, a lot of people have opinions about what should have, could have, might have been done. We're here to talk to you. I personally believe we've talked this into the ground. What do you think, Evelyn?"

"Let's give them one last chance to be heard. Then we're moving on."

"Before the break, we were taking a poll from listeners who had an opinion as to whether Dr. Jasmine was right or wrong. Let's go to the lines."

Jasmine sank to the floor in front of her television.

The equipment's fixed, she noticed as Malone tilted his head when he listened to Lee.

"Right or wrong?" Malone asked the caller.

"Wrong."

Malone pressed the next line. "Right or wrong?"

"Dr. Jasmine would be looking for a job and a new face if I was the senator."

"Got it. Right or wrong?" he demanded.

"Dead wrong, Malone. Hey, Evelyn," the caller said, conversationally.

"Hi."

Malone shoved the next button. "Right or wrong?"

"Fired. And wrong."

Nausea built in Jasmine's stomach. Malone didn't seem to care. They were blood cousins! He talked as if he hadn't been in that room with her. The next six calls were split evenly. According to her calculations, she should start looking for a new job before the sun came up.

Malone moved the levers while he talked. "I'm told our producer has a big announcement next week and it's going to blow the roof off Atlanta. Now that he's leaked it, everybody wants to know." Malone swiveled toward Evelyn. "You know something and aren't telling?"

"No, he won't say a word, only that it's big."

"I'll tell you what." Malone pointed to the cameraman. "Get a close-up on the bald guy. That's Lee, our producer," he told the audience. "He's the guy that makes pretty much all the decisions."

Lee was grinning, shaking his head no.

"Malone, he's much bigger than a lowly producer. He owns the place. He uses Mr. Sharpe as a figurehead," Evelyn chimed in. "I think we should give out his pager number. The public has a right to contact the black man in charge."

Evelyn sounded so logical, it was funny. They were having a good time without Jasmine. She couldn't believe how much she missed them.

Malone gave out Lee's number.

With a big grin on his face, Lee pointed to his fist, then his jaw, then to Malone.

Malone dropped his voice as if Lee couldn't hear him.

"Y'all, my boss looks like he's about to get violent. I'm not a punk, but I don't want to hurt the little guy. So don't call until we're off the air."

"We'd better take some more calls, because these lights won't stop," Evelyn segued.

"But first let's take a break and we'll be back on WKKY 104.9."

Jasmine sat still for a moment, but her brain screamed for her to get her résumé. She rummaged through her desk and found her laptop. It took the system a minute to power up, she hadn't used it in so long.

Malone's career had been ending and Evelyn's career moving in a lateral position when they'd come to *Atlanta Live*.

As far as Jasmine was concerned, they owed her for getting them where they were.

The phone rang and she jumped. "Hello?"

"J, it's me," Malone said. "Turn on your set, we're on with Channel Five."

She almost told her cousin she was watching, but changed her mind. "Sorry, kid. On my way out the door."

"Your ass is lying, but be that way."

"How am I doing in the polls?"

He chuckled softly. "Up two."

"They're taking this serious?"

"As a heart attack."

"Damn."

"Yep," Malone said. "Gotta go. Hey, come by my place tomorrow. We'll talk. All right?"

"Yeah. Bye."

"Later."

Ten

Malone rarely indulged in red meat, but every once in a while a juicy porterhouse put him in a good mood. He needed a good mood too, because trouble was on the way. Any time Jasmine was mixed with Evelyn and Carvel, there was always fireworks.

He stabbed the thirty-ounce slab, marinated and seasoned with herbed butter, turned it over, then closed the grill's lid.

He carried his glass of wine inside, sliding the patio door closed. His date, Rena from last night's late stop at 112, moved away from the counter where she'd been leafing through his mail.

She knew her ass was busted. That was why she added a little too much hip to her walk. "Hey, baby."

"Find anything interesting?" He put the mail in the kitchen drawer, turned up his glass, and finished the wine. He refilled, still looking at her.

"I was just looking for a magazine." She tried and failed to sound casual. "So, who did you say was coming?"

"Friends. Why? You need to go?"

"I was just asking." She slid her arms around his neck and shimmied her crotch against his thighs. "How about a little something before everybody gets here?"

Malone slid his hand over her ample butt. "What you got?"

Rena wasn't but about five-four, but she wore high heels that brought her to the middle of his chest. She started unfastening his belt.

"I can make it fast," she said, scooping his flaccid penis into her hand. Her knees hit the floor.

The doorbell chimed. She swore. Malone shrugged, nonchalant. Women were always talking about wanting respect.

All day she'd been listening to talk radio and whenever a woman called with a stupid story, Rena was spouting about how dumb the bitch was.

So how was she respecting herself by coming home with him, doin' it all night, and then gettin' ready to play herself to cover for getting caught going through his mail? When he climaxed, was her behavior supposed to be obliterated from his mind? She was good, but he'd never had any that could make him forget a damned thing. "I guess we gone have to save this for later." She looked up with hope-filled eyes. They both knew later would never come.

Malone fixed his clothes and opened the door. "Hey, bro," he greeted Lee. "Get in here. What you got there?"

"My mother's homemade potato salad and some greens Mama Mae made. She sends her best."

Malone reached for the bag. "Man, your grandma can put her foot in some collards!" He walked off, leaving Lee to close the door.

"Introduce yourselves," Malone hollered from the kitchen as he unpacked the Tupperware dishes from Lee's grandma and mother.

No Gladware or that other fake plastic crap they sold in the supermarkets. Old women knew how to treat a man and they did it right every time with Tupperware. He smelled the still warm food. "I know everybody else better get here in the next five minutes, or else I'm not responsible for what they don't get."

Lee came into the kitchen just as Malone finished washing his hands. "Who's your friend?"

"Nobody. Man, your grandma loves me. She sent some corn bread."

"That's mine." Lee reached for the bread, but Malone had already unwrapped a corner and pinched off a piece. "You're a dog, you know that?"

"Shut up. They live next door to you. It's not like you can't go get some more when you get home." Malone ate the bread and chased it with a swallow of wine. "That's the exact reason why you aren't ever going to get married."

"What does me getting married have to do with living next door to my mother and grandmother?"

" 'Cause it's against the law to marry your granny. You're spoiled, son. No woman is going to be good enough for you."

Lee wiped his bald head and shrugged his shoulders. "That's not true."

Malone ran his tongue over his teeth and peered around the corner to see what Rena was doing. She was flipping through his CDs, her purse on the floor next to her feet. Damn, he'd have to do a body check before she left. *No more chickenheads in the house!*

He stepped back into the kitchen and pulled out a freshly made iceberg lettuce salad with French dressing, and checked on stuffed potatoes that warmed at two hundred degrees in the drawer-size warmer. "I hope you aren't holding out for Jasmine to change her tune. She's not good enough for you."

Love as bald as Lee's head reflected in his eyes. "How can you say that?"

" 'Cause she dogs you just because you're a man and you're dumb enough to let her."

At work, Lee was self-assured, but on the regular asphalt of life, he was a complete wuss. "She's just acting up," Lee said about the woman he loved. "She's just been trippin' lately."

"Try every day of her natural life." Malone stacked wrapped dinner napkins and china on the counter. He popped grandma's greens in the warmer and added the corn bread before closing the drawer. "So what's up with the secret?"

"I can't say."

"Man, please." Malone got indignant. "You sound like a girl."

"I can't say!"

"You can tell a brotha if he's gone have a job come Monday. I got a kid to think about." He heard the soft clap of two CD cases touching. He looked around the corner and saw Rena shove them in her bag.

He shook his head. She was out of there just as soon as he finished with Lee. "So? Should a brotha apply for unemployment?"

Lee wavered a minute under Malone's intense gaze. "You got a job. But that's it."

"Cool. That's all I want to know."

The doorbell rang again. Malone rubbed his hands together. "Here we go. All I gotta say is don't play into Jasmine's shit."

"Don't say anything about work." Lee's hopeful look made Malone feel sorry for him.

Evelyn and her fiancé, Carvel, stood in the doorway. Jasmine stood a foot behind, her scowl leveled at the back of Carvel's head. He stood with his feet planted wide, looking pompous and too holy for Malone's taste. "Coming from a funeral?"

"No, from church. Been lately?" Carvel asked in that holier-than-thou way Malone hated.

"No, but God found me right here this morning."

"Ma—lone." His name was broken into a two-syllable warning from Evelyn.

"Hey, beautiful."

Carvel puffed his chest out a little more and Malone laughed.

While he and Carvel were the same height, Carvel was shy about fifty pounds in mass. Malone's midsection was rock solid, while preacherman's was soft, the churchwomen feeding him to death.

"Can we come in?" Evelyn asked, censure sparkling in her eyes.

"Sure." Malone watched the moody processional. This was going to be a fun time.

Jasmine brushed up against him, giving Malone a swift elbow to his midsection. He smacked her butt. "Ouch! Damn, that hurt." She rubbed, looking annoyed.

"Shut up. You're still on my list."

Jasmine saw Rena and cut her eyes to Malone. "I see why you were calling on the Lord. Is she out of diapers yet?"

Malone yanked a couple of Jasmine's braids. "She was just leaving. Rena, get your bag and come here."

The leggy dark-chocolate honey walked over, her gaze suspicious, and her shoulders slumped. "What you want with my bag?"

Malone acted like a club bouncer and went through her satchel, pulling out Lonzo's Michael Jackson and Sammy CDs. He dropped the bag into her shaking hands, opened the door, and escorted her outside. "Bye."

"Wait just a damned minute! Those are mine."

"Right. That's why the case says L.M. These are my son's. Now get the hell on before I lose my temper." Malone shook his head.

"You ain't about shit, anyway," she screeched. "You're washed up! A has-been! You just tryin' to get over like everybody else!"

She clawed his arms, drawing back and aiming for his face. Malone snatched her arm and twisted until her face was fully contorted. "Get out of my neighborhood. We don't like trash around here." He jammed two bills into her hand. She didn't argue, didn't say another word. Just ran, clutching her purse to her chest.

Blood glittered down his arm in four angry lines. He was going to have to give up women for a while. They weren't worth the trouble.

He walked in and everybody stared.

The clock in Lonzo's room clicked the five o'clock hour.

Malone didn't bother with an explanation. He threw the CDs on the counter, aimed the remote at the CD player, and went into the bathroom to wash his arm and hands.

Now he had to go out there and act as if he were having a good time. Not even his wife had ever left a physical mark on him. Damn Rena. Damn all women.

Malone suddenly wanted to be the one place where he'd always had fun and that was the football field. He missed it now more than ever. If there was ever a chance for a comeback, he'd take it in a heartbeat.

Nobody wanted to be here. But he had to fix things between them. He'd made a promise to Jasmine's brother, his cousin, ten years ago, and he intended to keep it.

In his room, he changed shirts and popped open a beer from the minifridge and downed it. By the time he was in the kitchen, he'd gotten another beer.

Lee came into the kitchen on Malone's heels. "You okay?"

"Yeah. Caught her stealing my son's CDs."

"What!"

Malone stared at Lee. "You do know people steal."

His expression changed. "She didn't look like she'd have to steal CDs from you."

Malone shook his head bitterly. He grabbed the cases off the counter and showed Lee Lonzo's initials. "This proves you wrong. Come on. Let's get this show on the road. Who's hungry?" he asked, heading around the corner. "We've got steak, steak, and steak."

Evelyn looked at Carvel, discomfort telegraphed in every movement. She did that thing with her eyebrows, where one went up and the other tilted in. "Carvel doesn't eat red meat."

"Evelyn."

The reprimand in Carvel's voice set Malone's teeth on edge. "Evelyn what?" he demanded. "So you don't eat red meat. Why is that her problem?"

"She didn't need to bring that up."

Malone saw the warning in Evelyn's eyes, the plea for Malone to be nice. Malone stretched his hands at his side and tried to imagine the tension leaving his body. "It's better to bring it up before you have twenty dollars' worth of meat on your plate. That's cool, though. We've got plenty of other stuff to eat." He smacked his hands together. "I'm going to check it now." The sliding glass door shut harder than Malone intended, but he didn't care.

Jasmine joined him, her hand full of chips, her jaws working. Malone took the fork from the cookie sheet. "You ain't got nothing to say?"

"I thought I had some time when I saw Carvel and Evelyn pull up. I figured you'd be too busy grinding Carvel to pieces and not bother with me."

"Oh, don't think I forgot I owe you a butt-whoopin'." He handed her the tray. "Might as well make yourself useful." He pierced the meat and a thin stream of blood ran over and hissed against the metal bottom.

"You could have called before Friday," Jasmine said. "You of all people should know I didn't mean for that girl to shoot herself."

"Didn't you?" Malone shifted, the sun on his back, a breeze in the air. "That day, *I* was scared of you."

"Oh, come on." Jasmine laughed and shooed flies away.

He looked at his cousin. She had on jeans and a shirt that crossed over and tied on the side. Her hair was braided, her face clean. She didn't look at all like the woman she'd been over a week ago.

"I pushed her, I admit it," Jasmine confessed. "But only so I could drag her back in, and I'd, we—"

"No, you had it right the first time. *You* could be the hero. Only, it backfired."

Evelyn stepped out on the deck and slid the door closed behind her. Her cheeks were flushed and her lipstick faded.

"What's wrong with you?" Malone asked her.

"Nothing." Evelyn took the fork from Malone and removed the rest of the meat from the grill. "Carvel had to leave. An emergency at church."

Malone and Jasmine exchanged knowing looks. "Good, he aint' a real brotha anyway."

"Malone, please."

Evelyn gave the fork back to him and took the tray from Jasmine.

"Look at you all dressed up in your cute shiny boots and your pretty red shirt. I mean, damn." Malone fingered the ruffle at her belly. "What kind of emergency would take him away from all this pretty, red-hot love?"

Evelyn and Jasmine faced each other, then burst out laughing. Evelyn's hair fell over her shoulder in a black silky curtain.

Her entire demeanor was different since her man wasn't there. And she didn't even see the difference in herself.

The meat tray tipped and steak juice plopped onto Evelyn's shoes. For a second, her face registered shock. "I'll bet he'll really want me now. Five-inch heels, patent leather boots covered in steak juice."

She laughed so hard, one of the steaks slid off and hit the ground.

Tears were running from Malone's eyes as he picked up the thick piece of meat and walked over to the water hose.

"You'd better not," Jasmine threatened, as she and Evelyn watched in disbelief.

Malone did something he'd seen his father do a million times. He rinsed the meat, kissed it up to God, and threw it back on the grill. He took the tray from Evelyn and dumped all the pieces of meat back on the grill and threw them one over the other until they could no longer tell which had been on the ground.

The girls hollered, dancing around the grill, laughing.

Malone laughed so hard, a stitch cramped his side.

Lee knocked on the glass, just like at work, and they sobered up one at a time. They'd become so used to him giving orders, they all paid attention. He walked off toward the bathroom.

Evelyn moved away from the grill and held her stomach, letting the sun caress her face. Jasmine joined her.

"Is it time to hang this up?" Evelyn asked. "We could have lost our jobs. We could have lost everything."

"One mistake doesn't make us failures," Jasmine said.

"But you—"

"I know. Nearly screwed it up for everybody. Didn't mean for her to get hurt."

"Yeah, well." Evelyn sat down on a lounge chair, her hands shoved between her knees. "There's going to be a big announcement next week. Have you heard anything?"

Jasmine shook her head no. "Not a word."

"I know you don't want to hear this." Evelyn sounded a lot like the woman she'd been when they'd graduated from college ten years ago. "But *Atlanta Live* was Ross's idea. He's been dead ten years. Why are we still trying to make this work?"

Malone stopped slathering sauce on the steak and cut down the heat. "You want to quit?" He sat in the chair beside Evelyn. "Is that what you're saying?"

"No, but I didn't want trouble either."

"Afraid of Mommy and Daddy?" Jasmine asked real low.

Everybody had an Achilles' heel, and that was Evelyn's.

"That's right, Jasmine. I happen to have people to answer to."

"What's that supposed to mean?"

Malone knew Jasmine was sensitive about her mother's poverty and never knowing her father. Evelyn did also, and although she'd never gone there, he wondered if she, too, had crossed the invisible line.

"It means somebody out there feels the repercussions of my actions. Or actions I condone."

"You don't control me. So you're off the hook."

Jasmine tried to pass Evelyn, but to Malone's surprise, Evelyn wouldn't let her. "I'm guilty by association. I can take the heat, but I won't be involved in a mess created because you want to be mean."

"I said I was sorry," Jasmine insisted, ready to get mad. "What more do you want?"

"Hey—" Malone stepped between them, but not before Evelyn, who was a head shorter than Jasmine, got right up under her nose. "For you to really mean it," she said.

He thought his cousin was going to explode, but tears glittered in her eyes. "I do."

The words diffused the anger, and although Malone wasn't sure Jasmine deserved a second chance, he gave in. "Let's put this to bed." He gathered them together, remembering a day ten years ago when they'd driven away from the cemetery after burying his best friend, Evelyn's fiancé and Jasmine's brother. They'd huddled against each other in the limousine bound in grief. Today was in strength.

"A long time ago, we were young and didn't have the power to influence a fly. Now we do and we said we'd empower our people so they wouldn't suffer like we did. We said we'd keep them straight when the rest of the world fed them crap stew. We're it. All they got. Are we gone walk away because it got a little tough?"

Slowly Evelyn's, then Jasmine's head shook against his shoulder. "Then we have to keep on bringing *Atlanta Live* to the public, giving them the real deal, no matter what happens next week. We can't ever give up."

"I'm in," Evelyn said.

"Me, too."

"Then let's make a pact. No more BS. We're doing this for a reason. We're the voice for people nobody listens to. If we keep it real, our work will take us places we never dreamed of."

They held each other, steaks simmering, the summer heat solidifying their friendship.

Eleven

The organist at Calvary Baptist Church was full of the Holy Spirit as he jammed Sunday morning.

Evelyn took the program from the church greeter, who then passed her off to a white-gloved usher, who escorted Evelyn to the first row, left of the altar to the seat traditionally saved for the pastor's wife.

She'd have a bird's-eye view of her husband-to-be.

She sat with her back erect, waiting for the head usher, a woman who telegraphed her disdain by the look on her face, to tap her on the shoulder and make it known she wasn't the pastor's wife, yet.

Then Evelyn would have to stand up in front of the entire church and be escorted to the rear because nobody would think of crushing their summer dresses in order to make room for her on a front pew.

The left hand of the white-gloved usher wouldn't touch her, but her hand would be stuck out in such a way that everyone would know Evelyn had just "got told." And that was worse than any words they could trade.

Her legs primly stuck together, hands folded demurely in her lap, Evelyn tried to slide her hips left, but a couple rushed down the pew and settled beside her.

"Mornin', sista," the woman said, breathless.

"Good morning."

Evelyn looked straight ahead, but from the corner of her eye she saw the woman's eyes shift sharply. In that quick glance, she pegged Evelyn and didn't waste any time in telling her husband exactly what she thought of the siddity, high-yellow princess sitting in the seat reserved for the pastor's wife, only he didn't have a wife, and that's why she was there to check him out so she could see if he was worth introducing to her sister.

The woman finally breathed and Evelyn looked at her and extended her hand. "I'm Evelyn Smith Howard, Pastor Albright's fiancée. And you are?"

"Oh, Lord." The woman's pecan-brown face turned ashen, and she leaned back against her overweight husband, who seemed to take an inordinate amount of joy in his wife's discomfort. "I didn't know you could hear me."

"I'm blind in one eye, but my hearing is just fine, praise God for that."

The woman's mouth fell open like an old cash register drawer.

Evelyn smelled the woman's syrup-sweetened breath when she leaned forward to see which eye was real, but Evelyn fluttered her eyelids.

Much to her relief, the prayer and praise quintet took the floor to start devotional, and the woman had to turn away.

Carvel ran service like a military officer did boot camp. He was in complete control of every facet from the recognition of visitors, to how long the choir could get happy, to the moment he stood at the pulpit and delivered a soul-stirring message.

Evelyn studied her man, warmed by the choir's praise-filled song, ready to hear a godly message. Carvel usually sought reassurance in her smile, so she curved her apricot-painted lips and waited. She watched him closely and her mind wandered.

For a preacher, Carvel sure could kiss. With her, a peck on the cheek wasn't his style. The moment they'd gotten engaged, he'd insisted on a full kiss on the lips. And always before they left each other's personal space.

At the podium, he adjusted his Bible and the pages of his sermon, and Evelyn waited expectantly for his acknowledgement.

None came.

"Church," he began, his bass voice singling out each person, yet drawing them all into a collective fold. "I come to you today, because the Lord has placed it upon my heart to forgo the teaching of the *Ten Commandments of Living in an Unsaved World* to teach another lesson.

"You know how I am," he said, and earned a few agreeing laughs. "When I start a series, I hate to deviate. But I contend there's a higher power than me at work here." The tone of his voice increased. "I contend that through my own self-aggrandizement, I was prepared to complete this series so we could move on to the other blessed work the Father has bestowed upon me to deliver this June. But—" Carvel wagged his finger toward the ceiling. "But God—" He grabbed the podium and shook his head.

"We-e-e-l-l," Deacon Kirk said, helping the pastor he'd served since Carvel had been ordained.

"The Lord stepped in and told me to teach today. So, I'm here in a capacity not only as a messenger from the Lord God Almighty, but as the son of the son of the son of the son of the son—you get where I'm going?" he asked, his voice building. "As the son of God, I come to you today as an instructor of the Word, and to God be the Glory, what a message it is!"

"Take your time!" Deacon Kirk hopped up this time, waving his hand as the crowd applauded. He hiked up his pants and sat down.

Evelyn's smile slipped. Carvel looked at her. Her lips trembled, but she lifted her head a little more as she'd seen her mother do thousands of times, and gave Carvel his nod.

There was no reciprocity. Not even in his eyes.

"Open your Bibles, with me, please. Today's sermon is *The Judas in All of Us. The Judas in All of Us. The Judas in All of Us,*" he repeated. "We fall down, but we get up . . ." he began to sing.

Evelyn couldn't join in. The Judas in all of us? What was he talking about? Was he saying that she'd betrayed Lindsey? Or that somehow she'd betrayed him or herself? Why hadn't he looked at her?

Evelyn's heart raced so quickly she had to fan herself to keep from perspiring. This wasn't at all what she had expected. Although they hadn't talked about the incident, she'd just assumed Carvel was on her side. What if he wasn't?

Here she sat in the front row of his church, with everyone's eyes on the back of her head. *They'll know if I falter, and they'll feel my guilt. Be still, be still, be still,* she told herself as she had a thousand times as a child. *This will end soon.*

Carvel's richly toned voice faded and he said a brief prayer to let the Lord's words come forth so that His people would be blessed.

Evelyn lifted her head and then straightened her spine another inch. It was hard to topple a child of Christ when He was your anchor.

"Family," Pastor Albright began, "I know that Jesus walks among us every day of our lives. From the time we open our eyes in the morning," he said conversationally, "to the time we close them in the midnight hour. I know because he's saved me more than once in my lifetime."

He grabbed the hand microphone. "How many times have we nearly walked—" He stepped away from the podium. "Or run or hopped—" Tall as Carvel was, he hopped like a child. To see him decked out in his black robe hopping was almost comical, but to Evelyn it felt as if a lid were covering her and Carvel's feet were stamping it shut.

"Or skipped into some sort of peril? How many times have we perched on the edge of indignity, stupidity, or embarrassment, only to be snatched back, caught up," he yelled and glared at her, "in the mighty hand of the Father?"

Evelyn withdrew into herself until she couldn't hear Carvel's voice. Here she was safe. In this quiet place. She stayed there until Carvel's raised voice shook loose the cocoon she'd burrowed into.

"How many times have we invited hell?" He paused and returned to the podium. "That's right, hell, right into our homes, and been delivered by our Lord and Savior Jesus Christ?"

He peered out over the congregation and his eyes rested last on Evelyn before turning to his deacons. "Mmm? Y'all don't hear me. It's okay if you don't shout today. I've got God on my side! Help me out, Deacon Kirk. How many times have we reached out to another and been betrayed?"

The deacon obediently stood and crossed his arms, giving his pastor an affirmative nod. "Take your time, son."

Carvel wiped the left side of his head with his handkerchief.

"Who's told a secret to someone, only to have it come back and not only slap you, but knock you down? Who," he breathed, "who told a friend about a job, only to have them go out and get it before you? Who shared a little pillow talk with your husband or wife, girlfriend or boyfriend, to have it pop up at the wrong time?"

He dared someone to answer.

"Who called a friend on the phone, only to have their business picked apart by people across the world?"

Each gasp Evelyn heard strung together like the sound of an eraser on a chalkboard. The gunshot went off in her head again.

"Tell it, pastor."

"Tell the truth."

Amidst the laughing, clapping, and affirmations, Evelyn heard, "*Tell her.*"

This was indeed intended for her.

"Go with me for a minute, church. I can just see you on your job, going into the break room, making sure your lunch sack is labeled with your name prominently displayed so nobody mistakenly takes your turkey and cheese sandwich with salad dressing and not mayonnaise, your Coca-cola, and your bag of chips."

The congregation laughed. "Uh-huh, I can see you bending down and stuffing your bag behind everybody else's, and while you're straightening the other bags out, two people walk in and they don't see you, but you hear the words you told your best friend in the strictest confidence come back and slap you down. Judas!"

He looked around. "I see you telling your best friend how much you like some man or woman and next thing you know, they're dating. Judas!"

His voice gathered steam. "I see you trying to save your hard-earned money to buy a house and as soon as you put a bid on it, your cousin's bid is higher and he gets it and you don't. Judas!

"Uh-huh, I see you coming to church, doing the right thing and praying to God to forgive your sins, only to have church folk talk about you behind your back and, some so bold, in your face. Judas!"

The church erupted with people laughing and clapping. Many were on their feet, shouting "Judas" with the pastor.

Evelyn's hand was over her mouth. The fat lady to her left elbowed Evelyn when she fell on her husband in a fit of laughter.

"Who hasn't had their confidence betrayed or their trust shattered by someone close to you?"

Hands went up all around the church. But Pastor Albright wasn't satisfied. "If you can honestly sit here and say you haven't, just keep on living. The devil is hard at work. You keep on living and you'll be betrayed by a husband, wife, cousin, girlfriend, boyfriend, whoever," he yelled. "They'll lie straight in your face and say they didn't betray you. Judas," he said, shaking his head.

"The Bible tells us how our darling Jesus was betrayed by Judas. That the Lord asked him three times, 'Are you going to betray me?' although He knew. *He knew!* And the Lord died upon the cross for that sin and *all* of our sins.

"Is there a Judas living in your midst? *Are you Judas?* You can act as sanctified and holy as you want, but many of us will betray or have betrayed our brethren.

"Change your life. Get off that false pedestal of sanctification!

Stop hiding behind your holiness! Stop saying you're helping in the name of Jesus, and admit your sins so you can enter into the Kingdom with a clean heart. It's time. Right where you are." He directed the musicians to lower the music.

"Right where you are, whisper a prayer of forgiveness. God is waiting. His arms open wide. *You can get back up again,*" he sang.

The music swelled as the musicians played Donnie McClurkin's "Get back up Again." "The doors of the church are open."

The congregation stood. Evelyn rose too, and swallowed the lump in her throat, the choir a blur because of the tears in her eyes.

She would not shed one.

Carvel walked down the stairs on her side of the church and Evelyn wondered, was he her Judas?

Twelve

At work Monday afternoon, Malone sailed in, rejuvenated from one night of peaceful sleep. He could have replaced Rena after Saturday's mess, but yesterday had slowly slipped from his hands, like a football covered with six-A.M. dew.

Whistling, he entered his office and started leafing through his messages. His boys, Zachary Tyson and Sash Bidwell, had left two messages each. They must have really wanted something.

Interview requests rounded out the next four. He dropped them into the garbage. Enough talking about old shit. The last one stopped him. His fingers trembled and his sight blurred.

The light slip of paper floated to his desk and skidded across the slippery surface.

Quinn Mourning, defensive coach of the Atlanta Falcons, had called.

Malone's blood pumped quickly through his veins and his mouth dried. What did he want?

The preprogrammed radio clicked on and Malone moved his shoulders to DMX.

Maybe the Falcons wanted to talk a comeback. Training camp had already begun, but maybe they saw what he'd seen. Their defense was weak. They needed a veteran in there to raise the bar for the young boys. He might not have the speed of the recruits, but he was football smart and that went a long way, especially now when some of the guys were more worried about endorsements rather than the game.

That had to be what they wanted, he thought, flexing the knee that had halted his career. No pain at all.

Dancing around his office, Malone noticed how smoothly he moved to the rap mix. *Dr. Dre is bad. I ain't bad myself.*

He slapped the message on his organizer and positioned it precisely in the center. He wouldn't call back today. Tomorrow would be soon enough.

His door opened and Malone grabbed Ms. Coretta's hand and waist and danced with the older woman. He gave her a sound kiss on the cheek.

She didn't say anything; just let herself be led around Malone's office. "When you gone marry me?" he asked her.

"Three thousand and one. Meeting, Lee's office, ten minutes."

"Do you love me, Ms. Coretta?"

"Yes, right after Payne, but before Ingram."

He stepped back, still holding her hand. "I finally beat out the Cockatoo."

"Boy, dance me back to the door so I can deliver these messages."

She walked out and Malone grinned. Ms. Coretta's ears were bright red. She needed a little love in her life.

Evelyn stuck her head in. "Hey."

"Hey," he greeted her. "What's up?"

"You know what this meeting's about?"

"The great unflappable princess worried about something?"

Evelyn looked around his office, as if her eyes were recording everything. Just when he thought he'd baited her, a smile spread across her face. "No, you?"

"Naw. You seen J yet?"

Evelyn shook her head. "You did a good thing Saturday. I'm sorry Carvel had to leave early."

It occurred to Malone that Carvel was rarely around for their get-togethers. He'd wanted to ask Evelyn how her man had reacted to the call, but there'd never been a good time. "He'd have ruined the fun if he'd stayed. He's so full of himself, I don't see how you fit in the car with his big-ass head."

Her grin grew wider. "You're not talking, Mr. bad girlfriend picker. Was she going to sell Lonzo's CDs or keep them in her private collection?"

Malone chuckled. "You got me there. Really, did he say anything about any of that?" Personally, Malone was tired of the entire subject. He'd done more talking in the past week than he had all last year.

"Not directly," Evelyn said, her usual evasive self.

He caught her eye as he was turning, and awareness shot up his body. Evelyn was scared. He grabbed her hands. At first she just held his until he shook them.

"What happened?"

She started to shake her head, but Malone wouldn't stand for secrets. He knew Evelyn well. Like brother and sister. He knew her now better than when they were in college.

For a minute Malone wished they were back in school where she had blossomed from beneath her parents' overbearing suffocation. For a minute he'd thought she'd made a clean getaway, but then she'd gotten engaged to the stuck-up preacher.

"We're having an early dinner. We'll talk about it then."

Malone saw where her carefully constructed response was going. That was Evelyn. Queen of the sound bite. "Yeah, you do that."

The phone beeped and Malone headed for the door. "That's Ms. Coretta's two-minute warning. We'd better head over and let these mo-fo's know who's runnin' thangs."

Evelyn fell into step beside him. "That's us, right?"

Malone grinned. "You know it."

Thirteen

Outside the boardroom, Lee stopped Malone and Evelyn. "The meeting's in here today."

Evelyn noticed his strained expression right before she did the drawn blinds in the room. "What's going on? Where's Jasmine?"

Lee waved down her concern. "She's inside."

"Let's see what's going on before we get upset," Malone said as he and Lee communicated in an unspoken language of raised brows and knowing looks.

Lee stepped back so she could enter. Tension greeted them.

Will Sharpe and several other people sat at the end of the table. Evelyn hid her surprise that one of the men was black. She pegged them for police or attorneys. At the end of the table, three chairs from the nearest person, sat Jasmine.

Evelyn's stomach jumped and she carefully took in a slow breath. "Good morning. I apologize for having kept you waiting."

"Not at all," Lee said in his easy manner. "Once you and Malone get settled, we'll start right away. Help yourselves to coffee and doughnuts."

Evelyn took the seat next to Jasmine. Malone sat next to Lee, who laid his hands flat on the cherry wood. "Now that everyone's here, I'll turn the floor over to Mr. Sharpe."

Heads swung in the president's direction.

"Good morning, one and all. The past two weeks have been tough. We made a name for ourselves because of 'the call.' Gained a lot of attention. Some good, but we also gained enemies. After much discussion and review with my attorneys, I've decided to sell Sharpe Enterprises to Jones Enterprises and Communications, Incorporated.

"Let me introduce you to some of the key players. Harris Bolden is VP of Communications. Cash Black is the station manager and a producer, and Laurie Quintero his right-hand consultant. I know this announcement took you all by surprise, but believe me, it's time for me to let you spread your wings."

Lee's face said it all. This wasn't voluntary. The three people that sat across from them had saved Will's butt, but from what?

Laurie sat back in her chair, folded her hands, and crossed her legs. Everything about her said she wouldn't be easily intimidated. When Laurie turned her blue eyes on Malone, Evelyn could feel heat wafting off Jasmine. This wasn't going to be a Miss Anne and Kizzy type of relationship at all.

Jasmine sat forward. "Will, you owe us a better explanation than that your advisers told you to sell. And," she emphasized. "You owe that to us in private."

"Jasmine, we came to a quiet settlement with the Kane family."

"They sued?" Evelyn asked, incredulous.

"Not exactly. In my experience, if there's money on the table, people don't leave it there." Will shrugged. "The insurance paid, but I can't afford another hit like that. The other factors are that I'm ready to retire and the money the Jones people offered wasn't something I could walk away from.

"*Atlanta Live* is about to be big. Bigger than I could make it on my own. For the first time ever, the show was number one in the region. Jones wants to take *Atlanta Live* places I can't." Will rose, looking every one of his sixty-eight years. The other men stood too. "If you have any questions after you've talked, come by my office."

Lee stayed stubbornly in his seat.

"The deal is done," Laurie said, once the door closed. "This meeting is a mere formality."

"Wasn't talkin' to you," Jasmine snapped.

"But I'm talking to you! You're going to be a problem, we know that, Jasmine," Laurie said pointedly. "But right now you have the luxury of having public sentiment on your side. However, let's understand where we all stand. You're not Star Jones. I don't think Simon and Schuster is going to hammer down your door with a book deal. Nor will you have Jones's TV show, or her endorsements, or her money."

Evelyn couldn't believe Bolden and Black were letting Laurie get away with this level of disrespect.

"You're good—" Laurie told Jasmine.

"It's about damn time somebody recognized that."

"But not that good." Laurie's smile faded, and Jasmine realized she'd been set up. "With a lot of work on your part, and a lot of help on my part, you could get close, damn close to having everything and more."

"Who says I want to work with you? Any of you?"

"Where are you going to go?" Harris Bolden said. For a VP, he was quieter than any Evelyn had ever met. "Ms. Winbury, right now you're more of a liability than an asset, but I've seen worse. Laurie, in her blunt way, is right. We can put you on the map."

"Where, in Poland?"

Bolden sat back. "I thought you were smarter than that. Innuendo-based race comments are ignorant. I make people famous. I don't care if they're orange." He waved his hands. "You can come on board, or we can execute the papers my people found when they audited the personnel files."

Only Evelyn saw Jasmine's hands shake. "We're in this together," Malone told them.

"I admire your loyalty, Mr. Malone, but your contracts are separate. One doesn't fall under the same umbrella as the other. The last thing we want to do is break up a successful team. But if you're let go, you wouldn't be able to work in broadcasting for a year."

"My lawyers could beat that," Malone stated matter-of-factly.

Bolden nodded. "True. But it's not worth it. We want to work with all of you, Mr. Malone. Ms. Smith Howard, it's a pleasure to meet you."

Evelyn didn't know about Malone, but she was uncomfortable with the whole arrangement. And Lee had been silent since they'd walked in.

"Mr. Bolden," Evelyn said, "we're sticking together. Jasmine didn't cry 'nuclear bomb' in a subway station full of people, and she didn't pull the trigger on the gun Lindsey Kane used to injure herself. So get it out of your heads that we're one of three and not a whole."

Evelyn wished her voice were louder, but now wasn't the time to worry. She made sure it was firm. "If this is how you're planning to treat us, I'll notify my attorney, John Steinhart of Steinhart, Carlisle and Drake."

Bolden's eyebrows twitched and Evelyn knew she had their attention. "Sir, we might not beat this immediately, but it'll be interesting watching you explain why you bought a minority-owned company and then fired their top employees."

Bolden's eyes never left Evelyn's, but she saw the shift from power to respect.

"Please accept my apology. I should have approached this situation differently. We're excited to become part of this team, and we want to support your success any way we can."

Bolden stood and extended his hand.

Malone got up, hulking, all six-four of him. He didn't move. Didn't blink.

Bolden shot Cash, then Lee an unsure look. "Mr. Malone," he said, "we'd be honored to work with you."

Initially, Evelyn thought Malone's posture reeked of rebellion, so he surprised her when he accepted the man's hand. "Thank you. Look forward to working with you, too."

Malone gave Cash a soul brother's welcome. When he finally took Laurie's hand, her dimples deepened.

Evelyn greeted everyone, too. At the moment she didn't see any other option.

"When is this sale effective?" Malone took his seat and quieted Jasmine's rocking knee.

"The deal is being finalized this week," Bolden said.

"I've never heard of Jones Enterprises and Communications, Incorporated," he finished, and sucked through his teeth. "Did you just rise from the dust?"

"Good question," Bolden said. "Jones began acquiring talk shows back in the eighties. We were a pretty low-key, regional enterprise, before we hit big with Jenkins and Rooster, in the early nineties."

"That was in the DC, Baltimore market," Malone supplied, and earned a withering scowl from Jasmine that he ignored.

Bolden's eyes lit up. "Correct. After we acquired them, we became more aggressive, and to date we have twenty-five stations across the West Coast. We're not trying to be CBS, or any of the corporations that own radio stations just to cross-promote their other business endeavors. We want to blow the lid off talk radio and we think with a little help, you three have what it takes."

"Why?"

"Beg your pardon, Ms. Smith Howard?"

Evelyn's head snapped up. "Call me Evelyn. Why do you think we can do any more than we've already done?"

"Because you have what it takes to handle any situation. You were so compassionate to Lindsey. Your nurturing personality reached out to her, and the public heard your sincerity. People eat that up."

"That isn't the way I want the world to remember me. I wanted to help Lindsey and women like her understand there are options out there." Evelyn almost didn't trust his sincere smile.

"We believe you, Evelyn," he said. "We believe in Safe Haven also."

"How do you know about my foundation?"

Cash quieted Bolden. "Don't be alarmed," he said. "We're interested in supporting you in any way possible."

"No. No!" Evelyn couldn't believe she'd raised her voice, but nobody was going to use her. "Safe Haven has nothing to do with WKKY. Nothing to do with *Atlanta Live*. If you think it's a package, forget about me."

"Of course we'll respect your wishes." Cash sat forward and raised his hand. "I swear."

Evelyn felt herself shaking. "Okay." She looked at Malone. "I'm sorry."

"Baby, speak your mind."

"Evelyn, your passion is what makes you so loved by the public. Malone, women and men alike listen to you. You took charge during the tragedy and everyone loves a hero.

"Jasmine, this looks bad for you, but you represent the other side. The side of man everyone has, but hates to acknowledge. Last week's incident wasn't your fault."

There was a shift in the silence. Where there'd been anger was now caution. "Then why am I being blamed?"

"The world needed a scapegoat. You were convenient."

"I won't be that anymore."

"That's where Laurie comes in. We'd like to see a big transformation. She will help you change your image. You can be on top in this business."

"I don't like Laurie."

"I don't like you either," Laurie cut in, attitude neck deep. "But that won't stop me from collecting my check. If you want to have staying power in this business and make a name for yourself, you'll do it with my guidance or you'll be a has-been"—she snapped her fingers one crisp time—"like that."

Evelyn knew Jasmine didn't like people telling her what to do under any circumstances, but a white woman to boot? They should have gone ahead and fired her.

"Excuse me," Evelyn said, "I'm not sure Laurie can help Dr. Jasmine, because there isn't anything wrong with her. The call was something we didn't expect. What are you going to do to ensure we don't get calls like that again?"

"Another good question," Bolden said. "You'll have a screener, producer, seven-second delay, sound engineers, and topics for each program. State-of-the-art computer system and test groups to show which topics are hot."

Laurie smiled at Evelyn. "I've worked with the best and I'm here as a favor to Harris and Cash. I'll offer suggestions to you two." She looked at Jasmine. "If you work with me, you'll land on your feet. You keep your attitude and you're out on your butt."

"Fine," Jasmine said unexpectedly. "We need more money."

"Excuse me?" Laurie said.

"For all this image changing, training, radio time—whatever, we need a raise."

The VP looked at them. "Ten percent is what we're prepared to offer."

Malone pulled his beeper from his waist. "Twenty-five is more to my liking. Nonnegotiable. And what about vacation that's already been scheduled?"

"Vacation has been suspended for the next three months. All other time will roll over."

"No deal," Malone said. "I've already made plans with my son. I get him two weeks in the summer, and I intend to keep our plans as they are."

"We can work something out," Cash said to Malone. "But we need your presence so we can keep the momentum. Maybe a couple long weekends."

"No deal."

"We could arrange for the company cabin for you and your son and he can invite some of his friends. We'll even throw in chaperones," he offered when Malone remained silent. "If you give me a chance, Malone, we'll do our best to honor your arrangements."

"I need a stronger commitment than that."

Bolden started to jump in but Cash raised his hand. "One week and then two long weekends before Labor Day."

Malone finally agreed.

"The three of us stay together," Evelyn told them.

Laurie's mouth twisted into a smirk and she played with her nails.

"Twenty percent increase in pay," Bolden offered, still negotiating, "with no permanent assurance on staffing. We can't afford too many of these liabilities."

Lee sat forgotten at the end of the table. His bald head seemed to leak oil like a busted water hose.

"We want Lee," Malone said.

Lee's eyes were closed as he pulled his head up. He gave a silent nod to Malone.

"No problem," Bolden said.

Malone slid his chair back and Evelyn and Jasmine formed an informal huddle with their heads together.

No words were said, but the agreement was made. Malone squeezed their hands and Evelyn derived strength from his touch.

They turned back to the table. "We accept."

"Excellent," Bolden rejoiced.

"Glad you're coming aboard," Cash said, and shook all their hands. "Shall we adjourn to the restaurant across the street to celebrate?"

"Why?" Jasmine's eyes shined bright, no doubt from knowing she was keeping her job. "Why us?"

"That brings me to the best part." Cash came around the table. "Now that everybody's on board, we have some big news. Prepare to work long and hard for the next month. We're taking *Atlanta Live* into syndication in four weeks."

Fourteen

The Atlanta Falcons Complex seemed larger than Malone remembered.

Funny how a few hundred days could change a man's perspective. He'd blotted out much about the Suwanee facility, having retired those memories of coming out here every day for nearly ten years along with his career. He'd been proud to be a Falcon, even in the losing years. Especially when players were traded or when the coach had gotten sick. Malone had been a leader on the team, a veteran men respected. But when his dislocated knee and subsequent damage had proved he was not invincible, with it snapped the fragile cord of his ego.

On the field he'd been crazy, thus his name maniac. But that last unceremonious, career-ending diagnosis in his doctor's office had reduced him to mere mortal. He hadn't realized until now how crushed he'd been not to have a say in how he'd leave the team and the game he loved.

As he drove through the winding complex, Malone knew this was his last shot at rewriting his final chapter in football history.

What he hadn't realized was how it felt to have a shot at that dream again. Familiar people at the complex made it real.

The welcoming smiles and the excited looks bolstered him, and he wanted to be there officially, worse than anything he'd ever wanted in life.

Malone sat before defensive coach Quinn Mourning and let the man study his day-old-health profile.

Mourning wasn't the kind of man that could be persuaded by the eager words of a player looking for a comeback. He'd looked men dead in the eyes that had just had their spines snapped, and told them they'd never play, much less walk again.

Mourning studied statistics. Whatever the doctors said, Mourning listened to.

Malone suddenly wished he'd taken better care of himself since his retirement two years ago. But he could get back in shape. He would if only to give himself one last stab at his youth.

Mourning looked over the assessment at Malone. "I haven't seen a better physical."

Malone's head snapped back in surprise. "Thank you, sir."

"For a man your age." Mourning's snake-eyed barometer registered Malone's dislike.

"What are you expecting—from a man my age?"

"When you were twenty-three you were at your best. At twenty-seven you were excellent until the knee. How's it feel?"

Malone smiled. He wouldn't get sucked into that false vortex. "How's it look on paper?"

"Better than good."

"Then it feels better than good."

Snake eyes caught him again. "I need a leader. Someone to line these men up and make them tough. They're in it for the money. Nothing more. They have no heart."

"And if I don't make it?"

"You don't play."

"What kind of assurance do I have you won't cut me?"

"None. This is one step better than a walk-on. You've been officially invited to practice with us. You'll have access to the trainers, and the complex. I'll get a weekly update from Salvatore, who'll be monitoring your progress. This is your shot, if you're interested."

Malone nodded, thrilled that even in the precarious position of having to prove himself, he was miles ahead of many men. "How soon will I know?"

"Four weeks—give or take a few days. In the interim, practice, train with Salvatore, the complex is open to you. If you make the cut—"

"I make the team."

"You'd have to give up that radio thing."

Malone didn't even blink. "I'll think about it."

Mourning nodded. "Four weeks then."

Malone didn't know which way to turn once he left the Falcons' office. Atlanta traffic was crazy, too busy even to attempt at rush hour.

He stopped off at Jeffrey's, a favorite sports bar and grill that catered to the players.

Before he could order food, his cell phone was ringing. It was Jasmine. He let it roll to voice mail.

Malone waited for the waitress to leave his food. She tried to get his attention by squeezing between him and the chair behind him. Her breasts ended up practically around his neck. When his phone rang again, he picked it up. "Yo?"

"Where are you?" Jasmine asked.

"Why? What's up?"

"Just wanted to hang. I'll meet you."

"Naw," he told Jasmine. The waitress stood against the bar, posing. She was young, too young, and he was glad he knew the difference. "Call me tonight. We'll talk then."

Fifteen

Evelyn left work floating on a cloud. Out of the rubble of this catastrophe, a rose. How could something so good come from something so bad?

God was rewarding them for saving Lindsey's and her baby's lives. He'd spared them all, even Jasmine.

Evelyn said a silent prayer of thanks as she climbed into her BMW coupe and pointed it in the direction of Carvel's church. They were redeemed. Carvel had to know that God didn't hold them responsible for what'd happened. He'd rewarded them!

She picked up her cell phone and dialed his office. "Hello, Carvel Albright, please."

"I beg your pardon?"

Evelyn tensed. "Good afternoon, Deaconess Jamison, this is Evelyn Smith Howard. May I speak to Carvel?" An old gospel song, "Lord Help Me to Hold Out," popped into Evelyn's head and she held her breath.

"I know who this is," the deaconess snapped back, unmoved by Evelyn's announcement. "But the pastor is busy. I don't know when he can call you back. Good-bye."

"Just a minute! Deaconess, I'm sure he'll make himself available if you'd just tell him it's me."

Evelyn rested her elbow on the steering wheel, mad that she hadn't avoided getting stuck behind a truck making a beer drop.

She flipped down her signal, but that only made drivers inch closer together. Sometimes she hated Atlanta traffic.

Help me, Jesus. "We have lunch plans and I wanted—"

"Your private life with the pastor is not my business. You'd do well to remember that. I don't want to hear about y'all's goings-on," the woman said in one long stream of words. "He's in a meeting and when he gets out, I won't be here. So call after five o'clock, after folk with church business have been able to get through. Good day, Sister Smith Howard."

Evelyn held the phone away from her ear and stared at it. What was *her* problem?

Evelyn tried to search for an excuse for the woman's rude behavior, but could only see jealousy and anger. She'd bet a dollar the deaconess would only act worse when she and Carvel married.

Carvel would just have to fire her. Evelyn had never seen such outrageous behavior of church employees until she'd become intimate with the women of Calvary. They ran roughshod over Carvel and he didn't even blink. Evelyn was her mother's child and she'd been raised around women who were always trying to catch her father's eye.

Deaconess Jamison might have lost her husband last year, but she was going to lose her job if she didn't get her act together.

Evelyn would see to that as soon as she and Carvel got married.

Carvel was well aware of the friction, but kept telling Evelyn to be patient. That having an outsider come in and sweep the church ladies' young bachelor off his feet and away from their daughters would take some getting used to. But Evelyn wasn't buying that anymore. She cradled the phone thoughtfully. Deaconess Jamison didn't like her, and Evelyn was tired of her nasty attitude.

She dialed Carvel's cell phone. After the second ring, he picked up. "Pastor Albright."

"Carvel, it's me."

"Hey, me. How's it going?"

"You didn't call today."

"I've been extra busy. I miss you."

Evelyn couldn't believe the intimately delivered words.

"That's funny. I thought you were angry with me."

"Why?"

"After Sunday's service, I thought we'd better talk. Why didn't you tell me you thought I betrayed Lindsey? Never mind that I didn't."

"Evelyn, I wasn't preaching specifically to you. If you feel something applied, then I've done my job as a minister. I can't water down the gospel for the sake of someone's feelings."

"I wasn't asking you to do that. But everything was different Sunday. Whether you recognize it or not, you hurt me."

"I didn't mean to."

"No?"

"No, never."

Evelyn wanted them to be all right. Although her feelings were still bruised, she moved on.

"We still meeting for dinner?" he asked.

Her smile faded. "I thought we were going to lunch. I'm five minutes away."

"Oh, baby. Didn't Deaconess Jamison tell you? I can't. I have to take a conference call. Dr. Lowery is being considered for an honorary degree at Georgia Seminary and Theological Institute."

"Weren't they sued by a group of ministers for not granting honorary degrees to qualified African-American ministers?"

"Yes."

"Then this doesn't mean anything. They're just considering him because he's black and they want to fulfill the obligation of the court's decision."

"Still, it's an honor."

Evelyn eased into traffic and ignored the angry honk of the driver she cut off. "No, it's not. It's a payoff. But fine."

"That's my girl. I'm sorry, sweetie. Same bat time, same bat channel?"

She giggled. "We don't have to go to the Cajun Crab House. We could stay in and I could cook for you. Let the evening go where it may."

"Keep talking."

Evelyn proceeded slowly, excited at the prospect of having Carvel all to herself. "I'll pick up some Cornish hens with wild rice and vegetables and some chocolate cheese cake."

"All my favorites," he said, his voice low and seductive.

"I've got some Will Downing and Rachelle Ferrell I'd like to play for you," she said.

"Mood music, too?"

"Mmmm. You still with me?"

"What time again?" he said softly.

"Our reservations are for seven, but I want to see you sooner. How about five-thirty? I could stop and pick up some wine and maybe tomorrow we could go to the mall and look at the bridesmaid dresses I liked."

"Evelyn."

Evelyn replayed the conversation through her mind and wondered what she'd said wrong. Her stomach flipped as it used to when her father would say her name in that same tight way. She kept her voice light to appease his irritation. "Honey, we can make it an early night. I know you have the meeting with the church council in the morning."

"I'm surprised you remembered."

The statement sounded almost accusatory, but she decided not to take it that way. "Of course I remembered. What you do and where you are is important to me."

"Wine, Evelyn?"

So that was it. Early in their relationship, he'd expressed disapproval of the fact that occasionally she enjoyed a glass of wine. Years ago after she'd moved into a place of her own, she'd have a glass of wine after work, but since becoming engaged, she only indulged every once in a while.

"Carvel, a glass of wine isn't going to diminish your abilities as a minister." When he didn't say anything, she pressed on. "Honey, the wine will go great with the hens. Just one glass is all."

"If it's just one glass, do we really need it?"

Evelyn rolled her eyes and massaged her forehead. Sometimes she thought he was a better lawyer than minister. She was trying to set a mood, not make him walk a DUI line. "It was just an idea, Carvel. I know what your problem is."

"I have a problem?"

She could tell he was seriously annoyed now. "Yes, my darling man, you're not accustomed to being spoiled. Everyone wants to feed you soul food, and tell you their problems. And there's nothing wrong with that," she hurried on to say. "But you need to know what it's like to come home to a quiet neighborhood, a beautiful house, and an adorable wife."

He chuckled and her stomach muscles eased. "Don't think I like to eat everyone's food," he said. "Sometimes I have to be polite."

"This evening I planned for us, darling. You'll have fun, I promise."

"I'd love to. I really would."

Evelyn's stomach bottomed out. He sounded so much like her father just before he delivered bad news. She wanted to tell him about her day, her week, but Carvel was so busy, they hadn't had time to see each other, much less talk.

"I really had my heart set on the swordfish from the Cajun Crab House. Do you mind?"

The gasoline light flickered on and Evelyn pulled into a service station and cut off the engine. She was a block away, but there was no need to get there now.

Although her plans had fizzled, she tried to remain upbeat. They would at least be off church property and could discuss their wedding uninterrupted by the numerous pastors, deacons, and church members. Evelyn had seen her parents' marriage from childhood to the day she left her father's church, and she didn't want to become her mother. Evelyn planned to demand a fair share of her husband's time.

"I don't mind not staying in as long as I'm with you, and you alone."

"I promise," he said, a smile in his voice. "No surprise guests."

"Good, then I'll confirm our reservations for seven. Pick me up at six-thirty?"

He made a negative sound. "I have an early morning tomorrow. As soon as I leave you, I've got to come back here and review the budget for the church council."

So much for that. Evelyn caressed the Rachelle Ferrell CD and stacked Will Downing on top. "Fine," she said. "I'll meet you there."

"Evelyn?" Carvel's smooth voice had the power to peel the clothes from her body.

"Yes?"

"I'm not blind, sweetheart, and I'm not immune." She heard rustling and his voice filled her ear. He must have cuffed his hand around the mouthpiece. "I can't wait to have you and touch you and . . ."

"And?" she said. She pressed her hand against her center.

"Taste you."

A thrill of pleasure snaked up her spine. She opened her mouth and exhaled. Evelyn didn't want to beg. Didn't want to have to ask him when, but her body was running the show. "When, Carvel?"

"Soon, baby. Do you think I don't know what it's like to yearn for something you can't have?"

"I'm not sure," she said softly. "I can't tell how much you're attracted to me when you constantly put me off."

"Evelyn," he admonished gently, "you are the sexiest"—he exhaled—"God, forgive me for saying these words in Your house—woman I've ever met. I'm so glad we're together and when we get married, it's on."

She sat up in her bucket seat. "Oh, is it?"

"Definitely. Every night in the bedroom, in the bathroom, in the kitchen, and in the dining room. I hope to God we have a big house because we'll christen each room. You hear me?"

His bass caressed the path her hand took, and her body leaped in response.

"I'll burst if it doesn't happen soon," she said. "You're going to have to peel little pieces of me off the ceiling."

He chuckled and the crest she was riding moved higher.

"We're stronger than the flesh. We can hold out a little longer," he said. "Speaking of which, I'd better go. I've got to take care of something before I can concentrate on my work. See you later?"

"Take care of what, Carvel?" she goaded, pushing him to reveal himself. He groaned, to her immense satisfaction.

"Don't do this to me, woman. Let me off this phone. I need some cold water, some cold air—something. Girl, if I let you—" His harsh breathing filled her ear. "Tell me you love me and let me off this phone."

An image of Carvel between her legs, his strong dark body driving into her, catapulted Evelyn to the edge. "If I say it," she whispered, feeling totally naughty, "something will happen. I want it to happen with you."

He groaned again. "Put your hands on the steering wheel."

Evelyn hated to release the apex of her body, but Carvel was right. They couldn't do this. He was inside the church!

Guilt as powerful as a raging wind consumed her and she hung her head. What was she thinking? Sins of the flesh had gotten her in trouble before, and now she was tempting Carvel to join her?

"You're right." She gripped the wheel until her hands hurt.

"Sweetheart, when it happens, it'll be for real." He didn't speak for a while as they mutually struggled for control. "You okay?"

No, she thought. "Yes."

Sixteen

Every time Jasmine watched *Inside Sports*, the reminder of Malone's interview returned as an uncomfortable flashback. So she flipped over to ESPN while Evelyn leafed through a black bridal magazine, taking notes.

"I like this one," Evelyn would murmur occasionally, her eyes dreamy.

Jasmine sat up on her couch and studied her friend.

"How did dinner go with Carvel?"

"Good," Evelyn said, but Jasmine knew better.

Unbeknownst to Evelyn or Carvel, she'd been seated on the slightly upper level of the Cajun Crab House. The restaurant had been remodeled to fit more customers, but really there wasn't more space, just the illusion of it.

Jasmine hadn't intended to listen in, but she'd been seated and had already ordered when she'd recognized their voices. If she'd shown her face then, Carvel would have accused her of interfering, which she'd never do for someone she cared so little for. "So, what did the minister have to say?"

"Soon," Evelyn responded with none of her previous night's passion. "He's got a lot on his calendar, so we still have to sit down and set a date we can both live with. You want to see a movie later?"

Jasmine watched Evelyn intently. She'd never once raised her head or seemed the slightest bit uncomfortable telling the series of half-truths.

"I don't know. I need to work out. Put that stupid book down. All you're doing is depressing yourself."

"I'm not depressed. There's a lot to choose from. As soon as I decide I like something, I see something else. I like that," she murmured, staring at the page.

"When's the date? That's what I want to know."

An unnatural groan interrupted their conversation and a shocking crash made them jump.

They scrambled over each other, heading to the dining room.

Shocked, they stopped in the doorway. A four-foot piece of white drywall lay fractured on the dining room table.

Jasmine stared at the wet gaping hole in the ceiling, not knowing what to do.

"Cut off the water, Jasmine. It's ruining everything!"

"Where would that be?" She ran to the kitchen, then upstairs to the bathroom.

"I don't know. By the toilets or in the laundry room." Evelyn grabbed towels from the laundry room on the main level. "Throw down more towels. Goodness, there's water everywhere."

Jasmine came in a minute later. "Water's off."

"Don't panic." Evelyn acted as if they were talking about mowing the lawn. "We have to call somebody."

"I know, but who?"

"A plumber." A stream of water ran off the table and ended in persistent drips. "I'll get buckets and you get the phone book."

The ceiling looked awful. And expensive. "Go!" she said, and they set off in two different directions.

Not knowing where to start, Jasmine called Ricky, her ex-realtor, a man who hated her guts. She didn't bother identifying herself. "My dining room ceiling crashed in."

"Sounds like a leak, *Ms. Winbury.*"

"Why did you sell me a defective house?"

"You picked it! I told you the builder had a questionable reputation, but you didn't listen." His muffled voice filled her ear. "All you cared about was the address and screwing me over. Now you're asking why you got stuck with a lemon? I'm surprised it didn't fall down long ago."

"Fine. Where's the builder? I'll go after him."

"He died two days ago. His company was bankrupt."

"This isn't fair!"

"You were so busy trying to play me, you got played. I hope for your sake you bought good insurance; otherwise . . ."

Panic seized her chest and Jasmine almost doubled over.

She'd bought house insurance, but when her bills had gotten tight a couple of months ago, she'd let it lapse. Now she had a hole that she could fit a big foot in, and no way to pay for it.

"Ms. Winbury," Ricky said, sounding official and cold. "I told you at the time of closing to transfer from your renter's to a home-owner's insurance policy."

"I did, but I mistakenly let it lapse—"

"Oh well."

"Don't give me that crap. I know you can do something before the bathtub lands on my damn head!"

Evelyn positioned buckets and garbage cans as if they were precious vases.

"I suggest you call a plumber, have him fix the pipes, and then hire a drywall person to fix the ceiling. Don't call me again." The phone went dead in her ear.

"Who was that?"

"Ricky."

"The realtor?"

Jasmine stared at the phone and sighed. "Yeah. I know I shouldn't have slept with his brother."

Evelyn folded her arms. "We won't even go down that road again. What did he say?"

"Same thing you said. But there's hundreds of plumbers in the book. How am I supposed to know who's good?"

"Maybe you should call Malone."

"Good idea." She speed-dialed her cousin. "Hey. Where you at?"

"Suwanee. Why?"

"What are you doing up there?"

"Handlin' my business, nosy. Why?"

"My dining room ceiling fell in."

"Damn, that's messed up. You okay?"

"Yeah. Evelyn's here with me."

"I know the ice queen is in full control."

"He called you the ice queen," she told Evelyn, who rolled her eyes and continued stomping on towels to staunch the flow of water from getting to the hardwood floor. "Do you know anything about plumbing?"

"Not a damned thing except how to turn off the water."

"Thanks, genius."

"I know how to write a check."

"You can write one over here if you're feeling generous."

"No, thanks, I've got an ex-wife who gets all my cash nowadays, so you'd better get off with me and call somebody that can help you."

"Thanks for nothing," she said, half sarcastic.

"Don't hate a brotha who knows his only talent is football."

"You mean radio."

"Right. I'll let you go before the upstairs and the downstairs are the same thing. Call me later."

"All right, bye."

Jasmine grabbed the phone book and walked back to the den, where Evelyn joined her. "Malone wasn't a bit of help, was he?"

"None."

Evelyn's cell phone rang and the quizzical look on her face turned to a smile as she listened. She snapped the phone closed. "I've got to run. Jodi thinks she's found me a building."

"For your foundation?" Jasmine knew the answer and couldn't help the surge of anger. She needed Evelyn, and she was abandoning her. But what could she say to stop her?

Evelyn picked up her purse. "I hate to run, but this place was just listed. I've got to see it before it's gone. Will you be okay?"

"Don't have a choice, do I?"

Evelyn kissed her cheek. "Don't be that way, you spoiled brat. If you want, I'll spend the night again and we can plan how to redecorate the dining room." She walked to the front door. "You've got your home repair nest egg, right?"

Jasmine didn't want to tell her that had gone with the insurance money to pay bills months ago. "I got it covered. No problem."

"I'll call you when I'm done," Evelyn said, with a final wave and click of the front door.

Another chunk of ceiling hit the corner of the table and exploded into powder and chunks of white drywall. Raising the phone's receiver, Jasmine dialed the first name on the list and kept dialing until she found someone.

Two hours later Jasmine sat at Gulliver's Tavern waiting for E.J. He'd said he'd be there at six-thirty, but it was already a quarter to seven and she didn't want to spend her evening in this smelly bar.

Jasmine thought of her raise and wished she'd had it in her hand right now.

Evelyn and Malone hadn't blinked at the twenty percent pay increase, but to Jasmine it was a gold mine. The repairs for the plumbing cost close to a thousand dollars, and the guy who'd showed up at the door to repair the drywall had been Mexican and acted like he didn't understand English.

But they both understood the numbers he'd written on the piece of paper. Four hundred dollars. Even with her raise, she'd still be in the negative. Angry, Jasmine pushed at the watery drink she'd been served and got up.

Just then E.J. sauntered in. He grabbed a chair, turned it, and landed his chubby butt on it. "What's up, Dr. J? What's the good word?"

"Money."

His brows shot up. "Sounds serious. How much you need?"

"Fifteen hundred. That's it."

"Fifteen?" He worked the toothpick from the side of his mouth to the center as he glanced at his large gold watch.

Jasmine had never seen anything more obnoxious. "Yeah, fifteen. Why, is that too much?" Anxiety pressed in on her. If he was in the money-loaning business, what was up? "Were you just talkin' trash the last time I saw you?"

"Naw, baby." He chuckled. "Nothin' like that. I just don't deal with that small an amount. I start at five."

She jerked. "Thousand?"

"You making an announcement for a reason?" His face grew hard as he looked around.

"No." She reached out, but drew her hand back. "No, I just need fifteen hundred. I don't need five thousand dollars. That's all. I was surprised. You caught me off guard. But that's okay. I appreciate you meeting me."

She got up and E.J. patted her arm, urging her to sit down.

"Come on, Doc. We go way back and you always been cool people. This is how things is in the street. You can get fifteen hundred dollars most anywhere. Some of these storefront loan companies will give you that. That's chump change. But I give loans that can change people's lives. Just think of what you can do with that money. Take care of your most pressing matter, then pay off or catch up on a few bills. I know you got debt, girl. As fine as you dress? I know your Rich's credit card is blowed up, am I right?"

She didn't know whether to breathe or not. "Yes, but I—"

"All right then. You driving a sweet Benzo, sweet crib. Your place look like it should be on *MTV* cribs. You're about to get large as the queen of talk radio. Anyway, all's I'm saying is that you can use this cash any way you see fit and then next month you pay me a deuce on top of what I loaned you."

"That's it? You loan me five thousand and I pay you back five thousand, plus two hundred or two thousand?"

"Hundred, baby. I'm fair."

It sounded fair to her. She leaned into E.J. "What do I have to do?"

"Meet me outside. I'm driving the black Explorer."

She wrinkled her nose. "You? An Explorer?"

"My lady's ride. Mine's in for new tires." They let his embarrassment fade. "I got what you need in the car along with some paperwork. Got to keep things legit for the IRS. Know what I'm sayin'?"

She nodded and followed him outside where she signed the papers and took possession of the money. "Thanks, E.J. I'll get this right back to you."

"I know you will. Later."

Jasmine got in her car and felt as if she'd just survived a near tragedy.

Seventeen

The buildup to syndication moved like an approaching tropical storm. Days slipped into nights, and with the emergence of each new moon, Jasmine's mood darkened. She and Laurie fought like two female gorillas over the affection of one male. Neither would back down and whenever they got started, Evelyn took cover.

Evelyn withstood the harsh critiques from Cash and Laurie, secretly thrilled that the show finally had a definite direction. Through long hours and hard work, they were getting better. Cash's presence had raised the bar.

They weren't just dealing with everyday callers about everyday situations; somehow Cash added a spin, and that made radio interesting. Even Malone didn't seem to mind, but over the last couple of weeks, his mind had seemed a million miles away.

The pressure to say more, do more, be funnier became the focus, and Cash left no stone unturned in his efforts to make them the best.

However, Jasmine suffered most. Although the scrutiny was the same for all three, she swallowed it about as well as she would razor blades.

Right now, she and Laurie argued about a red shirt Jasmine wanted to wear and the yellow one Laurie had chosen. Their disagreement had stalled the entire photo shoot.

"I like the red," Jasmine said loudly, her temper reaching the end of her patience limit.

"The yellow has a bright disposition. It makes a better statement than the 'fuck you' red you're always trying to wear."

Laurie's blond hair swayed as she tried in vain to get Jasmine to look at her. "Image consultant here," Laurie shouted. "I know what I'm talking about." She turned to the room of photographer assistants, wardrobe personnel, hairstylists, lighting techs, and WKKY staff, her face red with rage.

Jasmine stormed over, yanked the shirt from Laurie's hand, held it above her head, and ripped it straight down the front.

Laurie's mouth fell open. "That cost two hundred eighty-five dollars!"

"Wonderful! Any other questions about the shirt I'll be wearing?" Jasmine polled the room as had Laurie. Everybody, including the photographer, shook their heads. "Now if Ms. Booster Club will leave me alone, we might get out of here."

"How long till you get dressed?" Lin, the Asian photographer's assistant, asked Jasmine. A quiet woman with understanding eyes, she threw the yellow shirt into the trash without a second glance.

Jasmine appeared to have run out of steam.

Thank God, Evelyn wanted to say, but didn't.

Jasmine breathed in, appearing to see everyone watching her for the first time. "Five minutes."

"I'll get you some wine. You go change now. You're fine. The red will look nice on you. Go on in," she said, walking with Jasmine toward the changing area.

"Matt." Lin called the photographer and had his instant attention. "She'll be ready in five."

Once the door closed on the dressing room, everyone in the room sighed and the hectic confusion began again.

"Ever think she'd be this angry?" Malone asked Evelyn.

She shook her head. "Guess that crazy streak runs in the family, huh, maniac?"

"You aren't funny, pretty little rich girl."

"Stop calling me that."

He shrugged. "Shoe fits." He tilted up a beer bottle and drained it.

"The last thing you need is beer."

"Gotta get drunk to sit around for hours, waiting to get your picture made. It's almost a prerequisite. This shit is too boring."

The manicurist came by and touched up Evelyn's fingernails, then moved on to a small group of models.

Evelyn slid off the director's chair to sit on a white cube next to Malone. "Think Lee's okay?"

"Yeah. He's all right."

Atlanta Live had been moved out of the Southside of Atlanta to brand-new offices in Buckhead. The past three weeks had been traumatic and exciting at the same time, and Lee's role in *Atlanta Live* had noticeably diminished. They weren't a team anymore. Cash had taken over and Laurie had become his right hand.

Syndication was still a week away, and tomorrow the next phase of media would hit Atlanta with the rest rolling out throughout the next two months.

"What do you make of all this?" Evelyn tapped into Malone's quiet mood, and eventually the pace around them floated away. It was as if they were two people on an island with a lot of movement, but nothing that involved them.

"What? The fanfare?"

"Yeah. The call from Lindsey seemed so long ago. Almost like it didn't happen. I don't mean that how it sounds."

"I was there. I know what you mean. As for this, I enjoy the attention, but when you get tired and just want to sit around looking stupid, you want all of it to disappear. How goes the hunt for a building?"

She felt inexplicably shy. "I've found one that might do for a beginning."

He drew back, surprised. "You didn't even say anything. Why you holding back?"

"My folks are giving me a hard time."

"When haven't they?"

"I know."

"You gone let them run your life forever?"

"No, it's not that." Evelyn shrugged helplessly. "I still want their approval. I know it's stupid."

Malone got this faraway look in his eyes.

Evelyn felt like hugging him. She moved closer and rubbed his side with hers. "What's the matter? You've been distracted the past few weeks."

She felt his side tighten and noticed how close they were when he turned and breathed on her. "You telepathic or something?"

"No, but I know when something's going on. We've been friends too long for me not to know. What is it? You bought a new piece of gym equipment?"

He grinned. "You're stupid, okay?" With his arm, he nudged her whole body away. Evelyn scooted over again, just to get on his nerves. "If it's not gym equipment, it has to be Lonzo. How's my little boyfriend?"

"Guess he's aw-iight. Haven't seen him in almost a month."

Lin approached. "Lighting will take another five minutes. Have a drink to cool off. Those lights will be very hot." She held out bottles of water with straws in them.

They both accepted. "You think she'd come home with me?" he asked.

"Typical man. Always wanting somebody to wait on you."

"She seems to enjoy it."

"She's paid handsomely, Malone. I've seen her work in a small gallery in Buckhead. They did an up-and-coming revue. Right now she's gaining knowledge and money, but one day she's going to have the photographer's job."

Malone took another swallow of beer. "Can't hate her for that."

"So what's going on with little maniac Junior?"

His bottom lip jutted. "Don't know."

"What?" Evelyn wiped a stray hair from her mouth. "Why don't you know?"

"Look, E, don't ruin my good mood."

"I'm not trying to. I just wanted to know how my little friend is. Sorry I asked."

She read the apology in his eyes. "I got everything under control," he said.

Two wanna-be models, one anorexic beautiful and café au lait brown, and the other an exotic combination of black and Asian, eyed Malone.

He patted his lap, and they giggled, coming closer.

"Quit playing with children," Evelyn told him.

"They're grown enough."

"Jailbait. Trust me."

Finally the exotic girl came over, her facial expression saying she wasn't fazed by his attention. "What?"

"You've got a bad attitude," Malone told her.

"No man is going to run over me."

He gave her two seconds, then flicked her away. "Bye."

"So you didn't want nothin'?"

Malone eyed her anorexic friend. "Yeah. Tell her to come over here."

"Tell her your damned self." She stomped off. But before Exotic could relay what had happened, her girlfriend was already on her way.

"You're scandalous," Evelyn told him.

"I'm an example for men everywhere."

Anorexic slid into Malone's lap, her thigh snug against his groin. Evelyn pulled her eyes away, embarrassed. It had been so long since she'd felt the comfort of a man's arms, she was jealous. "Want something?" she asked, standing up.

"No. I've got what I need right here."

The photographer called them over and Malone's reluctant lap partner had to abandon her seat. He looked at Evelyn and laughed.

"Your face is red."

She touched her cheeks. "It's the makeup."

Jasmine joined them, quiet and composed.

Laurie was noticeably gone, as was Lin. Another assistant touched them up, and the shoot continued.

An hour later they were done. "I'm starving." Evelyn pulled her bag of clothes onto her shoulder, heading for the door, in full stage makeup. She didn't care. It was beautiful outside and she wanted to be far away from the stiflingly hot studio. "Anybody want to grab something to eat?"

Malone's little model friend was beneath his arm as if she'd been taped to his side.

"I got plans," he told Evelyn and whispered in the woman's ear, to which she responded, "What you gone do if I do?"

Evelyn tuned out the odd couple. "What about you?" she asked Jasmine.

"I don't have time. If Cash looks for me, tell him I'll be an hour late. Want me to take your bag?"

"No. I've got my wallet and other junk mixed in with the clothes, so I'd better keep it all. See you later."

The rush of pedestrians swallowed Evelyn and she walked with the flow, no direction in mind. The sun was high and warm, kissed by a rare breeze that gave the air just enough relief to have drawn people from the air-conditioned buildings.

Faint strains of a live band from Centennial Olympic Park caught Evelyn's attention and she headed over to take in the sights and sounds. She loved Atlanta, the rhythm of the people so mellow. Here she could get lost and not be Evelyn of *Atlanta Live*, or Carvel's fiancée, or Raynard and Marguerite's daughter, but an anony-

mous woman enjoying her afternoon in the park. She bought a ba-
nana and water from a vendor, and pulled an extra T-shirt from her
bag to sit on.

This was the first time she'd eaten alone in a while. Usually she
caught Carvel or Jasmine or Malone, but today she was alone and,
she realized, not at all bothered by it.

She needed to do more than think about Safe Haven, but make it
come true. The building was expensive at one hundred seventy-five
thousand dollars, but the location was great. Right in the city of
Atlanta on Piedmont Avenue.

When she thought of it, the price was great.

A tickle of expectation hit her and she pulled out a pad and began
to take notes. Her hand cramped and Evelyn stopped writing and
turned her face into the sun, her eyes closed. It was a glorious day.
Giggles from small children floated by and she took in a slow, deep
breath. The paper fluttered against her fingers and Evelyn was
drawn back to her notes. Wow, seventeen pages. The sense of ac-
complishment filled her empty well.

She finished her snack and was pulled away when her cell phone
rang. "Hello?"

"It's Mother."

Evelyn switched the phone from her left to her right ear. "Yes,
Mother?" She winced as the band struck up a tune using steel
drums.

"Good grief, Evelyn, you sound as if you're in a bar."

"I'm not."

"Come over when you get off work."

"Is everything all right?"

"Of course." Her mother always sounded impatient. "I'll expect
you at six sharp. I hope you're not wasting your day."

"Of course not, Mother. I was just having lunch in the park and
was about to head back to work. See you later."

Evelyn stood and brushed off her clothes. The small pad fluttered to the ground and she picked it up.

Marguerite Smith Howard could be intimidating, but she wasn't going to steal the tiniest bit of joy Evelyn had experienced all day.

Evelyn called Carvel's cell phone and left a message about dinner. If she was going to have to visit with her parents, she wasn't going to do it alone.

"Can you meet me in the lobby?"

Evelyn drew back at Carvel's tone. So different from this afternoon. "You can't come upstairs?" She'd planned a mini fashion show after the afternoon she'd had, and if he couldn't spare a few minutes now, what corners would he cut later on? A year ago, this wouldn't have been a topic of conversation. He was already taking shortcuts and they hadn't even set the wedding date.

He came back defensive to her offense. "We're late, that's all."

Evelyn's sleeveless pastel summer dress hugged her body in modest linen. "Hosea will let you park out front. See you in a minute." She hung up and raced up the stairs, removing her earrings as she went. Five minutes later the doorbell rang. Remote in hand, she clicked on her security system, and the image of Carvel filled the TV. "Hello," she murmured.

He adjusted his shoulders in his suit coat and ran his hand over his mouth. Good grief, he was handsome.

She released the lock, then got off her bed and walked into the hallway. "Make yourself comfortable, sweetheart. I'll be down in a minute."

Soft jazz colored the air in comfort and she heard him sigh and settle on the couch. Evelyn dabbed perfume on her wrists, then gathered her earrings off the bathroom sink.

Taking slow, deliberate debutante steps, she glided down the stairs, and made sure he knew what he almost missed. At the bottom, she affixed the earrings. "Hey, sweetie? How was your day?"

He unfolded his body like a lazy yawn, his gaze riveted.

Now that was more like it. Carvel's old-fashioned values had come in a close second to his voice, when she'd first met him. "You look beautiful," he murmured.

"You're not so bad either." She breathed peppermint-fresh breath on him. "How was your day?"

"Not as good as it is now. The traffic—"

Rising on her toes, Evelyn gave him a sensual kiss. Her arms circled his neck and she let her tongue dance across his teeth until they parted and she tasted him.

A moment dragged by before she lazily ended their hello.

"Hello, Carvel. How was your day?" she murmured.

His slow sexy smile brushed her lips. "Hello, Evelyn. My day was fine. Yours?"

She kept her gaze locked on his. "Now it's wonderful."

"Yeah?"

"You'd better believe it, handsome."

Mmm, the poke. She barely moved her hips, but he'd awakened against her.

"Are you ready?" he asked.

She traced his hairline until she reached his earlobe and earned a growl for her effort. "I could call and say you're sick and you need some tender-loving care."

She punctuated each word with kisses that ended on his ear.

"Evelyn." Carvel devoured her mouth for a full minute, then just held her close. "We're leaving before we get into some serious trouble."

"I want to be alone with you." She pouted and kissed his chin.

"We already said we were coming. If it's just us, they won't mind if we leave a little early."

Discomfort took hold and Evelyn stood rested on her heels.

"What's wrong?" he asked.

"Nothing."

They rode the elevator in silence. Every once in a while Carvel would look over at her, a worried expression on his face. A couple entered on the ninth floor and huddled together, the woman casting suspicious glances their way.

Evelyn had lived in this building for two years and was decked down in Versace. Why was she acting as if they were about to get robbed? *Idiots.*

She ignored them and caught up to what Carvel was saying.

". . . I enjoy your father's company so much. He's got such great insight."

"You're always so sweet to Daddy. He enjoys visiting with you too."

Hand in hand, they walked into the garage and Evelyn waited in her car while Carvel parked in her second space. When they had started dating, they'd agreed to always drive her car to her parents' house.

The entire drive, Carvel talked about church and conventions he planned to attend this year. A big conference was coming to Nashville that would bring together all the Southern Baptist Leadership pastors. He'd been tapped to make a twenty-year commemoration presentation to a minister from Florida.

"That's wonderful, honey. What an honor. You're a rising star. They don't ask just anyone."

"I know. I hoped to talk to your father about it this evening. Get his take on what I should include in my speech."

"Honey, you'll be fine."

Carvel talked the entire way.

By the time they'd pulled up at her parents' house, a headache had started behind her eyes.

She activated the remote to open the gates to the Howard estate. Sprawled across the white steel rods was an elaborately styled H. *No less than the best,* she'd heard again and again.

Carvel's reaction was the same every time. He always inhaled sharply as if surprised he'd been admitted into God's garden to rub elbows with a deacon of Christ.

They drove around the lane of paved driveway that ended nearly a quarter of a mile at her parents' estate. When Carvel pulled up, Evelyn let out a breath.

"Whose car is that?" he asked, referring to the navy Mercedes outside the five-car garage.

"I believe that belongs to the Kanes."

"I don't believe I know the Kanes." He got out, but she hadn't missed the disappointment on his face that he wouldn't have her father as a captive audience.

Carvel took her hand as they walked up the stacked cement stairway to the front door. Evelyn had a key, but she didn't dare use it. She pressed a button and they waited in agreeable silence.

The door opened and Karen, the housekeeper, greeted them. "Come in, Ms. Howard, Mr. Albright."

"Hello, Karen. How are you?" Evelyn asked.

"Fine, ma'am. Your parents are in the sunroom. Follow me, please."

The walls of the house rose to the majestic height of twenty-five feet, with floor-to-ceiling windows along two adjoining walls. Marguerite Smith Howard had never allowed her house to be trifled with by designers. She indulged her considerable taste for color and had the room painted cocoa brown with draperies in camel and brunette, flowing straight down the wall on either side of the windows.

Evelyn had to admit the style was unique, and it worked.

As did everything her mother had a say in. Evelyn led Carvel past a six-foot-tall giraffe that craned its neck toward heaven, ears perked as if God Himself were giving it instructions.

This was her parents' home. Evelyn hated every bit of it.

"I never get used to seeing this house. One day you and I can have this and more." Carvel's awe fed her headache.

Marguerite stood near the piano, speaking in hushed tones to Nora Kane, while Evelyn's father showed off a Bible from the early 1900s to Larry Kane.

"Mr. Albright and Ms. Smith Howard have arrived. Shall I prepare to serve dinner?"

Marguerite gave Evelyn an assessing look before answering.

"Give us fifteen minutes. I know we're running late, and I don't want to keep you from your family any longer than necessary."

"Yes, ma'am."

In the space of a few words, Evelyn had been reduced to a disobedient child.

Carvel hadn't noticed.

He'd already approached her father with his hand out. "Pastor Howard," he said with so much reverence in his voice, Evelyn wanted to drag him into a corner and check him for a spine. "Sir, it's a pleasure to see you again."

"Pastor Albright," her father blustered. "One of my favorite pastors in all of Atlanta."

Marguerite pulled Carvel in front of Evelyn, effectively blocking her out. She'd, once again, been dismissed in the only way her mother knew would hurt most. "Meet Nora Kane. My soon-to-be son-in-law."

Evelyn started to step back when Carvel brought her to his side with his left hand and shook Nora's with his right. "Ma'am, it's an honor."

Evelyn fell in love with him all over again.

"You must be so proud of your fiancée, Pastor Albright."

Carvel brought Evelyn within the protection of his arms and looked down at her with love in his eyes. "I am."

"Shall we?" Marguerite said and led the way.

Evelyn held back.

"You okay?" Carvel wanted to know.

"Yes. I'll be just a minute. Go ahead."

He put both hands on her waist. "I don't like the way your mother is treating you. What's wrong with her?"

"I don't really know."

"I wouldn't blame you if you wanted to leave."

Evelyn embraced Carvel so hard and quick, it took them both by surprise. "I just need a minute."

He cupped her cheeks. "Okay."

Evelyn headed into the powder room and sat in the vanity chair, her head in her hands. One minute she was out of the fire, and the next minute, flames licked at her heels.

She stared at herself to see what her mother and father saw. She was short with average features. Without the aid of makeup, she was as plain as the nose on her own face. Her dress was simple but elegant, the way her mother had always taught her, her purse and shoes the perfect complements.

While other women wore toe rings, she had French tips and un-scaled feet. She was the epitome of the daughter they'd always wanted.

Why weren't they satisfied?

"Evelyn," her mother barked, in a harsh whisper, "you're being rude."

Evelyn jumped. She looked at the door, and realized they must have an intercom in the bathroom. *Disgusting.*

"You were late, now Karen will have to have her son pick her up because she'll miss the connecting bus. Get out here now."

"Yes, Mother."

Evelyn rose and opened the door. Her mother was already at the table talking about her decorating hobby.

Carvel was deep in a discussion with her father and the senator.

No one acknowledged her presence as Evelyn slid into her seat. She ate the food served and prayed to leave before she exploded.

Eighteen

The sun hadn't started its assent into the sky, but Jasmine knew it was going to be a lovely day. Roses from two houses away flavored the dewy air as she climbed into her car for the drive to work. She would plant flowers too, as soon as she learned something about them. Since moving into the house she'd been living from day to day, but it was time for a little future planning.

This particular day of the month was especially sweet. Thank God it was payday. Jasmine hadn't felt this good in a long time. Her career was on track, and with the help of E.J., her finances had taken a turn for the better.

All in all, beyond her monthly sojourn into Blacktown, her life was good. Yet a sigh rippled off her lips. Sure, things were falling into place, but she didn't have the lead spot back.

Lately every decision was up to Cash's whims. His favorite line was "I don't want opinion, I want results." Cash got on her nerves, and she was going to let him know as soon as she got in.

And that was another thing. Five A.M. was too damned early to be listening to one of his rah-rah speeches.

Jasmine braked in front of her mother's house and gathered her courage. Last month she'd caught her mother as she walked home from her job. Adelia had wanted to visit with her daughter, and Jasmine wanted to be gone. They'd compromised and settled on a five-sentence talk through the sunroof of Jasmine's car.

After the obligatory niceties, they'd fallen into a stifling silence until her mother asked for a ride. Jasmine acted as if she didn't hear her. The five hundred dollars was as much as she was willing to extend, and Adelia knew that. But that didn't stop her from trying to wiggle her way into Jasmine's life.

This month, Jasmine felt it better to get here earlier.

Red dust billowed in a dirty cloud around the stoop, and Jasmine braced herself. She hated this place with a passion.

It was almost five. Not only did she have to give away hard-earned money, she was late for work. Sighing, she grabbed the envelope and her brand-spanking-new stun gun, just in case her stepbrother Wat tried anything.

The street seemed to awaken as soon as her door clicked open. King's vicious barks echoed across the quiet courtyard as lights in neighboring houses popped on.

She hurried up the walkway, and got to the front door when it was wrenched open and she was dragged inside by her neck.

Wat lay on the floor, bloody white nuggets that Jasmine realized were teeth beside his swollen face. She couldn't scream or move. A gun was pressed to her forehead and on the end of it, E.J. "Girl, you need to announce yourself before bustin' in somebody's crib," he scolded, as if he had the right.

King barked from the kitchen, barricaded with chairs and cheap furniture.

E.J. returned the gun to his waist. "What you doin' here?"

"I came to give my mother some money," she said, afraid he wouldn't believe her. Afraid he'd kill her just because.

She opened her palm and the crisp hundreds fell to the floor. E.J.'s henchmen looked at the bills as if they were meat.

"Those are mine," the guy said, who still had his hand around Jasmine's neck.

"Get off her," E.J. commanded. He looked at Jasmine. "You always had integrity, not like this low-life piece of shit." He punctuated each word with a kick to her stepbrother's ribs.

Most of her life Jasmine had hated Wat. Hated his father and hated her mother for bringing them into her life. Yet even though she wouldn't give him a morsel of food, she couldn't stand by and watch him get killed. "Stop. Please—"

E.J.'s foot was midair and her words seemed to steal the desire from him.

E.J. walked over to her as if they were saying hello for the first time. "Go home, girl. This place, these people, they too low for you."

Her head jerked in two movements as Wat stirred and groaned.

E.J.'s goons nodded as they passed, leaving her plastered against the wall, struggling to catch her breath.

When they were gone, Jasmine crept over to Wat and pushed him to his side. "Wat, you okay?"

"Where's my money, bitch?"

Her sympathy dried up like steam escaping a sauna. The room had been torn apart about as badly as Wat, and when Jasmine's eyes landed on the salt shaker, she didn't think twice as she unscrewed the cap and upended it over the gash in Wat's cheek.

His agonized screams faded with each roll of her tires away from the house.

At five-thirty, Jasmine opened the door to Cash's office. "Look, I don't appreciate having to park on the moon—oh."

Malone and Evelyn sat around the small conference table.

Cash looked like he was expecting her. "Nice of you to join us, Jasmine. You're fined five hundred dollars for being late to my staff meeting."

The words sucker punched her, especially after her morning. Five hundred dollars? Did he think she was made of money?

She hadn't even gotten her check, which was promised to E.J. Ain't no way she was paying him late. Her mind raced. "I didn't know the meeting was mandatory."

"Everyone received the same voice mail last night."

"I don't listen to voice mail after hours."

"Your mistake," he said without apology. "Along with a bigger salary and bonus comes additional responsibility. Check your voice mail every evening before nine and your e-mail before you come to work. Otherwise, the world could go to hell, and the morning hosts wouldn't know about it."

How did he think he was going to dictate how she spent her hard-earned money?

Men were a trip. Wat was stewing in his own juices and Cash was the coolest man she'd ever met. Yet, they both wanted the most vital part of her. "I didn't get your message. Sorry."

"Evelyn, where was the information regarding meeting dates and times?"

"Cash, don't drag me into this. *I'm* here and *I'm* prepared. That's all I'm worried about."

Evelyn's outburst surprised Jasmine and obviously Cash, too, because he immediately backed off. "Fair enough." Cash faced a wall of muted televisions that were tuned to six different local and national TV stations. Power exuded from him even with his back to her.

"You'll donate the money or you're suspended again, this time for a month. Trust me when I say the next time there's trouble, the company won't be so benevolent." Cash strutted past her and closed his door. His voice took on a more natural tone. "You can claim the donation back on your taxes. It goes to the Hartford House, a center for abused women and children."

Jasmine crossed her arms. "I'm not paying it. I didn't know about your meeting, which I think is ridiculous in the first place. It's five-thirty in the damned morning. What's so important it can't wait until ten o'clock when we get off the air?"

"Malone is lead until further notice."

A bomb exploded in Jasmine's head. "Why you playing with me?"

"No game. You're not ready. You don't have the discipline or the right attitude."

He turned to Evelyn and Malone. "Lee's in today. I won't see you later, so get a good night's rest, tomorrow's the big day."

Nineteen

Premiere day for *Atlanta Live* arrived with Malone wrapped around the tight body of Tela, his latest fling.

He separated his legs from hers and grabbed his clothes off the hotel room floor. He didn't take women home anymore. His block had seen enough damned drama.

Dressed, he dropped two twenties on the dresser so she could get home and looked over at the woman. She wasn't much younger than he, divorced and a mom of one.

For a change, she'd been nice to talk to and nicer to sleep with, but now the appeal of her and sex had lost its luster.

It was three in the morning. He had to go to work and after last night, talk wasn't his strong point.

Getting up this early was already kicking his behind, but he had to train, there were only two weeks left before he could officially try out.

If he made the team, his life would change three hundred sixty degrees. This would be a dream come true. He had a clarity he hadn't experienced since he'd been a Falcon. The routine, the strength he felt bolstered his confidence, different from how he felt on the radio. He felt better. Football mattered.

Malone didn't want to think about how he'd feel if he didn't make the team.

At the gym he worked hard, practiced the sprints, ran obstacle courses, and pushed his body to its limit. And when he left, he felt young again.

Malone walked inside the studio and saw the girls. They looked young, like they had back in college. "Hey."

"Malone," they exhaled and then started laughing. Some of the tension eased.

Jasmine, then Evelyn hugged him. "Y'all ready to roll?" he asked, noticing that the nervous habit Jasmine had of biting her cuticles had returned.

"I'm ready," she said, really cocky. She was going to show Cash nothing he did affected her.

Evelyn prayed, her head bowed and her hands folded. Her hair swung over her shoulder and she moved from side to side.

He and Jasmine stood off to the side, not messing with her or her God. When she joined them, they held hands.

"This is for us—" Malone began.

"Ross," Jasmine said.

"Us," Malone corrected her. "We're taking this to the country, and we're taking the truth to the people."

"That's right," Evelyn said. "For us. Ready?"

Jasmine finally nodded. "Let's go."

They sat down as they had for the past two years and pulled on new headsets, in a new studio with a new producer. And a new lead.

"Welcome to the first syndicated broadcast of *Atlanta Live*. I'm Alonzo, better known as Malone. My cohosts are the sweetheart of talk, Ms. Evelyn Smith Howard. Then there's the ball breaker, hip shaker."

Cash gave an enthusiastic nod when the girls started laughing. "Honey, I hope he's talking about me," Jasmine said.

"That's right, baby, Dr. Jasmine!" Malone pounded the console. "All I got to say is look out, y'all, *Atlanta Live* is taking over talk radio."

Twenty

After a week behind the desk, Malone slid into his intro as if the lead host spot were custom-made driving gloves, and the radio, his truck.

He spoke with an easiness Evelyn hadn't expected. He still bragged on himself, talked about football until her eyes crossed, and said things that made her blush, but he connected the Kenneth Cole and Tommy Hilfiger listeners to the Target, Wal-Mart shoppers with stinging honesty and humor.

Evelyn had to admit she'd had her reservations. Malone as a person was an egomaniacal man. But on the radio, he let her and Jasmine have their say. When he teased, it didn't hurt.

Malone had done the impossible. He made radio fun, and listeners grew by the thousands every day.

Jasmine sat beside Evelyn on the other side of the console, and had settled on an attitude that had only two temperatures: sarcastic and sullen.

But even as much as Evelyn enjoyed listening to Malone have his way, she felt good in the lead host chair.

This morning was no exception. "*Atlanta Live* promises to be hot today," Evelyn declared. "We received an e-mail from a woman who described a situation so unusual, we have to get to the listeners for your reaction."

"Only in Atlanta," Malone added, stealing a bit of Don King's famous line.

If Malone was shocked, the listeners would be wild. They fed off his moods, taking their cues from his tone.

"Don't you watch daytime TV? There's crazy folks in every city in the country," she tossed out.

"We seem to have more than our share," he said dryly.

Evelyn took over. "Let me read the e-mail and then we'll see how everyone feels. 'Dear *Atlanta Live*, my husband and I have been married for two years and I thought we were very happy, still making love and on our honeymoon. Six months ago, he went away for a weekend to visit relatives, and when he returned, he brought his cousin, a woman I'd never met before, to stay with us. He claimed she'd wanted to relocate to Atlanta and needed help getting on her feet. Although I was initially uncomfortable, she was a nice person, and I didn't want him to think I didn't want to help his relatives.

"I work as a flight attendant, and one day I ran into his sister, who was on a layover at the airport. I mentioned that their cousin Laverne was staying with us temporarily. I'm sure you know what's coming. They don't have a cousin named Laverne.

"I confronted him and he confessed. Now he wants me to live with him *and* his mistress as one. I still love him. How can I get him to choose me?"

Evelyn sighed. "Malone, I'm sure you have an opinion."

"If I ever met this man—I'd shake his hand. Bro got it goin' on!"

The men in and around the studio laughed. They'd taken to standing outside the booth and encouraging Malone.

"Why is she writing to us?" Jasmine asked. "Honey, if he didn't pick you straight out, he isn't going to pick you. He's trying not to hurt your feelings and offering you a way out of this mess, but you aren't bright enough to see it."

Evelyn balled up the e-mail and tossed it at Malone, who'd gotten the men outside stirred up. "I should've known you'd agree with this nasty man. He's a creep and she should kick *him* and *his girlfriend* out."

"For what?" Jasmine instigated. "This is the one time I have to agree with the men. Besides, what if it's his house? They've only been married for two years."

"Who cares? He disrespected the marital home. You don't think he's a perverted freak?" Evelyn demanded.

Jasmine gave Malone a sly look. "You know me. If he's swinging that club like that, then work it."

Malone howled.

"You're a dog, too," Evelyn said.

"I know," Jasmine agreed. "And I love me every day. If he pulled this off for six months, he should be the spokesperson for Viagra."

"He's a criminal," Evelyn said amidst the laughter.

"Baby sister, is that righteous indignation?" Malone baited her easily. She glared at him through narrowed eyes.

"Only you would think he's some kind of male role model."

"So what do you think, Ms. Archangel?"

Evelyn hated for Jasmine to use the Bible against her, but that was what made working with her equally fun and frustrating.

"I personally think he's crazy and lucky he didn't date someone that would burn his house to the ground with him in it. Let's take some calls. What do you think she should do?"

"Kick him out, but keep the girlfriend," the caller said.

"Keep her? Why?" Evelyn demanded. "Why not toss her out with the cheating husband?"

"She said in the letter that the woman is nice."

"Good-bye. You need Jesus," Evelyn said, and took the next call.

The show took off and finally wound down and Jasmine had to keep her gaze averted from Cash. Her desperate desire to have what was rightfully hers was so high, she might reach out and grab him by the throat. He knew he had her in the palm of his hand. And she hated it. One day, she'd be back where she belonged, and he'd be gone.

The mirror never lied. Jasmine knew the fiery-red corset and garter made her look sexy, yet she felt anything but.

Sex with Lee had been part of the deal. Any time. Any way. And he was waiting. She wanted to hate him for making her honor her agreement, but she couldn't.

Lee had done what men do. Taken a policy out on her ass to ensure she'd remember who was boss. He'd slipped, though, by falling in love with her.

On a basic level, Lee was a woman's dream. He was loyal, had a job, was heterosexual and drug-free. But he lacked drive and ambition. Factors she needed to fuel her dreams.

If they became a couple, she could see them slipping into the doldrums of black middle-class life, poverty chasing their asses around Decatur.

A nightmare, Jasmine knew. Poverty had beaten her behind once. Never again.

"Jasmine, how long does it take to put on lingerie? Damn! You just gone take it off, anyway."

"One minute," she called.

Her heart beat swiftly. Sweat pooled under her arms. She used to like having sex with Lee. So why was it so hard to walk out of this bathroom? She'd lost interest. The motivation, the hunt no longer existed. Lee was captured prey and therefore boring.

But she had to do this, if only to keep herself in his good graces. Before she changed her mind, Jasmine slid into the candlelit room.

"Hey, sexy."

"Hey." She walked toward him.

He reached for her. "I want to talk to you."

Jasmine wanted to scream. Talking wasn't what she had in mind.

She slid into bed and pushed her body against his. Her fingers tangled in the hair above his sex.

He brought them up and kissed her fingertips. "Hey, what's the rush?"

"Nothing." She looked away. "Just wanted you, that's all."

Love sparkled in his eyes as he got on top of her. "That's good news. We could be so good together. At work and at home."

"It's sex, Lee." Her patience slipped. She checked it. "Work is different." She tried to roll him, but he pressed his hips into hers.

"At work," he groaned. "You've got them on the run, baby."

Jasmine stopped resisting his thrusts. "Why?"

"Your numbers are high—too high for them to fire you."

"They hate me."

"You don't make it easy for them to like you."

"How high are they?"

He kissed her neck. "High enough that they're rolling out advertising with just you. Planning segments featuring you."

"When?"

"Don't know."

"Can you find out for me?"

"See what I'm talking about? You aren't going to find anybody else that will put up with your shit the way I do."

"Why do you?"

"Because you're that good. Controversy sells, especially when it's a black woman dishing it. But you can't grow in this business without somebody in your corner."

And somewhere else, apparently.

He rotated his hips and looked into her eyes, seeking the same level of devotion he felt for her.

Anxious, Jasmine tried to push away. "I don't want to get married."

"We could live together."

Lee would always settle. And that had never been her program. "Let's have tonight and let tomorrow take care of itself."

This time when she pushed, Lee rolled on his side.

Jasmine grabbed his member and pumped lightly. He groaned long and low. "I won't give up on you."

Lee would only be led around like a dog for so long; then he'd likely turn on her.

He braced his hands on her shoulders and guided her head down. "Yes," he moaned as her tongue snaked out and surrounded the head. "That's it, baby."

Everything in her life had always come back to this.

Twenty-one

The energy in the studio was palpable, infused with the excitement of knowing their show was a success. Evelyn could think of little else. *Atlanta Live* was a monumental hit!

Cash was the reason. He moved around them in quiet concentration, his expressions as deeply etched as the generals' in the side of Stone Mountain. She'd learned his technique and now all he had to do was gesture, close an eye, raise his eyebrows, and on those rare occasions, smile. She read him like a book, and now played off him.

He'd given her a chance at lead and she had no plans to let him down. Malone was cool with it, but Jasmine still had a burr up her behind.

"Welcome back to *Atlanta Live*, and I'm Evelyn, the sanest, coolest—"

"Please, y'all should see her knocking her head against the wall every day before we come in here," Jasmine told the listening audience. "She's as crazy as they come."

Malone just grunted. "For real."

"Don't listen to them," Evelyn said into the mike. "They're just jealous. That's our topic for the day. Jealousy. Our first caller has an issue with her sister. Welcome to *Atlanta Live*. What's your name?"

"Kennedy. Thanks for taking my call. I'm married, got a good job, house, one child. My problem is my sister. She's five years younger than me, been mixed up in drugs, the wrong men, and can barely keep a job. My problem is that my parents lavish all their time and money on her. My husband and I struggled to buy our house and we bought something modest."

"Did you get any help from your parents?"

"You mean with the down payment?"

"Yeah," Malone said. "Did they do anything to help you get started?"

"No," she said in a huff. "That's what I'm talking about. As soon as I said I was getting married, she announced she was getting married. Suddenly the money they'd put aside for me had to be split in half."

"They didn't have anything set aside for her?" Evelyn asked, feeling sorry for her.

"Yeah," Kennedy said, indignant. "But she ran through it for drug rehab."

Malone started laughing.

"We used to laugh, too," Kennedy complained, "but now it's played out. We have another baby on the way. I'm afraid to tell the family because the next thing you know, she'll be knocked up again with her hand out."

"The first thing you said that struck me was when you referred to your parents as 'my parents.' There are no other siblings, right?" Jasmine said.

"No, just she and I."

"Kennedy, you've been jealous of your sister from the day she came home."

"I was five years old," she said, disputing Jasmine's assessment. "Kids don't get jealous."

"I was with you up until that point," Malone told her. "If a dog can get jealous that his master has a new woman, pet, child, whatever, so can a person. You need to let go."

"What's that mean? I don't want to not see my parents. I love them."

"Then you have to be the bigger person," Jasmine said. "Only give your sister so much room in your life. Right now, all you're doing is reacting to everything she does. You need to put her in a box in your mind and don't let her go any further."

"What do you want from your parents?" Evelyn said.

"I want them—" She hesitated.

"You want them to yourself, right?" Evelyn understood Kennedy more than she'd ever know.

"Not all the time. But every now and then I'd like for my son to have their undivided affection without her hell-raisers stealing all their attention."

"She's jealous of you, too," Evelyn said. "You're educated, got a good job, husband, house. She creates situations so she can get attention. I bet at one time or another they probably compared her to you."

"The solution is simple," Malone told Kennedy. "When you're having them over, don't invite your sister and her bad-behind kids. Stop being so damned nice. The only other thing you can do is move out of state and don't tell her drugged-out butt where you are."

Kennedy started laughing. "Okay, Malone, I hear you. Thanks, guys, bye."

"Move?" Evelyn questioned Malone. He could be so outrageous sometimes. "She should abandon the job, family, friends, everything she and her husband built, and skip town in the dark to avoid her sister?"

"Yep."

"What happens if the sister follows her?"

"She won't. She's too broke."

They burst out laughing.

"You don't know how ridiculous you sound," Evelyn told him. Malone had that devilish glint in his eye that said he might say or do anything at this point. "What's wrong?" he went on. "I see it like this—people getting on your nerves? Move. Bill collectors calling? Move. Mama and Daddy just been paroled and want to start a drug-running business out of your basement? Move."

"Boy," Jasmine said, "you're just stupid. Be back in a minute. This is WKKY, 104.9."

The commercial cued and Evelyn removed her headset. "Jasmine, I take us into the breaks."

"Sorry. Just a habit, sweetie."

"No problem."

"Cash, I had a couple ideas about the series on men and women who're incarcerated, and how much parental rights they believe they should have. Parenting from behind bars," Jasmine said.

"Go ahead."

"I think we should hook up with incarcerated parents. We could get both perspectives about child rearing from behind bars. How they maintain control. Is that even possible or realistic?"

Cash stood with his feet planted apart, arms on his chest, chin on his fingers. "We'd have to get permission from both prison systems, and make sure there's no order from the court that the couples can't communicate with each other. I like it. We'll roll with it."

"Cash, I need the Fourth of July off," Evelyn said. "I submitted a written request months ago."

He nodded. "Denied."

Evelyn couldn't believe he'd turned her down. "I have to be at a function at my church."

"Denied."

Evelyn swallowed. "What if I don't come in?"

"A thousand-dollar fine."

"Expect my check then."

"Fine. Back on in ten. Evelyn, devil's advocate, caller on one."

She nodded, pulled her headset in place, and slid into her intro. "Welcome back to *Atlanta Live*, where you'll get the truth each and every day, each and every time. The topic for today is jealousy.

Why do we get jealous? What can we do about it? Vicky is on line one. What's going on?"

"Hey, y'all, thanks for taking my call."

"You're welcome," Jasmine said. "Who are you jealous of?"

"I'm not jealous of anybody. It's my best friend. We grew up like sisters and we've shared just about everything. We went to the same college, same major, same field of study."

"Sounds like you two might be a little too close. Know what I'm saying?" Malone's implication wasn't missed on Evelyn.

"Why does everybody have to be gay, Malone?" Vicky wanted to know.

Malone chuckled. "I didn't say she was. But you never know. Who chose their major first?"

"Me."

"And I'll bet you chose the college?"

"Yes, but we're not gay. She just wants everything I want."

"That could be the greatest compliment in the world or the biggest annoyance," Evelyn said.

Cash gave Evelyn the winding motion to pick it up. "I'm playing devil's advocate today, Vicky. Why do you care? Why not go on with your life and let her copy you?"

"I'm tired of it. I can't buy a shirt without her buying the identical item."

"Tell her she's getting on your nerves," Evelyn said.

"I don't want to hurt her feelings. We've been friends since the eighth grade."

"Women are emotional in a way that men don't waste time with," Malone told them. "We'd dog the other person so bad, he'd have to do his own thing or risk getting told off every day."

"When you go shopping, find items for her and tell her to buy them; otherwise you're stuck with a copycat."

"Hey, Vicky," Malone said.

"Yes?"

"I bet you'd do something if she were trying to share your boyfriend. Before it comes to that, you'd better take charge."

Evelyn slid in before another word could be said. "That's the last word for the day. Thank you for sharing *Atlanta Live* with us and come back tomorrow. We promise to get in your business and then tell how to get things done. This is Evelyn Smith Howard for *Atlanta Live*. See you tomorrow."

"Later," Malone said. Followed by Jasmine's good-bye.

Twenty-two

Malone circled the block for the third time, waiting for his ex to show up with his son. She used to set her damned watch to the minute he was supposed to pick up Lonzo, but lately, all Mohala was good for was playing games.

He swore. Women could be some vindictive creatures. He'd had plans to take Lonzo to an exhibition game at the Dome, but now the game was nearly over.

Malone raised his hand, but refused to check his watch again. It had been after ten the last time he looked.

He parked on the driveway and got out of the truck, his knee weak. He had to perform better than every other player out there to be considered. He'd been pushing himself at practice, the shot at a comeback days away.

He loved radio but he could taste football success.

He gathered newspapers off the driveway and threw them by the garage door. He'd dumped a career's worth of money into this house and his marriage. The lawn was dead. Weeds sprouted through the unkempt shrubbery, and the house needed to be painted.

Mohala got the house, the car, and his son. And he was left cleaning up the driveway.

The nose of the Lexus scraped the steep driveway and Mohala gunned the engine.

Gripped in the beams of the approaching car, Malone stood there a few seconds, then threw himself out of the way, banging his knee when he hit the ground.

Her laughter cut him deep in his heart. They might not have been married anymore, but until recently there'd still been a tiny level of respect. Now that was gone too. "I wasn't going to hit you, at least not on purpose."

She let the car door slam. Lonzo got out on the passenger side. "Dad, are you all right?"

Malone stayed on the grass, afraid if he got up he wouldn't stop choking Mohala until she was dead.

What had he seen in her?

His son yanked on his arm. Malone shifted to his knees, his son's small hands pushing with all their might. Lonzo wasn't helping, but the effort touched Malone.

"Thanks, man. I'm fine. Go get your stuff."

On his feet, Malone staggered.

Lonzo looked between his parents.

"Go on, son. We're leaving as soon as you get your stuff together."

"Mom said I can't go."

"What?" Malone bit back a curse. "Go in the house, son. Now."

Lonzo hurried away. When the door closed Malone turned on her. "What the fuck kind of game are you playing?"

"I'm not playing. I thought you knew that by now."

Malone wasn't buying her nonchalant attitude. "What is it? Money? You got every damn thing there was to have. Every time I come over here it's some shit."

"You were supposed to be here at five-thirty. I'm tired of you taking Lonzo for granted. My attorney said if you don't honor the terms of our custody agreement, I don't have to let him go with you."

"Your attorney?" Malone looked at the starless sky. "You're fuck-in' around because you want something. Does your attorney know you're poisoning my son against me? That you're negligent?"

"Prove it." She boldly stared him down. "I didn't think so." She went to the trunk and pulled out some packages. "Next time *be* on time."

"You think you're funny, don't you?"

"Am I laughing?"

"You don't know who you're dealing with."

"Are you threatening me?"

"I'm putting you on notice. Don't use my son for your vindictive shit! He's coming with me."

She gave a little shake of her head. "Can't have him."

Mohala started to pass, and Malone grabbed her arm. "You're not getting away with this."

She swung wildly, packages slapping him first. Malone tried to grab her, but she clawed him, screaming obscenities.

"Mohala, quit acting so stupid!"

Nothing he said stopped her. She was like an animal.

Malone quit trying to fend her off and grabbed her around the waist, her back to him, her arms pinned at her sides. "Calm the hell down," he growled.

Her answering buck and thrash showed she didn't care for him, herself, or their son. In response to her screams, lights went on in neighboring houses. It was only a matter of time before the police showed up.

Having black folks as neighbors was one thing, but fightin' black folks was too ghetto for Alpharetta.

His face stung and his knee throbbed where she'd kicked him, but he wasn't letting her go.

Malone pressed Mohala face first into the garage door. "What the hell is wrong with you?"

Just as quickly as her rage had come, she deflated and began to cry.

Years ago that would have worked, but nothing about this night was normal. "Let me go."

"So you can scratch my face again? Hell no."

"Alonzo Malone." The foreign voice came from behind him. "You let her go or I'll call the cops."

"Call the cops! I don't care," he said to Mrs. Chow, who hurried away. "Once they see how scratched up I am, they'll take her crazy ass to jail."

"Let go, please." Mohala cried softly. "I'm sorry."

"I swear to God, you better not . . ."

"I promise."

Malone shoved off her and wiped his face. Blood covered his fingers. "I can't believe your crazy ass scratched me."

His jeans were stained, his T-shirt ripped. He turned to his ex, who hovered by the garage door, looking demented and pitiful.

"My son is coming with me this weekend as we agreed. I don't want any bullshit out of you. No calling and hanging up on my damn phone, and none of your crying acts. I'm through with you, understand?"

She nodded.

"You pull this shit again, you'll regret the day you were born."

Her head jerked up and down.

He thought about leaving her outside, but he didn't know what the hell was wrong with her. For all he knew she could be on drugs. "Get in the house and clean yourself up before you scare the boy."

"Malone, I'm sorry—"

"Save it. I don't even hear you."

He walked to the front door and shoved it hard into the wall. "Son! You're coming with me."

Lonzo emerged from behind a fat leaf on the palm plant. His jacket was neatly zipped, his book bag secured on his back. His hair was brushed and his sneakers tied. His face was clean, his hands folded in front of him.

He was the most grown-up little kid Malone had ever seen. And the most sad.

"How's Mommy?"

"She's fine. She needs some rest."

"Did you tell her you were sorry the stick wasn't blue?"

Confused, Malone crouched down in front of his son. His knee popped and his back cracked. "Did you see it?" he said quietly.

Lonzo nodded.

"Was it pink?"

He nodded again.

"Okay," he said, wanting to get out of there now more than ever. "Let's go."

The water upstairs went on and Malone touched his son's shoulder.

"Did she say it was okay for me to go with you?" Lonzo looked up at his father with anxious eyes.

"Everything is cool."

"We can clean your cuts with peroxide, Dad. I have some in my bag with my inhalers." His son was whispering. He was afraid of his mother. And his father.

Malone's heart splintered. "Very good, son. Very good."

Twenty-three

Evelyn sat at her desk, had been there since dawn. The fourth day of July had arrived hot and dry, as had the past thirty-four days.

What had she been thinking?

She'd waited until the day of, the very last minute, to tell Carvel she had to work.

And now he'd be angry. He'd wanted so much for her to make a good impression upon those that disliked her.

Evelyn closed her eyes to fight off a knot of pain in her stomach. Disappointing Carvel affected her in the same manner as when she'd upset her parents. *Only because he cares*, she told herself. *His love is unconditional. He'll understand*, she convinced herself and dialed his number. "Carvel?"

"Hello, Evelyn." The affectionate way he said her name had such sensual overtones, Evelyn wished the day were over and they were in her condo, dancing to something slow, her name a whisper on his lips. "How are you?"

"I'm fine." She mustered her courage. "Honey, things are crazy here at work. I thought I could get a replacement for today, but things just blew up when I told Cash I couldn't come in for the early broadcast. Now, don't worry," she rushed on, feeling worse with each word. "I'm going to be there, but someone will have to fill in for me for a short period of time."

He didn't say a word.

"Can you think of anyone who can substitute for a bit?"

"No."

Harsh. Cold. Quiet. Her false sense of security crumbled. "Sweetheart, I *have* to do this. I tried to get out of it, but I can't."

"Evelyn." Now when he said her name, the intensity felt as if the July heat had melted the walls and found her bare skin. "You said you'd be in charge of making sure the volunteers were where they're supposed to be. Everyone is counting on you. I can't believe you'd fall down on the first job the church asked you to do."

"Carvel, I know you're disappointed, but we all have to make sacrifices."

"What about honoring your word? A sacrifice is something that's going to hurt, but you do it out of a sense of responsibility."

"I understand." Evelyn tried to be reasonable. "You have duties that come up all the time and I don't give you a hard time."

"You can't compare the good work of this church to the nonsense you do. While we're feeding the hungry, you'll be judging a wet T-shirt contest. I want an honest answer. How long have you known about this?"

Evelyn felt as worthless as lint. The transgressions kept piling up. She leaned her head back. She'd lost this fight.

"A month. I was hoping something could be worked out. I'd hope you'd understand."

"I've got to stop what I'm doing to fill in for you."

"Wait. Don't hang up. I—"

"Can I depend on you, Evelyn? Are you coming?"

Her throat closed. "I'll be a little late, Carvel. Just a little late."

"We don't need the leftovers," he said adamantly. The phone went dead in her ear.

Evelyn dropped her head, short shallow breaths making her

chest rise and fall. She'd been wrong yet again. Would she ever learn?

Cash stuck his head in her office. "Ready?"

The recorded telephone message to hang up zigzagged through the air. Evelyn dropped the phone home and with practiced ease, she draped her purse over her shoulder and got up.

"You okay?"

"Fine," she said.

The blinds against the window clicked as cool air flushed the room.

Evelyn gathered her sunblock and a water bottle. When she was at the door, he handed her the company baseball cap. "Got to represent, right?"

They started walking. "Right. How are you today, Cash?"

"Love trouble?" he asked.

"Not a bit. You?"

He watched her closely. "You seem upset."

Evelyn kept her composure. Was she that transparent? "I'm great. What'd you come to see me about?"

"Just wanted to feel you out about how things are going. My job is to keep the talent happy."

"I'm fine. Thanks for asking."

He held open the elevator door. "I think you should crank it up. Get controversial. Get the church folk angry."

They walked outside and Evelyn drew on sunglasses. "I don't know if controversy is the best use of my talent. I'd like to think about it and come up with some ideas."

"What if I said just do it?"

"I'd insist we develop a better plan."

He grinned at her. "I hope you're not always this unflappable, Evelyn."

"I don't like people who intentionally try to aggravate me."

He got close. "Am I one of those people?"

Heat rushed to her cheeks. "No, but you're blocking my way."

He stayed rooted in place. "I've met charming men, but you have a dangerous side. Once upon a time, your flagrant attempt to upset me would been enough for me to fall to pieces, but I've learned how to handle you."

"How's that?"

Evelyn deliberately stuck out her arm, moved Cash aside, and kept walking.

He laughed hard and long. "You're something, you know that?"

"Yes, I do. I'm leaving early."

"That'll cost you a grand."

"You are consistent. I respect you, Cash."

"And I you. Don't get mad when I try to shake you up a bit, okay?"

"Do your job. I'll do mine."

Evelyn climbed into the van and reached for the door.

Cash reached too, looking and smelling good, but not the man for her. "Back up before you get your head smashed in."

"You're definitely some fire," he said, low.

She was still grinning until she saw Carvel's car and his stony face.

Twenty-four

The pure white cross of Calvary Baptist Church rose above the earthy backdrop of four razed acres of red Georgia clay. The church's brown brick building sat in the middle of the vast space, the dream of expansion loftier than recent tithes and offerings.

Evelyn told herself to slow down, not to worry, but her foot responded to internal fear, and she pressed the accelerator nearly to the floor.

She sped into the lot and drove all the way to the back by the Dumpster, and hopped out.

The thousand dollars didn't hurt as much as not knowing how Carvel would react to her being late. She tried to calm down, but couldn't.

In the glass of her rear window, Evelyn saw the shadow of her WKKY baseball cap, snatched it off, and threw it in the car.

She took a deep breath and regarded her enemies, the women who wouldn't verbally malign her right now, but would channel their dislike through scathing looks. Yet Evelyn wasn't worried about them. She needed to have the approval of her man.

She pulled her hair into a knot and jogged to the serving line. "Good morning, everyone. Sorry I'm late. What can I do to help?"

Of the twenty women at the table, not one answered.

Evelyn donned gloves and gathered two plates of warm butter biscuits. She moved through the cafeteria-style seating, and fed the hungry.

Deaconess Jamison and the other mothers of Calvary watched her like a hawk, but Evelyn didn't break.

Soon, they tired of watching. Tired of holding their faces in ugly sneers. Tired of her getting praised. And they began to work hard, too.

They hustled on flabby legs to fill the guests with false support and goodwill. But Evelyn had learned one thing. The poor were more adept at spotting sincerity, because they had nothing to lose.

Carvel sat with the children, two mother lieutenants keeping vulturous eyes on Evelyn. She didn't dare get too close, his abrupt greeting upon her arrival was enough to chill the air.

When there was no more food to serve, Evelyn found the garbage bags and cleaned any- and everything. Her arms ached as she trekked bags to the Dumpster, but she never sat, never stopped. If Carvel couldn't measure her dedication by her actions, then he didn't really know who she was.

Evelyn grabbed another bag and Mother Hunt spoke up. "The children will get the rest of the trash."

"I don't mind," she said, and kept moving. Her father had been a tough punisher. These ladies couldn't hold a candle to him.

Every so often, Evelyn caught Carvel watching her. First with anger, but as the day slid by and the sun shifted from blazing to pleasant, so had Carvel's eyes.

Once he even smiled.

Her heart pounded with joy.

Although she wanted to run into his arms, she stayed put.

Finally, only one table remained unattended. Evelyn moved toward the mothers.

They huddled together the way old women do.

No one lifted a finger, but watched like Olympic athlete judges, searching for one mistake. When there were none, their scrutiny cooled into indifference. She knew a whole lot about being invisible.

"You want something to drink, Sister Evelyn?" Mother Hunt asked, rising on thick legs.

"Thank you. I'd love anything cold."

Evelyn sat.

One by one the other mothers began to leave. No one spoke directly to her, but just as her heart lay trampled under their feet, two nodded, showing her the barest form of respect.

When the last one had gone, Evelyn let out a sigh. She had nothing left to protect herself with. If Mother Hunt and Carvel decided she was prey, the jackals would win.

Evelyn blinked dry eyes.

Mother Hunt sat down and gave her a sweating bottle of water, which she drank until it was gone.

"How have I offended them?" Evelyn wanted to know.

"Besides being beautiful, young, successful, and rich? You're who they were forty years ago."

"What does that mean?"

"Church is all most of them had in their day, and even now. They wanted a good man like Pastor Albright, but there's only so many like him to go around." Her nostalgic smile touched Evelyn. "Now we're mothers. If his attention is on you, what do we have?"

"I didn't mean to—"

Mother Hunt patted her hand. "Would have been any woman he chose. You're a hard target because you don't make it easy for them to hate you. Still." She shrugged. "They find a way."

"Why aren't you like them?"

She laughed. "Once upon a time, I was you."

Carvel's long-legged stride brought him to Evelyn's side. He hovered, shifting in and out of the sunlight. She and Mother Hunt finished their drinks in companionable silence.

Mother Hunt took Evelyn's empty bottle and the hand Carvel offered. "Well, Pastor, I'm gone be on my way."

"I'll walk you to your car," he offered.

Mother Hunt smiled. "Now if I can't walk from here to the car, that don't say much for me, does it?"

"Whatever you say, ma'am."

"Nice talking to you, sister. Take care."

Evelyn reached out a dignified hand and was engulfed in a hug that filled her. "Thank you."

"Love yourself. God will bless you with all you need." The words were whispered into the wind for Evelyn.

Mother Hunt drew away, but the closeness they'd shared stayed between them. "I guess I could use a hand back to my car."

Soon, Evelyn stood alone on the driveway with the man she loved but didn't understand. "What happened today, Carvel?"

"I don't know."

"Your job has demands, so does mine. Why couldn't you understand?"

"I was wrong for that. I shouldn't have judged you. I came to apologize; then I saw you. Smiling up at him like he hung the moon."

"Cash is my boss. Do I try to come between you and your boss?"

"Evelyn!"

"Really, Carvel. Answer me," she said, hearing the plea in her voice.

"No." His shoulders lifted helplessly. "Never."

"I've always been respectful of you and the things that take you out of the pulpit. Why couldn't you extend me that same respect?"

He looked off then, at the traffic, a thousand things he didn't say passing over his eyes. She wanted to know his thoughts. She wanted to know his heart.

"I got scared." He was finally being honest. "Wrapped up. You don't know the effect you have on people. Since that call, life hasn't been the same."

"What?"

"You're famous. Well known. I wanted you to choose me over the radio station."

The tortured days and nights she'd spent worrying over how to tell Carvel flipped through her mind. Knowing his behavior had nothing to do with God and everything to do with man made waves of anger sweep through her.

She took in the man who claimed to love her, but had manipulated her, more than anything. Could he love her as Christ loved the Church? Or would power struggles be the cornerstone of their relationship?

Evelyn simply couldn't imagine this life as her own. "You can't ever put me through that again. Or I won't go through with—"

Carvel caught her to him in a fierce hug. She didn't yield, couldn't, but she heard the word "Please."

Her insides crumbled and she gave herself to his embrace.

"Okay."

"I'm sorry. I love you." Carvel choked up and her heart moved for him.

"Set our wedding date."

"Evelyn, we're going to get married. I need a little more time."

"How much? How long should I wait?"

"Very soon."

Her body ached and her head pounded. She took one, then two, then three steps away. His "soon" wasn't today and if she didn't leave now, she'd stay for all the wrong reasons. "I've got an early morning."

He shadowed her, then seemed to know he couldn't stop her as she got in and started her car. "I'll call you tomorrow."

Carvel motioned for her to roll down the window. "The church is looking for an office manager."

The pieces didn't fit together in her tired mind, but Evelyn couldn't decipher anything anymore. Today was over. She put the car in drive. "If I can think of anyone, I'll e-mail you."

"Sweetheart, you'd be perfect."

An airplane streaked the sky overhead. At the moment she'd go anywhere. The car engine rumbled. Evelyn pressed the accelerator.

"We'd make an excellent team."

Carvel walked beside the moving car and she gave the accelerator another push. "Think about it," he said and started to jog. "What? No kiss?"

She pushed the accelerator and the car flew into the street.

Light as a bird, she left her troubles behind.

Twenty-five

Jasmine didn't know what to expect from the new accountant, but he'd made her nervous, not wanting to talk about the status of her tax returns over the phone. She stood in the lobby of the CNN building and pressed the button for the elevator when her phone beeped. "Hello?"

"Hey, baby. How are you?"

Impatient, Jasmine let the first elevator go without her. "Lee, I'm on my way to a meeting."

"Anything important?"

"I'm in a rush." She didn't care how impatient she sounded. Lee had been over to her house three days this week and she was tired of being his sex toy. "I miss you. Can I see you later?"

"I've got a three o'clock with Laurie. Maybe after that."

"I won't be here when you get back. That's why I called. I've officially been demoted."

"What?" This time, Jasmine stepped away from the bank of elevators and back into the brutal August sunshine. Damn! Lee had been feeding her info all the time he'd been at WKKY. Without him, who'd give her the inside scoop? Who'd watch her back? "Did they say why?"

"They want me to produce a couple A.M. shows."

A.M.? She was offended for him. "What the hell's wrong with them? What happened to 'No changes are going to be made'?"

"I don't know."

Jasmine glanced at her watch and heard the depressed drone of his voice. She couldn't do a damn thing for Lee. "I've got to go."

"Tonight. I'll come over."

Lee's power over her had just expired. "I don't think so. Gotta run. Bye."

She cut off the phone and rode the elevator up.

Twenty-six

Another show had been put to bed and Evelyn felt good. Everything was finally working together. She stored her headphones, gathered her newspapers, and headed out the studio door, Jasmine and Malone not far behind.

"Guys, can I get you in here for a minute?" Cash said.

"No," they replied in unison.

Cash's minute-long talks always turned into hour-long meetings. "Ten minutes, I promise."

Reluctantly, they strolled into his office. Nobody sat. "Sit down," he offered. "Anybody want me to order in breakfast? Doughnuts or coffee?"

Evelyn couldn't help but laugh at his unusual gaiety. "Get on with it. I'm trying to get out of here."

"All right, Evelyn, I hear you. I wanted to find out if you're interested in doing a TV show."

"As a guest? What is it, an interview with Monica Kauffman for *Up Close and Personal*?" Jasmine wanted to know.

"No." He was still smiling. "This would be a show called *Atlanta's Own*, and one of you would be the host."

"Would the person have to leave the radio show?" Evelyn asked.

"That's a distinct possibility, but we can discuss that a little further down the road."

"I'm the most qualified for the job," Jasmine boldly announced. "I conceptualized *Atlanta Live,* and then sold the idea to Sharpe Enterprises. I brought Evelyn and Malone on board, knowing what a good combination we'd be. I also have the persona needed for a TV show to be a hit."

"Go ahead and act like we're not sitting here while you stick the knife in our backs, Jasmine," Malone told her.

"Facts don't lie."

"Nothing you've said gives you an advantage unless the others aren't interested," Cash quickly pointed out.

"I'm interested." Evelyn looked at Cash only.

"Why?" Jasmine demanded. "Because it's something I want?"

"Excuse you, but I came from television. Besides, I think I'd be good at it."

"Malone?" Cash jumped in before an argument could escalate.

"Sure, why not?"

Jasmine sucked her teeth and slumped against the door.

Evelyn couldn't understand why she'd been in such a piss-poor mood lately, but now she was acting as if they'd stolen something from her.

"If you have a few minutes more," Cash said, "the executive producers are upstairs and would like to meet each of you."

No one had any objections, but Evelyn noticed the way Jasmine rushed out the door first.

Evelyn refreshed her makeup and took in a few calming breaths before going up. Jasmine wasn't going to ruin her good day.

Atlanta Live had grown from fifteen cities to thirty. The executives upstairs were more than pleased. She'd received more accolades than ever in her entire career. The great thing about Jones Enterprises was that they put their money where their accolades were and gave bonuses when a new station was added.

160

Evelyn had managed to save a nice nest egg. And Cash had finally pared down the daily morning meetings to two per week.

Upstairs, she sailed through her impromptu screen test and sucked on a throat lozenge as she headed for her office.

A nice quiet lunch was the only must-do on her list today.

As Evelyn rounded the corner, she noticed a woman outside her office. "May I help you?"

"I was looking for Alonzo Malone."

"And you are?"

"I'm DeDee Garr. I'm here to deliver some papers from the attorney."

"Can I take them?"

Ms. Garr pulled them back. "No, I have to deliver them in person."

The woman looked like a Malone kind of woman. All legs and breasts. This one had intelligent eyes, which could have ruled her out of his fan club, but she could be slumming. "Malone isn't in his office. I'm not sure where he is."

"I have to get these to him right away."

Evelyn walked into her office and offered Ms. Garr a seat. "Let me see if I can get him on the phone."

The woman hung back by the door. "I don't want to disturb you. I can wait in the hallway."

"No, please. It'll only take a minute."

Curiosity piqued, Evelyn tried Malone's office, then called the receptionist to have him paged. She leafed through her phone messages and prioritized them. A converted house in the Highland Park area was available, the asking price a quarter of a million dollars. The last building had fallen through, unable to pass inspection. This one was almost double the price, but had more room. Evelyn cross-referenced the house to the real estate book and put a red circle around the photo.

"Looking for a house?" DeDee asked.

"Not really."

"I've heard some interesting things about Safe Haven. That home would do nicely. In my opinion."

"You're an awfully perceptive messenger. In fact"—Evelyn assessed her carefully—"you're too intelligent looking to be just a messenger."

DeDee smiled. "I relocated to Atlanta six months ago with my boyfriend. When he got a new girlfriend, I found myself without a place, or a job. Now I've got an apartment, and a job—of sorts, so this is just temporary."

"There're a lot of opportunities in Atlanta. What's your specialty?"

"I was an office manager in Detroit. If you find the need for one at the foundation's headquarters, I'm available."

Evelyn liked DeDee. "Thanks. You make it sound so formal and official, but I'm nowhere near having a staff yet. But I'll keep you in mind. Have you got a card?" DeDee hesitated and Evelyn wondered why. "Something wrong?"

She gave Evelyn the card. "I just hope you'll give me the opportunity to prove myself."

Malone stuck his head in Evelyn's office. "Hey."

She stood and walked around her desk. "This is DeDee from your attorney's office."

The woman stood, an apologetic look on her face. "Mr. Malone?"

"Yes?"

"I'm sorry to have to do this, but I'm with Stein and Berkshire Attorneys at Law. You've been served."

Malone took the envelope she thrust at him.

Stunned, Evelyn watched Ms. Garr leave the office.

"I'm sorry. I had no idea." Evelyn's phone rang, cutting her apology short. "Malone," she said, to his immobilized frame. "For you."

He took the phone. "Yeah?" He listened for a moment, and then dropped the receiver into her hand.

"What is it?"

"I tried out for the Falcons."

"Wow." Evelyn's heart skittered. Was Malone leaving? What would happen to them? "Well, what happened?"

"I was just released."

Evelyn thought he'd fall down, and did the only thing she could. She wrapped her arms around him and told him everything would be all right.

The papers were like a death sentence. They spelled out Mohala's desires in a few sentences. She wanted full custody, no visitation for him, and an increase in support to ten thousand dollars a month.

The restraining order she'd executed against him was worse.

He was prohibited from coming within two hundred yards of her or Lonzo.

The words on the paper still looked harsh as he sat in his attorney's office an hour later. "How can she do this?"

"She claims assault. Has pictures to prove it."

"She tried to hit me," Malone argued. "Thought it was funny that I ended up ass first on the ground."

"Why did you go over there?"

"To pick up my son."

Ethan leafed through the custody agreement. "You were supposed to be there at six o'clock. What were you doing there at ten-thirty?"

"She hadn't been home! That's what I'm talking about. She's been messing up for months, but I thought we could work it out."

Ethan leaned back in his chair, his ice-blue eyes steady. "Give me some examples."

Malone recounted the incidents with the school and Lonzo.

"Any more?"

"Besides her being negligent? That's not enough?"

"We're a long way from negligent. But we can build a case against her. My investigators need time to gather evidence."

"How much time?"

"Might be a few weeks, maybe longer."

Malone shot out of his chair. "I can't wait that long. She can't keep me from seeing him."

"She claims to be afraid for the boy, stating if she's not around, you'll use him as a punching bag." Ethan threw the graphically misleading photos on the desk for Malone to see.

He couldn't deny they'd had an altercation, but these bruises looked as if he'd beaten her when all he'd tried to do was restrain her. "Where'd you get these?"

"From her attorney. Did you do this?"

"No. You should have seen me!" Malone banged his hands on the desk. Ethan looked annoyed, but Malone didn't care. He was fighting for his life.

"I was on the driveway picking up all the newspapers and she nearly ran me over. Then she got out, claimed I was late, and said I couldn't see my son. We got into it because she went crazy! I was scratched up all over my arms. She even scratched my face. I finally had to restrain her crazy butt to keep her from tearing off the rest of my skin. That's when she broke down, crying and apologizing. My son and I left and when I brought him back on Sunday, she acted like nothing had happened."

The horrific night came back in slow motion. "She acted like she was possessed. I swear, I never hit her. Never would."

"Did anyone see the altercation?"

"No." Malone's voice caught. "Mrs. Chow, the neighbor, saw some of it. She threatened to call the police. I let Mohala go after she promised not to go crazy on me again."

"We'll get an affidavit from the neighbor. Sounds like Mrs. Malone might have been on drugs. Any knowledge of that?"

"No, but she might have been on something. Her behavior has been erratic. She was chain-smoking, frustrated that she'd forgotten the parent-teacher meeting at the school and that they'd called me."

Ethan scribbled furiously. "This is all good information. Anything else?"

"Before we left, my son asked me, did I apologize to his mom because the stick was blue?"

"Pregnancy stick?"

"I believe so."

"Have you had an intimate relationship with her?"

"Hell no! But she's been trying to mess with one of the rookies on the team. Lonzo also said that he'd gone to sleep in his mother's bed and hadn't seen her."

"Who got him ready for school?"

"He's very independent. He gets himself ready."

"At eight?"

Malone didn't like his tone. "He's smart. Smarter than both my ex and me put together. He was such a tiny boy at birth. Four pounds. Lonzo has asthma, but as he gets older, he's getting healthier."

Silence hung between the two men.

With his having lost his mother and father in his early twenties, family was important to Malone, but now he was staring his worst fear in the face. He might lose the ability to see his son for good. A thousand ways to reach out to Lonzo raced through Malone's mind. He could have listened to the boy more. Been there for him more.

"I've never hurt him. Never hit him. He's a sweet boy, a good boy." His voice broke and he struggled to see Ethan. "She can't do this."

"Alonzo, you're going to be with your son again."

"How?"

"If she's up to something, the investigators will catch her. In the meantime, stay away from them."

"But she attacked me!"

"Not according to the police report."

"Well, can I file one against her?"

Ethan's doubtful expression said it all.

"So I'll be the lying, no-good, ex-wife-beating asshole, and she's the fairy fucking godmother? That's bullshit!"

"Anything you do at this point will make you look guilty and vindictive. Anybody see your injuries?"

"No, yes, no. I didn't tell anyone the truth about how I got the scratches."

"Can you think of any reason why she'd make up these allegations?"

"Money. That's the only thing she consistently talks about. She knows the only way to get to me is through our son. Child support is one thing, but I shouldn't have to subsidize her playtime. It's been almost three years since the divorce. She knew she was coming off spousal support in a couple months."

Ethan gave a tentative nod. "Good. Go on."

"Do I have to pay her ten grand a month?"

"I've already asked for another hearing to have that decreased, but the assault charge isn't going to endear you to the judge."

"How much is this whole thing going to cost me?"

"Right now, five thousand, and we work from there."

"Damn." Malone wrote out a check and slid it to Ethan. "Call me. Let me know what the investigators find out."

"I know you want to see your son, but you have to stay away for your own good."

Malone nodded, but knew he couldn't make any promises.

Twenty-seven

The summer heat tended to push everyone inside, and Jasmine was no exception. She worked late, not wanting to look at the administrative stuff tomorrow.

After seven, she left her office and headed down the quiet corridor when she heard Cash's and Laurie's voices.

She almost walked past when she heard Laurie say something about *Atlanta Live*.

"Malone is awesome and Evelyn's come a long way. But that other one—she's more trouble than she's worth."

Jasmine slipped inside the secretary's cubicle and waited. Cash and Laurie had always thought Malone hung the moon. Their opinion hadn't dimmed any by his embarrassing stab at youth. She'd have to find a way to take a little of the shine off his star.

"Is that Laurie the consultant talking, or Laurie the woman?" Cash said.

"Look, whenever we're here, I'm the consultant. Besides, it was you who didn't want to revisit 'us' again."

Jasmine drew back, never guessing that there'd been more between the pair than a professional relationship. She should have guessed. Although she'd hinted at an interest in Cash, he'd never taken her up on her offer. There were intimate possibilities still unexplored.

She edged farther into the cubicle, grateful the administrative staff had been given half days off every other Friday.

"She's worth it, Laurie. Dr. Jasmine might be a bitch on wheels, but she causes controversy, and that causes conversation. If everybody in radio were nice, nobody would be listening. The differences between them is what sells this show through the roof. You were supposed to help her, not make her do dog tricks."

Jasmine braced herself for Laurie's stinging response.

"The show has to cut overhead somewhere. She's the logical choice." It was Laurie who sounded too logical. She hated Jasmine and obviously worked constantly to undermine her work.

"We'll cut from other shows before we touch *Atlanta Live*," Cash said. "It's bringing in consistent revenue and holding its own. I only wish Bolden hadn't started by giving them all that twenty percent raise. He just made our job harder."

Laurie made a sympathetic noise in her cheek. "Especially now that he's whining about controlling costs. I bet Dr. Jasmine would shit a brick if she knew she made ten thousand less than Evelyn and Malone."

Cash's voice sounded tired as he yawned. "She'll never know that confidential piece of information, will she, Laurie?"

"Not from me. I am ethical, even if I am a bad-ass white girl."

Cash chuckled. "Yeah, you are. Ready to go yet?"

"Let me shut down my computer and get my jacket. How about dinner?"

Jasmine crouched lower, furious. Why were Malone and Evelyn earning more than she? She'd built the show from dust. She moved and the chair squeaked. "Hello?" Laurie called.

Jasmine held her breath. She'd heard enough. How could they entertain the thought of getting rid of her? If someone had to go, why not Evelyn with her too-cute ways or Malone with his "keep 'em barefoot and pregnant" mentality?

"I'm hearing things," Laurie said to Cash. "Give me two minutes."

"Okay."

She walked past the cubicle, her high heels silent.

Jasmine hated them all. No wonder Malone and Evelyn had no worries. They were making an extra eight hundred dollars a month.

She'd been getting screwed, but not anymore. Jasmine waited until after Cash left before going into his office. She dialed a media contact, then leafed through the unlocked file drawers.

She'd get them. All of them.

Jasmine stood outside the studio and watched the interview with Malone and Josh. How had he been able to get a TV crew to the station by six A.M.?

She'd made sure to make her interview look as if it had been spur of the moment. The reporter had come by late last night. How had Malone scooped her?

Cash. He was like a human information factory. Somehow he'd gotten wind of what she'd done and had circumvented her.

Malone sat in the studio laughing, wearing his Atlanta Falcons jersey, cameras rolling, Evelyn all smiles. Malone looked like a real hero.

Josh turned to him. "Tell the kids out there what it means to shoot for the same dream twice."

"I was on top of the world. I had fallen back into a time in my life when I felt good about being a man. I trained, I practiced, and I learned. I felt good for the first time in a while. Maybe it was the exercise. I pushed my body in a way I haven't since I was actually on the team. When I first retired, I was glad not to have to train every day. But this time, I was grateful that I could complete all the drills and still be standing. I was at my best, but as I look back over this past twenty-four hours, I know why I got cut."

"That's quite an announcement. Tell us."

"In practice, I was giving my best."

Josh smiled. "I understand where you're going."

"I couldn't have given any more during a game and we both know you must have that inner reserve of strength so that when the time's right, you tap that and give your all. I was giving that every day during practice. I didn't have any extra, and ultimately I would have gotten injured and wouldn't have been worth anything to the team or myself."

"We all know that hindsight is twenty-twenty. Would you do it again?"

"Definitely. You have to know what it's like to compete on a professional level to know what you're giving up. No, it didn't feel good getting cut, but I'd feel worse if I let fear stop me from trying in the first place."

Josh gave him a soul-brother shake. "You're a good man for telling it like it is. This is Josh Cavallaro in the *Atlanta Live* studio, with newly retired Atlanta Falcon Alonzo Malone, and his cohost Evelyn. We'll be right back on Channel Five."

Jasmine stopped trying to get into the studio, and walked down the hall alone.

The Atlanta skyline faded in a final burst of orange and blue, and Malone sat outside, alone. His phone rang a second time and he debated answering. After the third ring, he snatched up the receiver. "Hello?"

"Don't sound so friendly," Josh said. "You do know answering the phone while in a bad mood is optional."

Malone laughed. "What do you want? I've already told the world all my business, and you still won't leave me alone. I'm going to have to report you to your superiors."

"Great, while you're at the golf course, can you tell them to kiss my ass since I have to work so they can play? Can you do that?"

"Right, man, you love being in charge."

"True," Josh agreed.

"So, how's it really going?" Malone asked, glad to be talking about something besides himself.

"Good, that's the reason for my call. We've got a show in the treatment stage that the president, Ken Mannix, wants to rival SportsCenter and ESPN. It'd start as a local show, and then go national. The slant is comedic and there'd be guests, interviews, contests. We'd find players from everywhere and profile their lives from high school to the pros. Maybe do pre- and post-*MTV* cribs-type things." Josh finally stopped. "How's it sound?"

"Young. Like you're appealing to the young male athlete or wanna-be. That's cool and all, but they lose interest very quickly. You'd have to go to the hood and find the bad boys. Mexico and find the best soccer and baseball players. Then again, you'd find the next Moses Malone, Spreewell, and others. Now that's an interesting show."

Josh went on. "You'd have to host parties and invite some of these guys to come watch the game at your place. The crew would shoot footage and we'd air it."

"Man, not another talk show. That is so played out. It'd be better if you only show clips from the games and the reaction of the guests. That shit would be so funny."

"That's what I thought," Josh said.

"Josh, you never could come up with original ideas. You've been stealing from me since college," he told him, laughing. "I want your boss to know this whole thing was practically my idea, so when I come up there trying to collect my check, they don't have security wrestling me to the ground."

"Okay. You're hired."

Malone stopped. "What are you talking about?"

"I thought you'd be perfect for the job, so you're hired."

"Fool, don't you know I have a job already?"

"You're a sports guy at heart, Malone. After the interview, I hung around a bit, and I gotta be honest, that show is a stick of C-Four waiting to blow."

"It's a little intense right now, but trust me, it's cool."

"Look at the signs right in front of your eyes and when you see reality, call me. This job won't start for a couple of months, but there's a lot you can be doing in preparation."

"Josh, I'm glad you thought of me, but I'm not ready to jump into something else."

"It's a contracted job. I don't know what you're making over there, but I believe we can comfortably double your salary."

"Well, damn."

"You don't have to answer now. Just know that the offer is on the table for the next few weeks. After that, we have to go to the next person on the list."

Malone was more than flattered. "I—I'll call you soon."

He hung up, his bad mood replaced by the unsteady rhythm of his future.

Twenty-eight

Malone stuck his head into Jasmine's office. "I need the money I lent you."

"When?"

"Now." She got this look on her face and Malone's mouth twisted. Here Jasmine was acting as if they were cool, when all she'd been doing was stabbing him in the back. "You got it?"

Her head jerked. "I didn't think you'd need it so soon."

"It's been a month."

"I know. What's going on?"

"I need the money, that's it. When can you get it?"

She threw up her hands. "Tomorrow I'll have half."

"How much do you have now?"

"Right this minute?" She started to laugh, but there wasn't a damn thing funny. "A hundred dollars."

She was lying. Jasmine didn't travel light. On any given day she had at least two hundred dollars on hand. He came around the desk. "The money, Jas?"

She knocked his knee with her wrist and he moved. She pulled her shiny red purse from the desk drawer, and made a point of turning her back and getting her wallet.

Malone's frustration level peaked. Between Mohala, Jasmine, and the women he'd been picking up, they were all trying to drive him crazy. "Jasmine, would you come on?"

She jumped and dropped three one-hundred-dollar bills onto the floor.

For a second Malone saw red. In his book, Jasmine had hit an all-time low.

Malone scooped up the bills before she reached them.

"Malone, I need that." She sounded like a crack head.

"Yeah, well. So do I."

He walked out, pissed at her, pissed at the world. His life felt as if it were the timer on a ticking bomb. But he couldn't lose control. He had to stay focused and get to the bank on time, because if a deposit wasn't made before one, his mortgage check would bounce. It wasn't like he didn't have IRAs, but if he liquidated, the penalties were so high, he'd jeopardize his financial future. This money would tide him over until payday.

Malone got into his car and stomped on the gas at every green light.

Beautiful women lined the streets, but he couldn't garner any interest. He was what Evelyn termed morbidly mad.

She was the only one he could stand talking to lately. He wondered how was she doing. She'd been quiet, unusually so. Maybe her creep of a fiancé had finally left her alone. Malone couldn't explain why that lightened his mood a degree.

He drove into the bank parking lot and his pager vibrated. The school had called. Malone checked his cell phone and cursed. Off again. He really needed to get his act together. "Damn it. What now?" he said, as he called them back.

Inside the bank, he scrawled the deposit slip and hurried over to the teller just as the secretary answered.

"Malone, returning your call regarding Alonzo Malone Junior."

"Just a minute," the secretary said.

"Can you hurry?" he said to the teller. "My son's school is on." She did as he asked and handed him the receipt.

"Mr. Malone, young Mr. Malone was taken to Egleston Hospital for an asthma attack."

Malone's knees went weak and he grabbed the counter. "How do I get there from here?"

Out of nowhere two security guards were beside him. "Is there a problem, sir?"

"My son," he managed. "Egleston."

The tall blond man's eyes changed and he escorted Malone through the front doors. "I can get there faster than you. My name is Tim."

"Don't you have to stay and guard the bank?"

"I'm on lunch. Hop in. We'll be there in ten minutes."

Tim was a man of his word.

They entered the hospital, painted in bright primary colors, and Malone was escorted to another ward. He saw Mohala first. "How is he? What happened?"

"You're not supposed to be here. I have a restraining order against you."

The words were like ice-cold water in his face, but he couldn't reconcile them with his fear. "How's Lonzo?"

"Security," she called loudly. "Arrest him. He assaulted me. I've got pictures to prove it."

Nurses hovered because Mohala was making a scene.

Malone moved toward the most official-looking people, the women in white coats. "I got a call from my son's school. An emergency. How is he?"

"Sir, you have to leave. You're causing a disturbance."

"That's right," Mohala taunted. "He's the problem. Arrest him," she yelled at Tim.

"He hasn't done anything but ask a reasonable question. How is his son?"

Malone held his hands up. "I'm not trying to cause any problems. I'll stand over here." He moved to the end of the nurses' station, hoping Mohala would come to her senses. She was loud, her hair unkempt, just like the last time he'd seen her. "Doctor," he said, not looking at his ex-wife. "I just want to know if Lonzo is okay."

"Sir, I'm Dr. Albert." He could tell she didn't know whom to trust, but she made a judgment call in Malone's favor. "Will you come this way, please?"

The elevator doors opened and two orderlies exited. He knew the police were on their way, and if he was going to see Lonzo, he had to do it now.

"Are you his attending physician?" He followed her down the hall. "Has he been checked in?"

"Yes."

"Don't talk to him! I'll sue you if you give him one piece of information about my son. Let me call some real cops. Malone, you're in violation of the order of protection. You're going to pay for this."

"Mohala—" He started to say something, then thought better of it. The doctor spoke to a nurse and an orderly outside a room, and Malone's heart quickened.

"Lonzo," he said, as they pushed the door open.

"Dad?"

It felt so good to hear his voice, weak as it was. Malone saw him, so small in the big white bed. Two nurses attended him, and one leaned over to listen to Lonzo, who took fast, shallow breaths.

She patted his hand. "Mr. Malone, he said he's proud you tried out for the football team again."

Malone smiled through his tears. "Thank you, son. You know I love you, right?"

Lonzo leaned back exhausted, and Malone watched as his small hand waved. The nurse leaned down once again.

"He said he loves you, too."

The nurse had returned the mask to Lonzo's face. His son gave him the terminator. The thumbs-up. Tears spilled.

They were closing the door and Malone begged for the first time in his life. "Please, just keep the door open. Please?"

"Get out of there! You don't have the right to be here."

"Mrs. Malone, stop screaming," Dr. Albert ordered. "I don't care what's going on between you and Mr. Malone, but right now, you're the problem. Until the police get up here, both of you are to be quiet." She hesitated and looked at Malone with sympathy-filled eyes. "And the door will stay open."

Malone wiped his face.

Tim came to stand next to him. "Can I be frank?"

"Tim, today you're my best friend."

"If there's an order of protection against you, you're going to be arrested. Call your attorney now, and I'll stick around and get statements from the folks here as to your ex's and your behavior. You're going to need all of that. How can I reach you later?"

Malone had never felt so grateful. In the rush to find out what was wrong with Lonzo, he hadn't thought of the repercussions to himself.

The elevator doors opened and two officers walked toward them.

"Get a drug test."

"I'm not on drugs."

The man's eyes shifted toward Mohala, and Malone understood. His lawyer had told him to do that before, but Malone hadn't thought any more of it because he still couldn't believe the relationship had deteriorated that much.

But it had. They were here because of her. Malone shoved his card into Tim's hand. "My home and pager. Don't know what's going to happen."

But he knew.

Mohala started trippin' and the cops pulled out their cuffs.

"I want her tested for illegal drug use."

Mohala choked on the surprisingly fast turn of events.

"I don't have to prove nothin' to nobody. You're going to jail, not me. Nobody can touch me."

The police didn't need further encouragement. One took her by the arm and Mohala's eyes grew wide, and she started begging.

Malone was cuffed and looked into his son's eyes until he was led away.

Twenty-nine

One phone call wasn't enough. Malone tried Jasmine's number again. If she didn't pick up, he'd have to try Evelyn. It was bad enough that'd he'd been in jail a whole day and night, but he was sure Cash had sent out the hounds since he hadn't come to work this morning.

The reason he was still in the Fulton County lockup was so stupid, he couldn't rationalize it. The vitamins he'd put into his pocket had dissolved into a white powder and because the police couldn't verify they weren't an illegal substance, they kept him.

They'd given him a little leeway, by letting him use a desk phone, but he had to put up or get locked up for another night. Knowing this was his last call for the night, he prayed as he dialed.

"Jasmine," she said. "Who the hell is this?"

"Hey," he said, relieved to hear his voice. "Where you been?"

"That's the million-dollar question. Where you callin' me from?"

"Fulton County lockup."

"Boy, quit lyin'!"

"I wish I were. Can you come and get me?"

"Oh."

An uncomfortable feeling twisted his stomach. The desk sergeant walked by and told him time was up. "Look, can you come now?"

"Yeah. Sure. See you in a bit."

"Thank you, cuz. I owe you big time."

Malone didn't hear her response, just the dead phone line.

Jasmine counted the money in her hand one more time, as if handling it would make it grow. She was five hundred short of what she owed E.J. There was no ducking him. Making him run after her would be like taunting a pit bull.

She sat in Gulliver's and waited, nervous and scared. She'd brought this on herself. How could she not have his money? Especially after the beating he'd given Wat?

The IRS took every dime of her paycheck, Cash wouldn't give her an advance, but it was Malone who'd screwed her last.

The bartender shoved another shot of tequila her way. "I can't drink that rotgut."

"Drink it. You need it."

Her bladder quivered. Fear seized her. Had he said, "You'll need it," or did she just look like she needed a drink? What would E.J. do to her?

She would have the money in a day or two.

She was a professional and he was a businessman. They could work something out. She threw back the shot and the bartender sighed, a sorrowful expression on his face.

The door pressed open and summer heat blended with the thick funk of the bar. E.J. walked in. "What's the good word, Doc?"

"I'm short five hundred dollars," she whispered.

He rolled the splintered toothpick over his tongue and lodged it in the side of his mouth. "Meet me outside."

"Please!" Jasmine couldn't believe he was going to beat her up. "Please, give me another day." There were only five people in the place, but Jasmine had to save herself. "Are you going to kill me?"

His hand snaked up her neck and her eyes grew large. "If you keep frontin', yeah," he said. "Now let's go outside and discuss the terms of your extension."

"Where?"

"In the truck." He turned to the bartender. "She'll be in the truck with me. Feel better?" he asked Jasmine.

She nodded and E.J. let her go.

Jasmine followed him to his pristine white Escalade and stood a safe distance from the door.

"Get in." He climbed in the rear passenger door behind the driver's seat.

She got in the opposite door.

"These are the terms. The fee jumps five hundred a day or—"

Jasmine thought she'd have a panic attack. "Or what?"

"That's the million-dollar question. What you got to trade?"

"Nothing."

"Your car."

"For five hundred dollars? Come on, E.J. We go way back."

"That's right, we do. I always thought you were cute, but you never gave a brotha the time of day."

Chills ran over her skin. "I never knew."

E.J. was a hood rat and she'd been too interested in getting out of Blacktown, not bringing trash with her. "I thought you were married or something."

"That ain't got nothin' to do with this. Five a day or you can cut the fee in half by proposing a little somethin'. You got a doctorate degree 'cause you're smart. What can you do with this?" His finger traced her lips and then down the front of her body and stopped at her vagina. "Two hundred fifty dollars is a lot of money."

"Why not the whole five?" Even as she said the words, her stomach rolled. She wasn't attracted to him in the least little bit, but she'd given up ass for less. She tried to detach and tell herself that she'd survive and life would go on, only her mind revolted. "Be a friend, E.J."

"Pussy ain't worth that much," he said. "I'm giving you the house break and it's a onetime offer. Next time I decide."

Jasmine knew she didn't want to put her mouth on him. Not with him looking in her face as he came. "Doggie style."

"Sign this." He thrust papers at her.

Jasmine tried to read by the overhead light, but E.J. sucked his teeth. "Stalling ain't gone do you no good."

She scrawled her name and gave them back to him.

He initialed a couple of places, signed, then tore her copy from the stack. He folded it in threes and handed it to her.

"Put this up."

She shoved it in her purse.

"Give me the money you already have."

With her bag open, she handed over the cash.

"You should never pay in cash. Always check or money order. So you have a paper trail." He still gave her a receipt and twisted his pen closed.

Jasmine wanted to gag. She didn't need a business lesson. She needed to be far away from here. She stayed on her side of the truck. E.J. smiled. "What you lookin' so terrified for? I'm not gone hurt you. Come on, girl. Just think of this as something long overdue between friends." He scooted over a bit. "Unzip me."

E.J. was fat. Larger than any man she'd ever dealt with. She could immobilize him with a self-defense move, but he'd get her. He had all the power right how. "Get it hard," he told her, his tone much cooler. "I'm not going to be accused of rape later."

Jasmine touched his warm member and wanted to vomit.

Pee ran down her leg. She closed her eyes as she drew her hand up and down his shaft in a rhythmic motion.

"Shit, that's starting to burn. Wet it."

"What!"

"You got to do somethin' better than that. I don't care if you spit on your hand, but you're not about to rub the skin off my Johnson."

His half-hard penis looked like a one-eyed monster. "Can I turn off the light?"

"Take care of business. I'll worry about the light."

She spat into her hand and started massaging him again. He grew to a respectable length and she hoped he would erupt before she had to pull her pants down, but he stopped her. "Now you."

The cotton capri pants Jasmine wore were easy to slip off, but she couldn't do it with the light on. She didn't want him to know her weakness when he saw her wet panties and pants. "Use a condom."

"I am. I don't know where you've been."

She squeezed her eyes shut at his nerve.

Jasmine managed one more request. "Please, the light."

He turned it off. "It's not like I haven't seen it in all shapes and sizes. I was there for the birth of my two kids, so I've seen the best and the worst."

She fumbled with the waist and finally got the pants around her thighs. Jasmine had never wanted to beg so badly in her life. "Please, let me do something else. Please, E.J. Please."

"We had a deal, girl. On your knees. I ain't that bad."

His paw-sized hand wrapped her torso and before she could plead again, he filled her up and started a steady rhythm. Jasmine breathed through gritted teeth. Her head knocked against the passenger door and she shoved back and E.J. grabbed her thighs. "That's it, girl, get into it. This is good stuff."

His thrusts became stronger until he was bucking, and shaking the truck. Finally, he cried out and shuddered long and hard.

Jasmine didn't wait for him to finish. She scrambled out and barely got her pants up before she ran to her car, crying.

The fifth brandy was the charm, Jasmine decided, her head way past hazy. She'd cut off her cell phone and unplugged the house phone. She didn't want to hear from anyone, especially Malone. It was his fault that she was in this condition, and for all she cared, he could rot in jail. She adjusted her maxi pad, her bladder releasing every few minutes. If she didn't calm down, she'd have to buy some Depends.

She sat on her bed, staring at the TV. The late news came on, a camera crew in Blacktown. *Somebody dead, what else is new?*

She started to turn when she recognized the jacket of the victim and took the TV off mute. *Watson Graves, dead at thirty-one.*

Jasmine started screaming and couldn't stop.

Thirty

"**R**atings have tapered off, so we need to get controversial. Step further out on the limb and get people talking."

"I thought they were talking. The prison segment, the baby's not living with Mom, and the jealousy shows were hits," Evelyn supplied, unfazed as she usually was when Cash told them they needed to do more.

"We have to get bigger."

"How's that possible? Word of mouth is the only thing that will increase ratings."

Cash stalked around the table. "That's right, Evelyn, so we have to get people talking."

"They're talking about how crazy our producer is. Lighten up. The show's doing great."

Cash rubbed his head. "We are doing great, aren't we?"

"So he can hear," Jasmine finally jumped in. "But do you care more about how many advertising dollars are rolling in or us?" Jasmine demanded.

"Both."

"I'm glad you're being so honest, because a little birdie told me there's going to be a cutback."

Evelyn looked up in surprise.

Cash was good. Only his eyebrow rose slightly. "What little birdie was that? I might need to get my hands around its neck and squeeze hard."

Jasmine shrugged. "The who isn't as important as, is it true?"

"No."

"No?" Jasmine clearly didn't believe him.

"You heard me the first time."

"All right," she said, knowing different.

"I'm backing off. Anyone heard from Malone?" Cash asked.

Evelyn shook her head and so did Jasmine.

"I'll try his cell phone again. Have a good show."

The table was set, candles lit, and Carvel on the other side of the door. Evelyn checked her hair once more.

Everything was perfect.

She opened the door. "Good evening, sweetheart."

His eyebrows shot up, taking in her snug white dress, silver earrings, and the silver and diamond choker around her neck. Evelyn wore her high silver sandals so she was taller, closer to his mouth. She gave him a sensual kiss.

"Good evening," he said. "To what do I owe this reception?"

Evelyn took his hand. "Because I love you, and since we're planning to spend our lives together, I want you to know what's in store for you."

She led him inside past a grouping of mirrors and caught a glimpse of herself and Carvel.

She tugged his hand. "We're quite an attractive couple."

Carvel stepped behind Evelyn and held her around the waist. "We are attractive."

He nuzzled her hair and his hands roamed up and over her breasts.

Evelyn leaned into Carvel, relishing his touch. She'd wanted to have a mature relationship with him for so long, she couldn't believe they'd finally reached the same point emotionally.

He devoured her neck, his hands trailing the shape of her body.

Evelyn whispered consent for him to take as much of her as he wanted. He'd been the one not wanting to breach their sedate level of intimacy, but today was a new day.

She tipped her head, giving him better access. "I want you," he breathed into her neck.

"I'm here." She could feel him struggling, but he couldn't hide his arousal any more than she could hide the fact that she wanted to make love. Now.

Evelyn stepped back, her bottom grazing him. Carvel pulled in a shaky breath. "April seventh."

Evelyn had been waiting to hear their wedding date almost as much as she wanted to make love. "April seventh at what time?"

"Seven o'clock."

She didn't object when he sank to his knees, taking the top half of her dress with him.

"The honeymoon?" Evelyn held Carvel around the neck, her breath coming in short, choppy bursts.

"Aruba." His mouth closed over her breast for the first time. Evelyn rocked, her legs wanting to give out. She'd waited so long for this day, she didn't know what else to do but bask in the glow of his lovemaking.

Her skin chilled from the trail of his mouth and expectation. Carvel still wore his suit coat, so she tried to nudge it from his shoulders.

His lips left her breast and she moaned from the loss. He pulled her down in front of him and kissed her with such precision, his lips made promises her body wanted fulfilled.

"Let's slow down."

"Oh, Carvel. Please, honey?"

"Stay right here," he said, guiding her onto her back. "You'll stay, right?"

"Yes." He got up and started a fire in the fireplace and Evelyn smiled. It was a hundred degrees outside, but her condo was cool. He returned from the linen closet with a blanket and the kitchen with a bottle of wine.

Evelyn pushed up on her elbows. "Wine? What's gotten into you?"

"You. I don't want to lose you."

He shrugged out of his jacket and led her to the fireplace, where they lay down. The earlier passion was gone, no matter how hard Evelyn tried to rekindle it.

Somewhere between Carvel tasting her breasts and starting the fire, he'd regained control of himself.

"What happened?"

"Nothing, baby."

"Carvel, I want you. Don't you want me?"

"Like crazy." He kissed her hand. "Before I got saved, I was a womanizing fool."

"I just can't imagine that being you."

He looked down at her and Evelyn basked in the glow of his adoration. "I did that and a whole lot more."

"Like what?"

Carvel had never talked so openly about his life before becoming a minister. Evelyn was more than curious. She suddenly had a thirst to know everything she could about him.

"Have you ever been in love before?"

"No." He kissed her lips tenderly. "Not until I met you."

Evelyn drew back. "Really? Not even in high school?"

He chuckled. "Well, there was Sarah, and Brenda and Jaime and Teri and—"

"Hey." She playfully punched him on the shoulder. "I hope you tore up your player's card, because I'm all the woman you need."

He trailed his finger through her hair. "You sure are."

Evelyn turned into him. "I predict April seventh is going to be a glorious day."

"I do too."

Carvel snuggled her into his chest. "There's only two good things that resulted from my player days."

"What are they?"

"I found the Lord."

"And?"

"I didn't have any children."

All the passion and joy fled her body in one breath.

Carvel sensed her withdrawal. "What did I say?"

Evelyn could feel tears building up. "Nothing."

He looked totally confused. "Children—" he stammered. "Evelyn, I don't have any—"

"I heard you."

She struggled to get up. She needed space.

Carvel sat up, "We can have children, Evelyn. I thought we'd wait a couple of years—"

Evelyn just shook her head until the words came out. "That's not it. I—I—"

"You what?" Carvel sounded scared.

"I had a son."

"No, you don't."

"He's ten. I gave him up for adoption."

"Evelyn, you don't have a child. You can't." He got up and walked around the living room, his hands on his head.

"Yes, I do. His father, Ross, died of cancer a week before he was born. Ross was Jasmine's brother, Malone's cousin."

"So you were married?"

"No, Carvel. We found out about the baby too far into the pregnancy for a few months to matter. Then Ross got ill. When we found out, he lived only a few more months. I knew I couldn't raise him by myself, so . . ."

Silence hung between them until each passing moment stripped away her esteem, confidence, and trust.

"Why didn't you tell me before now?"

"I didn't know how. I didn't think it'd matter."

"Of course it matters," he shouted, glaring at her. "I've got to get some air."

"Carvel, please stay. We can talk."

She trailed behind him as he took his jacket and walked to the front door. "Don't call me. I'll call you when I can talk about this reasonably."

Carvel closed the door behind himself. Evelyn walked two feet into the room and sank to her knees.

Her chest lifted and fell, lifted and fell, her heart ripped out with his rejection. Evelyn needed water, something for her mouth and for her eyes. She felt as dry as the wood beside her fireplace.

Tears wouldn't come, so she lay there, her body succumbing to the spasms of grief.

Thirty-one

Evelyn watched Jasmine over steaming plates at the Waffle House. Her eyes were red lined and tired looking. While at work, she'd been popping eyedrops, but now the need to disguise herself was over.

Evelyn wasn't all that hungry, but the combination of stress and worry robbed her appetite further. "Fight with Lee?" she finally asked.

"I wish it were that simple."

Evelyn almost didn't want to know. Jasmine had a way of making her problems seem like world crises, and it didn't matter if anyone else had a situation, they could just go to hell. Jasmine had been hateful lately, and an apology just wasn't going to cut it.

Evelyn forced herself to bite into her french toast.

"Do you have five hundred dollars I can borrow?" Jasmine asked, stirring her grits.

Offended, Evelyn opened her cell phone and dialed. "Let me try Malone again. I can't believe he hasn't called me back."

"Did you hear me?"

"No, you can't borrow any money. Don't you already owe me fifteen hundred?"

"I know, but I really need this."

"Jasmine, why don't you listen when *I'm* talking? I just closed on my building for Safe Haven, and you haven't once asked me how's it going, what's going on, nothing. Every time I talk to you, it's all about you."

"I need the money for something important."

"I don't have it." Malone's phone rang for the fifteenth time and Evelyn ended the call. "Maybe something's wrong with Lonzo. Do you think Mohala would know where he is?" A headache started at the base of Evelyn's temple and spread like syrup on pancakes. "I've got to go."

"We just sat down," Jasmine protested, looking suddenly scared.

"I'm tired. I've got lots to do; besides, I've got an appointment with a lady who's going to help me apply for a grant."

"I've done grant writing. I can do yours for five hundred dollars."

"Why are you so hung up on that? Who do you owe?"

Jasmine bit the tip off her bacon. "Nobody you know."

Fed up, Evelyn snapped open her phone again. "Maybe Malone's at Zachary's."

"He's not! Damn! He's in jail."

The phone slipped from Evelyn's hand and hit the hard plastic seat. The battery came off and the front landed on the floor. "He's where? Since when?"

"A couple days."

"How do you know this?"

"He called me yesterday."

"And you didn't go get him?" Evelyn heard derision in her own voice and could only blame her parents for the disapproving reprimand that made Jasmine jerk. For the first time in her life, she wanted to slap her best friend across the face. "Why not?"

"Because I have problems of my own, damn it!"

Evelyn scrambled off the bench, grabbed her purse and busted phone. "You selfish—monster! Where is he?"

"Fulton County, but he'll probably get out today. "*I'm* the one who needs to be rescued. I need this money or something terrible will happen to me."

Evelyn stopped in her tracks. "Are you on drugs?"

"No."

"Then dig yourself out of whatever you got yourself into." Evelyn threw a twenty on the table, and ran out the door.

Changing her mind, she hurried back in and snatched the money from Jasmine, who was tucking it in her pocket.

She turned to the waitress. "Here, Margo. Keep the change."

Evelyn worked the legal system as if she were a sitting justice. She called in favors and finally got Malone released. She waited for him in a dull gray room filled with plastic chairs and other dejected women.

The events of the day played through her mind and she still couldn't believe Jasmine. She'd been acting too bizarre for words, but intentionally leaving Malone in jail? That was crazy.

If Malone didn't kick Jasmine's butt, Evelyn would be surprised. A buzzer sounded and the women flooded the doorway. Bonding agents picked up their newly released clients, and handed them packages full of their personal effects.

The men were then released to go home with their rides.

Malone walked out, his face covered with stubble, his eyes black and storming. When he saw her, he lifted his arms. Evelyn went to him and held tight. He kissed her hair. "Thank you."

"I'm so sorry. Had I known, I would have come yesterday."

Inside her car, he reclined the seat and closed his eyes, his right arm wedged behind his head, his left hand on her back.

In all the times she'd ridden in the car with Carvel, he'd never so much as held her hand. "You want to go my house?" she asked him.

"Home. I need to sleep in my bed."

Evelyn made one unscheduled stop at the grocery store before pulling up in Malone's driveway.

His house looked desolate with the newspapers for three days tossed carelessly onto the grass.

Evelyn grabbed the orange plastic bags that held the papers and threw them in the garbage as soon as they got inside.

The house smelled faintly of aftershave and Pledge. The house-keeper had come regardless of the fact that her boss had been in jail.

"Hungry?" she asked him.

He hit the button on his machine and listened to Cash's concerned voice. The last message was pleading. They could hear the fear in his voice. "I'll square things with him tomorrow. Look, you don't have to take care of me."

"I know. But I don't mind fixing something for you to eat. If you want me to leave after that, I'll go, okay?" His hand grazed her shoulder and Evelyn felt a swell of compassion. "Go take a shower. The food will be ready when you come out."

"What man in his right mind wouldn't appreciate you?" He kissed her softly on the lips and left her standing in the kitchen.

Piping-hot food sat on the table and Evelyn tried to keep her thoughts focused. Malone had kissed her. Not in a sexy way. Not in the way a man kisses a woman he wants to be intimate with.

But that wasn't how she'd reacted.

Confused and afraid her emotions were too scattered, she did what she knew was right and dialed Carvel's phone number.

"Pastor Albright."

"Hi, it's me, Evelyn."

"Oh."

Words failed her.

"Evelyn, I can't talk now."

"When? I have to know what you want to do. I only told you because I didn't want there to be any secrets between us. That was the past. A different time and place. Ten years ago. I was practically a baby."

"Apparently not."

The remark hurt deeply. Just as much as it had to give her son away. "I know it was wrong, but that isn't my life anymore."

"I can't talk now. Not while I'm here."

"When, Carvel? You never have time for me. When?"

He hesitated and she prayed he'd say whatever was on his mind right then. The truth would almost be welcome. "I'll call you. Soon. Good-bye."

He didn't let her hang up first. The phone clicked in her ear.

Evelyn closed her cell phone, only to have it ring right away. "Hello?"

"It's Mother."

"Mother, I'm kind of in the middle of something right now."

"I hope it doesn't have to do with that foundation," her father said, his voice surprising her. "Evelyn, this isn't at all what we intended for you. Now, we let you do the radio thing, hoping you'd work it out of your system, but you're being stubborn for no reason. You need to get on track and do the job you were meant to do."

"Father, what I'm meant to do is live my life for God, not you or Mother. If you have a problem with that, then I can make it really easy for you, and step out of your lives."

"Now you're being irrational. You live in a place that belongs to me. So who do you think you're threatening?"

"Father, the deed for the condo is in my name, and I pay all the fees and taxes associated with living there."

"How dare you talk back to me? You know your problem? You've forgotten your place in this family."

"That's *all* I've got. You treat the hired help better."

"Evelyn!" her mother said.

"Hush, Mother!" Evelyn shook in anger. "I was so naive, I didn't know Grandma would tell the church and I didn't know you'd treat me like an inconvenience for the rest of my life. I was a child! So don't shake your morality tree at me. If you don't like me having anything to do with Safe Haven, don't have anything to do with me. Good-bye."

Malone walked in and took the phone from her hand, cut it off, and dropped it in the bottom cabinet. "I think you've talked on the phone enough for one day. Come on and eat."

He gathered another place setting and took them both to the patio where he sat down, and shoveled half the food from his plate to hers, and then pushed it across the wrought-iron table.

"Why are you hollering at your parents?"

Evelyn crossed her arms and ankles. "Because they get on my nerves."

He stopped eating to laugh.

Evelyn fought hard, but Malone's laughter coaxed a smile to her lips and then a full-blown laugh. When she stopped, she felt free. "I wish I was little again."

He ate his Cream of Wheat and then finished hers. "Why?"

"Little people are so innocent. I used to sit on my father's lap and he'd tell me I was his special girl. I knew of his love then. Now, I'm not sure of anything. People protect children from all the mess adults go through."

Malone sat back and wiped his mouth. "Not really."

"Come on. So far, being a kid looks really appealing."

"What were you arguing about?"

"Mother and Father want me to abandon Safe Haven and do what it is I'm supposed to being doing."

"And what is that?"

"Being a Stepford daughter of the BBS."

A grin spread across his mouth. "BBS, huh? What's that stand for?"

"Bourgeois Black Society."

Malone grunted. "And you don't want to be a BBS clone."

"That's right."

"Good for you. Is this the first time you've stood up to them?"

Evelyn shook her head. "This is the first time they knew about it." They both laughed again. "God, I'm so glad we're friends."

Malone took her hand in his. "Me, too."

She looked into dark brown eyes. "Tell me what happened."

"I got a page from the school—no, let me back up. Jasmine borrowed money from me."

"Me, too!"

"How much?"

"Fifteen hundred. What about you?"

"Three grand," Malone said.

"What's she doing with all that money?"

"She said something about plumbing—but, she's into a thug named E.J. for some money."

"How much?"

"I really don't know," Malone said. "All I know is I went to her office and asked for the money back, and she acted like she didn't remember that she'd promised to have it back to me last week."

"She made me ask her for the money she owes me, too. Go on."

"When I told her to give me what she had, she lied and said she only had a hundred, but she dropped three one-hundred-dollar bills on the floor. I took the money and went to the bank."

"I was with her earlier and she mentioned she owes somebody and if she doesn't pay, she might get hurt. I thought about loaning her the money, but when I went back into the restaurant she was stealing the money I'd left for Margo."

"No damn way. Are you for real?" he muttered in disbelief.

"The twenty was almost in her pocket. I was so shocked, I grabbed it and shoved it in Margo's hand and told her to keep the change. Then I came to get you."

"You mean to tell me Jasmine wasn't trying to raise the bail money?"

"No. All she talked about was her situation and that she needed money because she owes somebody."

197

"Shit, she owes me." Malone got up, angry. He stood with his back to Evelyn, looking over the yard. "She's trippin'. I stayed in jail an extra night thinking she was getting the money together."

"How'd you end up there?"

"The school called and said Lonzo was in the hospital for an asthma attack."

"On my goodness, is he all right?"

His shoulders heaved up and down in a helpless shrug. "I really don't know. I went to the hospital with a man named Tim; he's a guard at First Union. Mohala was acting a fool. Screaming and hollering that she had a restraining order against me."

"Does she?"

"Yep. She claims I beat her up and bruised her when she attacked me."

"Malone, stop. She's too little to be trying to attack you. How did this get started?"

"She's been acting funny." He shrugged again and Evelyn's heart went out to him. "Unreliable, mouthy, skittish. I don't know. I feel like she's got something up her sleeve, but I don't know what it is."

"Have you talked to your attorney?"

"Not lately. While I was locked up, I couldn't catch up with anyone."

"What happened next?"

"Well, worse gets worse, and finally the doctor tells her to shut up. I finally see Lonzo hooked up to a machine. But he gives me the thumbs-up. Seeing him for just those few minutes, I didn't mind sitting two days in jail."

"Did you beat her up?"

"Evelyn, I wouldn't ever hit a woman."

"You could have called me."

"I thought about it, but I figured if you were with His Holiness, you'd take a bunch of unnecessary grief."

"He's not speaking to me right now."

"Why?"

"I told him about the baby." It was her turn to get up. "He walked out."

"That guy is a first-class—"

"Malone, don't say it. If it's God's will, we'll be together. But that's beside the point. I would have come for you."

"Just like you did. When's the reception for Safe Haven?"

"Supposed to be in two weeks."

"No, damn it. We've got to keep living. It's *going* to be in two weeks and damn the rest of the crap in our lives. I don't care if it's just us and Cash. You know his behind will be there. Safe Haven is going to open and you and I are going to survive this mess."

"All right. Yes," Evelyn said, feeling strength in her spirit.

"Some people are going to catch hell, though," he said, and she knew what he was talking about.

"Can't you just let it go?" she asked him, as she watched two cardinals play in the tree. Evelyn looked back at Malone and knew the answer before he spoke.

"No. Jasmine's going to regret screwing me over."

Thirty-two

Malone stood before the judge.

"You are hereby fined one thousand dollars and twenty-four hours in jail."

"Yes, sir."

Mohala gloated in her victory, the pictures she flashed like credit cards worth a thousand words. By all accounts, she looked as if he'd hurt her, but they both knew what had happened that night on the driveway.

"Your Honor, by error, my client has already spent two and a half days in jail. Can we have the sentence reduced to time served and a fine of two hundred fifty dollars?"

"Granted. The court hereby extends the order of protection for another thirty days until Mr. Malone Sr. can get a psychiatric evaluation. You are also ordered to attend a mandatory four-hour parenting class. There'll be no visitation until such time that the court is satisfied the child is in no danger."

Ethan gently interrupted. "If it pleases the court, we have the principal of St. Timothy's School present and he is prepared to testify to incidences of inappropriate and erratic behavior demonstrated by Mrs. Malone. He's an impartial third party, Your Honor, and has no vested interest in slanting information to either client's advantage."

The judge fondled the gavel, considering. "Proceed."

"We also have a signed affidavit from Dr. April Albert, the attending physician the day Mr. Malone Jr. was admitted to Egleston. Again, information contained in the affidavit supports allegations that Mrs. Malone was the aggressor, and Mr. Malone was only acting in a manner of concern for his son."

Mohala's attorney tried to cut in, but Ethan pressed on in a louder, more authoritative voice. "Dr. Albert clearly states that Mrs. Malone was disruptive, confrontational, and demonstrated behavior that could suggest impairment of some sort."

"Objection!"

"I'd like to offer this information as evidence," Ethan said quickly. "I have a copy for Mrs. Malone's attorney."

Malone held his breath and could see that Mohala's attorney wasn't pleased that they'd been set up. Once the affidavit was entered as evidence, the judge would have to read it.

The judge scanned the paper. "Overruled."

Excitement coursed through Malone, but he kept it contained.

"Your Honor, we have witnesses that are here to testify that Mr. Malone was notified while at the bank making a deposit, that Mr. Malone Jr. had been taken by ambulance to Egleston.

"The guard, Retired Captain Tim Wilcox, is prepared to testify that he observed a distraught Mr. Malone and personally drove him to Egleston. Captain Wilcox stayed with Mr. Malone until his arrest. Captain Wilcox acquired statements from persons who witnessed the entire incident and behavior of both parties."

"Is Captain Wilcox in court today?"

"Yes, sir."

The captain stood. The judge nodded and Mohala's attorney shook his head and threw his pencil on the table.

"I'll hear from him, too," Judge Butler said. "I don't need the statements. I've got enough here. Have the captain come forward first, then the principal. Does Mrs. Malone have any witnesses?"

Her attorney stood. "No, Your Honor. This is a contempt hearing. We're not prepared to present witnesses. The pictures prove that Mr. Malone is a violent man."

"Since I'm the judge of record on both cases, I'll hear this testimony and determine what's what. I'll see the attorneys and witnesses in my chambers."

An hour later, Malone felt as if he'd been through a hurricane. The judge took the bench and looked over at him.

"Mr. Malone, the earlier sentence and fine are set aside. You will have two hours of monitored visitation with Alonzo Malone Jr. per week. Sundays from two to four o'clock."

Malone's heart jumped. "Thank you, sir."

"You are not to speak or contact Mrs. Malone for any reason. A social worker will handle the exchange of your son, and you will get that parenting class and a psychiatric evaluation so the court can determine your mental state."

Judge Butler turned to Mohala and her attorney. "Mrs. Malone, the evidence presented against you is alarming. According to testimony presented from all sources, your behavior is such that I'm ordering you to get a toxicology screening today. You are also ordered to get a psychiatric evaluation and attend forty hours of parenting classes in Fulton County. I don't want you having any contact with Mr. Malone."

Mohala stared in defiance at the judge, who became sterner. "I want the drug tests done before you leave this building. If you do not adhere to the terms of this ruling, the minor child will be taken into the custody of DFACs. We will reconvene in four weeks." He lifted the gavel. "The officers at the back of the court will escort you, Mrs. Malone. Adjourned."

Malone stood next to Ethan, drained, but excited.

Two hours a week. Evelyn was always talking about praise God for this, and praise God for that. This was the first time he'd ever wanted to say praise God.

Ethan and Malone walked into the corridor. "Don't be upset," his attorney said.

"No way, Ethan. This is our first victory."

His attorney patted him on the back.

Mohala walked over, fury distorting her face. Her attorney tried to pull her back, but she wouldn't budge.

"You're violating the order of protection against me," Malone told her.

"This isn't over. You'll never get him, because I know that's all that matters to you."

Ethan pulled out a microrecorder and pressed REWIND. "Shall we have a listen, or should I play it for Judge Butler in his chambers?"

"I hate you," Mohala whispered to her ex-husband.

Malone didn't show the pain he felt. "I see you at the top of a house of cards. Your world is crumbling, and when it comes down, I'll drag my son from the debris, and run like crazy."

The officers walked up and led her away.

Thirty-three

"Hello?"

"Jasmine? It's yo' mother. 'Bout time I found you. Your number isn't listed, and it's not like you gave it to me."

Jasmine sat up in bed, aggravated. "It's not listed for a reason."

"You been out of this house for twelve years and you still ain't learned no manners."

"What do you want?"

"Your brother was killed the other night."

"Wat was *your* stepson. He wasn't ever my brother."

"You grew up in the same house as him! He was more brother to you than anyone I know," Adelia said, defending him as if the same blood ran in their veins.

"What is it, Adelia? What do you want?"

Her mother sucked up mean words and got to the point. "I need money. The funeral is expensive."

"No."

"You'd let your brother be buried in a pauper's grave?"

"Why do you keep referring to him as my brother? He wasn't any kind of brother I'd ever claim. He abused me! Molested me! Hated me! What about that?"

Jasmine hoped her mother remembered this conversation until her dying day. "You claimed a nasty molester as your son, but wouldn't lift a hand while he and his father raped me. How dare you ask me to do anything for him? I don't care if the skin falls off his bones, I wouldn't ever spare a penny for him. Never!"

"I didn't know," Adelia cried.

"Mother, you always turned a blind eye. Now I can't see you."

"I shouldn't have expected any different from you," Adelia said, no longer hopeful Jasmine would give her some extra cash. "You always were impossible to love. Nothing ever satisfied you. I'm your mother and I guess in some part of my heart I'll always love you, but I'll never like you."

"I don't even feel that much for you."

"I got one thing to say. E.J. came by, and I know that man ain't up to no good. He's dangerous. If you don't do nothing else I say, take heed to this. If you're mixed up with him, you'd better figure a way out before you end up buried beside Wat."

"Don't call here again."

"Don't worry. I won't."

Jasmine disconnected the phone and let the fear of her mother's final words invade her.

She owed E.J. big time. He was probably already looking for her, and the last thing she wanted was for him to find her without the money. She rummaged through her purse, pulled out her wallet, and started calling her credit cards to see if she could get a cash advance. With each card that landed on the bed, Jasmine's trepidation grew. There wasn't a way out of this unless she begged, borrowed, or stole the money.

She'd already covered the first two and dropped her head into her hands. Stealing. The natural thought was to steal from someone who wouldn't miss the money, but who?

Jasmine's mind worked until it ached. She'd love to steal from Laurie, but the woman was tight-lipped about her personal life, as if she had anything worth stealing.

Evelyn had a safe. Buried in her closet. A thrill danced through Jasmine and she paced, planning. Somehow she'd have to get up to Evelyn's condo unnoticed.

Maybe act as though she were delivering something. Jasmine tore through her purse and found the key card that activated the front door. Evelyn always had rainy-day money, and as far as Jasmine was concerned, it was raining cats and dogs.

She just needed to bide her time, and she'd get what she needed real soon.

Thirty-four

The fragrance of lilies scented the air and Evelyn moved the flowers, the smell overwhelming. She was anxious and excited at the same time.

Safe Haven was days from opening. DeDee Garr sat across from her and Evelyn put the woman's résumé between them. "Why do you want this job? There's no money, no glory, and no clients." She laughed. "Right now I almost wonder why *I* want it."

"Because all that you wish for, *we*," DeDee emphasized, "wish for, will come true. The people will come, funding will come, work will come. Am I still going to keep my high-paying messenger job?" She wrinkled her nose, being funny. "Yes, because I have to eat and pay the bills. Eventually, Safe Haven will fill some part of that role."

The woman's self-assurance bolstered Evelyn's confidence. The negativity she'd experienced from her parents and lack of support from Carvel had left her feeling isolated, but even then, she wouldn't give up. She believed in Safe Haven, and that's what mattered most. "Why not go back into the field that was paying you so much money, DeDee?"

"I fell out of love with corporate America. The games, office politics, and shenanigans of an unsavory boss cured me of my thirst for the almighty dollar. Now I do things I believe in. When I heard about Safe Haven, I knew I had to be involved. The capacity didn't matter. What you're doing by empowering women with answers to the hard questions is what I believe in."

A warm spirit enveloped Evelyn. She felt at ease with DeDee and in this home. When she'd walked through the home with her realtor, Jodi told her that the owners hadn't occupied the place for over ten years, and had never expressed an interest in selling. Out of the blue, they called and told her they'd sell if the house were used to help women.

Evelyn had felt their generosity was a godsend. This place was meant to be hers. Meant to be for the women of this city.

Evelyn extended her hand. "You're hired." They laughed as they shook.

DeDee then rubbed her hands together. "Let's plan the most awesome reception Atlanta has ever seen. First, we need sponsors. Since this all began with the call into the radio station, what is *Atlanta Live* willing to do?"

Evelyn pulled a list from her bag. "This is a beginning. Why don't we draft a form letter and see who's ready to put their money where their mouth is?"

"Yes, ma'am," DeDee said with a smile.

"*Atlanta Live* welcomes to the family two affiliate stations from Dallas, Texas," Malone said. "We're talking today about office politics. Not the kind where you vote on who's going to buy tickets for the office lottery pool, but the kind that can ruin friendships. Check this out. 'Dear *Atlanta Live*, I was cool with most of the other black attorneys in the firm, but now that I've been promoted to partner, they started treating me differently.

" 'We used to hang out on the weekends and now they claim I'm acting like an Uncle Tom. Yes, I go to the partners' houses, and have taken golf lessons, but the partners don't hoop, so sometimes I have to be where they are. How can I make my friends understand I'm still the same guy that I was before I got this promotion?' Evelyn," Malone said, "you got any advice for this strugglin' brotha?"

"He's not the same guy. The sooner he realizes that, the better. To make partner, you have to work long, hard hours and win cases before a firm will consider you. Obviously, his friends weren't doing that or they'd have been vying for the position," Evelyn said to Malone.

"That's worse—" Jasmine said, cutting in.

"But, Evelyn," Malone said, taking control again, "have his boys lost him forever?"

"I don't think so, but he has to take steps to preserve their relationship. When he makes plans to hang with them, don't flake out and not show; eventually they'll come around."

"What about the fact—"

"We'll take a break," Malone said, leveling Jasmine with a cold stare. "*Atlanta Live* will be back on WKKY 104.9."

"You're so childish, it's embarrassing," Jasmine told Malone at the top of the break. "And stupid, too, if your feelings are still hurt about the whole 'getting arrested' thing. It was you, not me."

"I guess that's what sitting in jail does to a man. Don't ask me for shit again, you hear? And I want the rest of my money."

"Guys, deal with it after work." Evelyn could tell this wasn't going to blow over like a regular Malone/Jasmine argument. They needed privacy and time to duke this one out.

"Don't give me advice when out of three hundred sixty-five days, you can't decide which one you're getting married on."

"Don't take your bad mood out on me," Evelyn snapped. "I don't have anything to do with it."

The phone inside the studio rang and Jasmine grabbed it before Malone. She listened a minute, then said, "Hold on."

"Save it for the air," Cash instructed from the booth. "Back in three, two . . ."

"Welcome back to *Atlanta Live*, where truth is our trademark." Malone looked at the computer screen and took the first call. "What do you think Mr. Attorney should do?"

"Find some new friends that aren't going to be jealous of his success. People are crazy," Leslie from Ohio said.

"Hot line for you," Jasmine said to Evelyn. "An emergency."

Evelyn's heart thundered in her chest. She slipped off her headphones and took the long-corded phone away from the console. "Hello?"

"It's me, Carvel."

Relief encompassed her. If he was all right, then it must be her parents. "Has something happened to Mother or Father?"

"Nothing like that."

"Then what's wrong? Are you all right?"

"No." He sounded sad. "I didn't want to tell you this way. But since you were on a commercial, I thought I'd just get it over with."

"What is it?"

"I don't want to marry you."

"What?" she said in disbelief.

"Evelyn?" Malone's panicked voice echoed in her ear, but she plugged it, and faced the wall. She couldn't deal with Malone. Carvel was too busy breaking her heart.

"It's because I had a baby." The whispered words still had power to resonate, if only in her head.

Carvel sighed. "Yes. And being with you just isn't good enough. You're an unclean woman."

"No, I'm not," she said, feeling as if her skin were being pulled off in strips.

"Evelyn, the wife I choose must be a pinnacle in the community, and a role model for young women. A woman other women respect."

A loud crash caused Evelyn to jump, but she tuned out Malone's and Jasmine's raised voices.

"Evelyn," Malone barked. "Stop!"

"Carvel—" Evelyn's voice caught. "I'm such a good person."

She leaned against the wall and Cash banged on the glass. She couldn't look at him, couldn't do any more than stand against the immovable surface. "Why can't you forgive me?"

"You did an honorable thing by placing the child up for adoption. But I won't ever be able to forget that you've had a child."

"Or that I've been with another man."

"Yes," he said.

"That's why you never touched me."

"I want my wife to be a virgin."

Malone tore the phone out of the wall and the receiver from her hand. Evelyn stared at him in shock. "He said I was unclean." She took in gulping breaths of air as her heart splintered into a thousand pieces.

Malone moved toward her and Evelyn put her hand out. "I'm not good enough for him."

"Sweetheart—"

Malone looked so sad, years of anguish, pain, and tears unlocked inside Evelyn and she started to cry. "Help me, Malone." The studio turned black. Tiny silver stars sprinkled the darkness and she felt herself falling. Carvel's words found her in the dark. *Not good enough.*

"I just wanted him to love me." But he didn't and Evelyn let the darkness win.

Evelyn awoke in her bed, everything out of place. Her hair wasn't tied up, but splayed across her face. Her tongue stuck to the roof of her mouth and her head pounded.

A sliver of sunlight pierced the curtains, letting her know it was the wrong time of day to be sleeping. But her limbs ached and overwhelming sadness kept her on her side.

Evelyn turned her head a fraction and caught a movement. She wasn't alone. Before she could get scared, Malone's face slid into view and with it a flood of memories.

Evelyn reached out and by sheer will, pulled him down beside her. "I'm cold." Tears slid down her face.

Malone drew the comforter around her back.

"I haven't cried in sixteen years. Now that I've started, I might never stop."

"Cry as long as you like, but don't waste good tears on that asshole."

"He was the asshole I thought I wanted."

Another first, Evelyn knew. She hadn't said a profane word in years.

Malone touched her chin.

"Don't look at me. I'm a wreck." Evelyn tried to hide her face. "I'm ashamed, Malone."

He used a fraction of his massive strength to separate them. With a downy-soft cloth, he dried the path of her tears, although they continued to flow.

"There's nothing to be ashamed of. You are a remarkable woman. Don't let him steal that."

Malone was right. There'd been so much wrong with their relationship. They were two mature adults, yet Carvel treated her like a child.

She'd tried to impose her heart on a man who had never loved her for who she was. Now her heart was fractured and she didn't know how long it'd take to be whole again.

Evelyn focused on the steady thump of Malone's heartbeat. The slightly salty taste of her tears and the quiet. "How long have we been here?"

"Since yesterday morning."

She sniffed, her chest rising. "Why don't I remember coming home? What happened?"

"Shh."

"I've been a clueless idiot for sixteen years, Malone. I don't care how much it hurts, I don't want to be in the dark anymore."

He took a deep breath. "You fainted in the studio."

"What else aren't you telling me?" she asked quietly.

"Some of the time you were on the phone, we were live."

The phrase jogged a memory and her stomach sank. Evelyn held on to his arm. "Did everyone hear?"

"Yes, sweetheart, they did."

She started crying again, long soul-wracking sobs. Malone let her weep until she was exhausted.

"The devil sure has been busy," she tried to joke. "How did that happen? Was it an accident?"

"No, Jasmine did it."

"Why does she hate me?" Malone wiped Evelyn's eyes and nose.

"She's sick. That's the only way to explain her behavior. You were upset," he said gently. "Cash phoned your doctor and he prescribed a mild sedative."

"Have my parents called?"

"No, just some lady named DeDee. She wanted to come over and help, but I didn't know who she was. I cut off the phone last night so you could rest."

"Thank you. Will you call DeDee for me and tell her I'm okay? Just tell her I'll trust her judgment on things right now until I get my bearings."

Malone stroked her cheek. "Get some rest."

Somewhere long past dark, Malone shifted and Evelyn realized she'd dozed off again. She tried to move, but her legs felt like spaghetti.

Malone awoke. "Stay put," he told her. "I'll get whatever you need."

"I'm going to the bathroom, but really, I'm better."

Malone pushed her onto her back. "Evelyn, I'm not putting up

213

with any of that 'I've got my shit together' crap, okay? Tomorrow is soon enough to act like nothing happened, but I'm here and I'm going to help you."

He extended his arms and Evelyn knew he'd carry her by will or force. She started crying again. "Just this once," she said.

"Until I say so," he said back. He lifted her as if she weighed no more than a feather.

Evelyn went to the bathroom and when she walked out of the toilet room, he'd left clean pajamas hanging on the clothing tree. She showered and slipped into the fresh clothes.

"I'm decent," she called. "Malone?"

"Right here." He walked her back to bed and helped her lie down. "I talked to DeDee. She said not to worry."

Evelyn was almost afraid to ask. "Anybody else?"

"Your mother is on the phone as we speak. Are you up to talking to her?"

"Better now than later."

"Are you sure?" His dark brown eyes captured hers.

"I've put this off long enough."

Malone handed her the phone and slipped out of the room. Evelyn pushed the MUTE button and put the phone to her ear.

"Hello, Mother."

"What do you mean, 'hello, Mother'? Do you have any idea what kind of shame you've brought on your father and me? We've been fielding calls from our friends all day. The snide remarks are almost unbearable."

"That should tell you they're not your friends."

"Don't sass me, girl. How could you have been pregnant and I not know?"

"I was invisible, Mother. You never paid attention to me."

"Oh, stop with the 'I'm so pitiful' act! You got all the attention you needed, but you were such a handful, you required the strictest discipline," Raynard spat.

"Including withdrawing your love? You call that discipline, Father? I call it abuse, and I'm not taking it anymore."

"You're not taking it? You'll need us long before we need you. I think it best if you don't contact us again."

What was left of Evelyn's heart threatened to dissolve, but she held on to it for dear life. "Good-bye, Mother."

"Raynard, she's all we have. Don't do this! Evelyn," her mother sobbed, and Raynard barked, "Marguerite!"

Evelyn's mother hung up, leaving the two alone.

"Did God ever forgive you for your sins, Father? For the infidelity and the abuse? Did He ever forgive your mean spirit?"

Her father choked, unable to formulate words. He grunted and damned her to hell. Evelyn waited until he caught his breath. "Father, I'm so happy I was in love when I conceived my child. I would have loved him as Christ loves me. But we all lost, didn't we?"

"How dare you?" Raynard said brokenly.

"Because of you." Evelyn lowered the phone before she could hear another word from her father's mouth. Malone walked in and unplugged the phone. Before she could object, he said, "Tomorrow, dragon slayer."

Evelyn ate the soup he'd brought and then lay down. "It's time to go."

"Not tonight."

"Yes, I want to leave. I don't know where I'll go, but this isn't my home, it's theirs."

"Your name is on the deed."

"But I don't want them to have anything over me. I'll go to a hotel."

"Come home with me."

"I don't want to jeopardize your suit for Lonzo."

Malone folded his hands over hers. "You're coming home with me. You're my friend and I won't leave you alone. Things would look worse if I stayed at a hotel with you, so if you're bent on doing this tonight, I'll get you something to wear and we can hit the road."

Evelyn lay back against her pillow and wondered why God had blessed her with such a good friend.

Malone had been everything to her and she'd never been able to see past his ego to the real person inside.

He was the kind of man a woman could fall in love with.

Her heart fluttered and, while shocked, Evelyn didn't panic. Her life had been chock-full of disappointment, pain, and loss. Why not discovery as well?

Malone brought a mismatched outfit out of the closet.

"Are you color-blind? That doesn't even go in the same season."

Evelyn swept her braid over her shoulder. "I can find my own clothes, you know."

He went back inside. "No, I'm having fun. You have a lot of crap for a woman who isn't very tall."

She smiled against the softness of her pillow and waited.

Malone kept talking about "all the crap" in her closet and she applied the metaphor to the rest of her life.

Her emotional closet was just about clean.

They drove to Malone's and soon Evelyn was tucked in the guest bedroom. When Malone later tucked the blankets under her chin, she held his hand until he lay down with her. Only then could she rest. "I love you."

His fingers grazed her cheek. "Aw, shucks, ma'am. Thanks."

Her lips moved as if she wanted to smile but weariness dragged her back to sleep.

Thirty-five

Jasmine dialed the number to the bank and followed the prompts for the bank balance. "The available balance is two hundred forty-five dollars and seventy-five cents. To repeat this balance, press one, to exit the system, press nine."

That couldn't be. Today was payday.

She dialed WKKY. "Put me through to HR."

Jasmine waited, nervously checking through tiny slits of space in the curtains. She hadn't been home in a while, knowing E.J. had been looking for her. Despite the fact that she didn't like her mother all that much, Jasmine did know when to heed a warning. She was playing with fire.

"Good morning, this is Melanie."

"This is Dr. Jasmine Winbury. Is there—was there a problem with the automatic deposits? My account doesn't reflect that I received my paycheck."

The woman began whispering to someone else. "I asked you a question!" Jasmine exploded. "I don't appreciate you talking to someone else while you're supposed to be helping me."

"Ms. Winbury—"

"*Doctor*. I'm *Doctor* Winbury, in case you don't listen to the show that brings in all the revenue."

"Dr. Winbury," the woman corrected herself. "Your paycheck was garnished *again* by the Internal Revenue Service," she said, no sympathy in her voice at all. "I hope that answers all your questions."

Jasmine drove as far as an eighth of a tank of gas could take her and had to stop before she ran completely out.

She pulled into the QT gas station and couldn't decide what to do. She'd screwed up everything. Her friendships, her love life, and her job. She had one of the most dangerous gangsters in Atlanta looking for her and all she had was two-hundred forty-five dollars to her name.

A car horn blasted and Jasmine jumped, scared for her life. She was going to get killed. E.J. had killed Wat and he'd kill her.

If she could redeem herself, she had to do it here in Atlanta, but she couldn't owe E.J. at the same time. He wouldn't let her live.

She peeled ten dollars from the dismal stack of bills and ran inside the store. She'd get gas and something to eat and figure a way out. There had to be a way.

Jasmine grabbed her phone and dialed.

"Hello?"

"Lee, do you have any money I can borrow?"

"Gotcha! I'm not here right now, but leave a message and I'll get back to you when I feel like it. Later."

"It's me, Jasmine," she said, after the beep. "I need your help, desperately."

The low battery tone echoed in her ear. "I don't have much time on this phone, so I'll call you when I can. Maybe we can talk about us. I didn't mean what I said when I told you I didn't want to see you anymore. I've been thinking—"

The phone beeped five times and died.

"Lee—"

Dry, wracking sobs shook her chest. She had to get some money and a way out of this life.

She had to go home. She could hock the VCR and TV. She could give E.J. a down payment on what she owed.

Jasmine gripped her keys and started the car when she remembered the one thing that was better than finding a wallet on the sidewalk.

She still had the spare key to Evelyn's, and Evelyn was at Malone's, thanks to Cash's informative conversation with Laurie last night. Looking over into the passenger seat, Jasmine grabbed the bags of snacks and ran into the store for a refund.

Evelyn kept a fully stocked kitchen.

She drove over and pulled into the store next to Evelyn's building and snuck into the parking garage.

Taking the elevator to the sixteenth floor, Jasmine eased into the corridor and entered Evelyn's condo with relative ease.

They'd been friends for so long, Evelyn had probably forgotten Jasmine had a key. On tiptoe, she headed for the stereo first, but it was built in and she had no idea how to unhook it. She didn't have any tools. She needed things she could carry in the crumpled grocery store bag in her pocket.

Jasmine hurried up the stairs to Evelyn's closet and found the built-in safe. The dial shifted like a sleeping baby, and with the final twist of Evelyn's birthday, Jasmine guided the handle down. "I need this money way more than she does. Please, don't let me down."

She slid the door open and gaped at the stacks of bills. Jewelry boxes surrounded the money and Jasmine grabbed all she could carry.

She ran down the stairs and didn't look back until she'd driven inside her garage and lowered the door.

Inside the house, Jasmine moved through the dark kitchen grateful Cec hadn't bothered her lately. She didn't have time for her overweight ass, anyway.

Jasmine threw the bag on the table and grabbed the cordless phone. She dialed E.J.'s pager, pushed in her number, then hung up.

In her rush to get out of Evelyn's, she'd forgotten to get something to eat. She opened the refrigerator and in the silence heard three steady beeps.

Terror shot through her body and she tried to run, and got snatched back by her braids. "E.J.?"

"Surprise, surprise. Where you been?"

"Nowhere. I was looking for you. I paged you."

"Don't matter. What happened to paying me on the agreed-upon date?"

"The IRS took my check," she whispered brokenly.

"Now I've heard it all. I can't believe someone with a Ph.D. couldn't come up with something more original. Where's the money now?"

"On the kitchen table in the grocery bag."

He walked her over and fingered the bills. "What'd you do, rob somebody?"

"Why does it matter where I got it?"

He slapped her hard across the face. "Don't get smart with me."

"Don't kill me, please."

"You're seventy-five hundred short."

"E.J.," she pleaded as he pulled her toward the living room. "That's interest. I gave you what I borrowed, please don't." She sank to her butt, digging in her heels. "Don't kill me," she begged.

"I don't kill women. Just no-good, dog-loving men who don't pay on time."

Jasmine kicked and her foot landed. E.J. yelped in pain and she got to her knees and was almost to her feet when he caught her by her braids. "Now I'm really going to beat your ass."

Before she could react, E.J. had her on the floor, dragging her by the ankle. He wrestled her pants off and stood over her. He started unfastening his belt. "You bitches never learn."

"Please don't. E.J., I'm good for the money."

"Naw. Not this time."

He shoved Jasmine to the floor and she thought he was going to rape her. She heard a whistle one second before a searing sting lit up her thighs. Jasmine screamed.

E.J. held her down by her neck and beat her behind until he was tired. Jasmine screamed until he shoved her pee-soaked pants into her mouth.

Her butt and thighs were on fire and her throat was raw. She wished she would just pass out, but any time she felt she was losing consciousness, E.J. brought her back with a few more well-placed licks and kept swinging.

E.J. finally stopped and Jasmine could do no more than whimper. Her hands hurt from trying to block the belt, but they hurt more when E.J. shoved a pen in her hand and told her to sign over her Mercedes Benz. "You're a disappointment to your kind," he said. "I thought you were different. I'd take this house too, but the IRS owns it."

He folded up the papers and threaded his belt through the loops. "Don't bother me again. Your credit is no good with me."

He stepped over her and walked out the front door.

Thirty-six

The backlash against the station was tremendous. Malone hadn't anticipated how much the rest of the country would want a piece of Jasmine for hurting Evelyn.

He'd expected to take heat for how he'd blasted her over the air, but just about everybody that called, e-mailed, wrote, or stopped by the station expressed the same sentiment: Get rid of Jasmine.

Malone drove to her house and banged on the door, but got no answer. He hit all her old hangouts, but couldn't find her. He finally gave up and dialed Cash.

"Man, where the hell have you been? We need you in the studio today!"

"No. Evelyn's not up to it, and I'm not doing a damned thing with Jasmine. I don't care what the contract says."

"She's MIA, too."

"Her ass better be hiding deep under a rock, and I'd better not find her."

"I know," Cash ruminated. "We've been playing the best of *Atlanta Live* tapes for the past two days. How's Evelyn?"

Malone turned his truck onto his old street and squinted to see if he could make out his son in a pack of boys on the neighbor's driveway. Lonzo wasn't much of a basketball player, not much of an athlete, but that didn't stop him from trying.

Accept your children for who they are. The parenting class had made him understand a lot about himself. He was too tough, and his son was still a sensitive child. He and Mohala had forced Lonzo into their adult world and he rightfully couldn't handle it.

A surge of pride hit Malone as Lonzo tried a layup. Malone couldn't stay on the street or he'd be in violation of the protection order, but he sat for another minute and then turned his truck around.

"Malone, I'm begging you, come to work."

"I'll be there. But Jasmine better not be."

"I don't see how Atlanta Live *perpetrates like it's for us, when you allow Jasmine to dog out Evelyn."*

"Evelyn doesn't need to be ashamed. Atlanta Live *needs to be ashamed. Y'all could have cut that off."*

"I'll never listen to Atlanta Live *again. I was embarrassed for you."*

"Evelyn should have been brought out of the dark. She was a phony and we at Calvary Baptist always knew it."

Cash stopped the tape and Evelyn sat beside Malone in Cash's office. "I quit," Evelyn said.

"No, Evelyn. We'll work it out." Cash tried to reassure her, but she wasn't buying it.

"What she did was cruel and—" Evelyn couldn't find the words and Malone watched her give up. He'd been afraid she'd have a setback. For two days he'd shielded her from the media, creating an airtight cocoon so she could heal. But today she'd insisted on going to Safe Haven and then to see Cash.

Malone had been comfortable leaving Evelyn because DeDee would take care of her. But now Evelyn had entered the fire a little too soon.

"Evelyn," Cash said, "you made a decision that was right for that time in your life. No one is ashamed or angry with you. I thought that was what Safe Haven was all about."

"It's about helping women. Cash, I can't do *Atlanta Live* anymore. I don't want to talk about what happened or argue with people. I don't want to defend myself. I just want to be left alone."

Evelyn walked across the room. She'd lost weight, and still had that shell-shocked look about her. Malone could only watch.

Their lives had intertwined in a way that was more personal than ever. Somewhere along the bizarre and twisted road they'd traveled, he'd fallen in love with her.

Malone started toward her.

"No, I'm all right."

"I know you are."

"Don't quit," Cash pleaded. "Take some time off and let me work on a few things. Promise me before you make any decisions, we'll talk."

Malone took Evelyn's hand and led her toward the door.

"Cash," Evelyn said, "will you come to the reception tomorrow?"

"I can't think of anything I'd rather do."

Evelyn walked over and hugged him.

Cash looked startled and Malone understood his reaction. Malone had grown accustomed to Evelyn touching him and sleeping with him. He didn't know what he'd do when she was finally strong enough to handle her life on her own. He guessed he'd have to handle his.

"Come on," Malone teased. "You're scaring the man. He thinks you want a raise."

Cash laughed and Evelyn stepped away and folded her hands in front of her. She was retreating again to that place where she'd hidden in plain sight for years.

I'm here, his heart cried, but he kept his mouth shut. He didn't say a word when she laced her fingers with his and left the office through the back entrance. Nor did he comment when he took her to her condo and she hesitated before getting out of the truck.

"I can come up with you," Malone offered.

"No," she said. "I'm home. I can get up there by myself, and get some clothes, and—" She stopped talking for a few seconds. "I'm going to be strong again."

"You don't have to be by yourself. I just worked out for the past six weeks. I can share a little bit."

Her small hand ran up his arm. "I guess you can. One hour?"

"Forty-five minutes."

She was almost out of the car when she brought her legs back in and leaned over nearly into his lap. They looked at each other eye-to-eye. "What are you doing, little girl?"

Evelyn pulled the sunglasses from her eyes. "Right now, what do I look like?"

Her hair was pulled back into a loose ponytail that swung down to the center of her back. She had on a skirt that showed off her tanned legs, and a shirt he was sure she didn't know accentuated her breasts.

Malone brushed a tendril of hair from her cheek. "A woman playing in a man's sandbox."

"Maybe I like the company. How about you?"

"Evelyn—" He had to warn her. He wasn't Carvel. He'd been in love before. He knew where the looks, touches, and feelings were leading, and he wasn't sure she could handle it.

"We're two grown people. Good friends. Better than friends. Okay?" she said.

He didn't try to speak. He just nodded.

"Forty-five minutes?" she confirmed.

"I'll be right here."

Malone couldn't help himself. He watched her walk into the parking garage elevator and disappear.

Evelyn was through her front door and in the center of the living room when she realized someone had been in her home. There were footprints embedded in the carpet small enough to be a man's, but dainty like a woman's.

The cleaners had come, but the woman she employed always vacuumed her way out the door. She took pride in never leaving footprints.

Afraid, but determined to be strong, Evelyn followed them up the staircase and to her closet door. She grabbed the universal remote in case she needed security in a hurry and eased the door open. The lights flickered on. Nothing looked amiss, but there was definitely something wrong. The footprints stopped at the right place.

Evelyn knew before she opened the safe that the money was gone. She just prayed that her grandmother's jewelry was still there.

When Malone arrived, Evelyn thought he would have a coronary.

"What the hell happened?" he demanded.

"My place was burglarized."

"What?"

She eased him down beside her. "My condo was burglarized," she said calmly. "While we were away. Probably last night."

A detective questioned Hosea, who looked anxiously at Evelyn.

"I believe we have all the information we need," the officer said. "Once the security tapes have been reviewed, we'll have you in to see if you can make an identification."

"Thank you, Officers." Evelyn shook hands with the men. "I appreciate your coming. Thank you."

The condo security chief and two of his officers tested her security system. "Ms. Howard, we're sorry this happened but believe me, we'll get to the bottom of it."

Reed had been in charge of security since she'd moved in. A

quiet man in his fifties, he knew his job. A call came on his cell and he stepped away.

Evelyn gathered a dress bag and her purse.

"That's it?"

Malone took the lightweight leather bag.

"This is all I need," she said. "We're done here."

Thirty-seven

Evelyn reviewed the menu and marveled at DeDee's efficiency. She threw down the list. What had she been thinking, planning a twenty-thousand-dollar reception?

Cash didn't know but she was going to leave *Atlanta Live*.

Leave her job security and the job that paid her bills. *Atlanta Live* was going to be a thing of the past.

Unlike a few months ago, Evelyn knew she wouldn't miss it. The show belonged to Cash. It hadn't been theirs since it had been sold. A part of her regretted Lindsey's call because it had changed her life so drastically.

Friend had turned against friend. Family against family.

Evelyn used to consider Jasmine the sister she'd never had.

But Jasmine had pimped the most vulnerable moment in Evelyn's life all for a job. All for nothing.

Carvel had hurt her.

But Jasmine had nearly destroyed her.

Evelyn looked at herself in the full-length mirror. If there was any good that had come from this, she'd learned of the depth of God's love and how to love herself.

She bowed her head and folded her hands as she'd done many times over the past week. "Father, I know You haven't forsaken me. Whatever comes, I know You'll be there to protect me. You didn't make a mistake when You made me, Lord, and I'll do my best not to disappoint You. You gave me life and from this life, I give it back to You. I will do Your good work for the rest of my life, and so I just want to thank you in advance for my blessings. Use me to the glory of Your kingdom, amen."

Evelyn left the guest room at Malone's and walked into the hall. He was just leaving his room when he saw her and grabbed his chest. "Evelyn, baby . . ." he said with nothing but male admiration on his face.

A blush crept up her cheeks. "You look nice, too."

"Are you ready?"

She nodded.

He offered her his arm. "Then come on. We've got a town that's going to light up just for you."

DeDee had arranged for a limousine, but Evelyn sent him away. She couldn't arrive in a beautiful stretch limo when most of the women who'd come to Safe Haven would be walking.

The thirty-minute ride passed in silence, but once they hit Piedmont, Evelyn grew anxious. "I can't sit here any longer. Let's walk the rest of the way."

"Are you sure?" Malone flicked down his signal. "We'll be parked in a few minutes."

"I feel like it. Please?"

Malone pulled into a lot down the street from Safe Haven and paid the man.

He rushed around the truck and helped Evelyn down. She'd done her hair up in an elaborate bun and looked absolutely regal. They strolled down the quiet street arm in arm. "No matter what happens tonight, you'll always be a success."

"Malone," she said, calming him. "We haven't failed yet. Even though there's nobody outside the center. And even though we're the only ones on the street. We can eat six pounds of Beluga Caviar by ourselves, if nobody shows."

They walked up the steps and Evelyn entered a fantasyland sprinkled in cream lights and symphony music.

There were people everywhere and it was all Evelyn could do not to break down.

DeDee stepped up on a stage and the four-piece ensemble quieted.

"There is a special woman who conceived from pain this wonderful center called Safe Haven. We're here tonight to christen this facility, but also to pay homage to its founder.

"At the time she conceived Safe Haven, we had no idea the pain of her life, the turmoil, or the trials, we just knew that the hand that she reached out with had been dipped in the blood of the Holy Spirit. That hand reached out to all of us on that fateful day and with the power of the Lord, changed each and every one of our lives.

"I know we know that God is good, so we know Safe Haven is His blessing to us. And He used a wonderful person to bring it to us. Ladies and gentlemen, Evelyn Smith Howard."

The applause was deafening. Tears of joy streamed down Evelyn's face and she felt the Holy Spirit around her.

She took the tiny stage and couldn't speak, she was so overcome. As she looked into the faces of her guests, she heard the Lord when He said, *Go and lead.*

"Thank you," was all she could manage. God would take care of the rest.

"Our next special guest is here because her life was touched in a special way by Evelyn," DeDee said. "Ladies and gentlemen, Ms. Lindsey Kane."

Smiling, pregnant, crying, Lindsey came forward.

Malone went to help Lindsey onto the stage, but she captured him in a strong hug. "Thank you."

Tears ran unbidden from Evelyn's eyes and when Lindsey turned toward her, belly and all, Evelyn reached out and aided her sister in spirit. They rocked in an embrace that bonded them for life.

Malone pressed a handkerchief into Evelyn's hand, but she didn't care how she looked. She was Evelyn. Just fine. All by her natural self.

She took the microphone. "I wasn't sure what God had intended for me, but I never expected this blessing. Never this. But God has a way of bringing people into our lives and working with us to see the real thing He means for us to do. I'm so blessed to have been at work that day. To have my very best friend at my side. Even in the dark times he was there for me. Thank you, Malone."

He blew her a kiss and her heart fluttered.

Evelyn reached back and took Lindsey's hand. "But this young lady had to come into my life so I could learn the purpose of my work here on earth. I started Safe Haven because I was once Lindsey Kane. Afraid of what I'd done. I felt alone and ashamed. There's only one decision I made at that vulnerable time in my life that I'm proud of and that was to have the baby."

Evelyn couldn't speak for a moment, the crowd warm with support. "Before I leave this stage, I want to say that I'm honored that Senator and Mrs. Kane have supported Lindsey."

Evelyn wiped her eyes. "This is a night of celebration. Thank you to my right-hand woman, DeDee Garr, who put this reception together when I took a moment—"

Evelyn swallowed, not wanting to revisit the wound left by her parents' defection. "Honor each other," she said when she found her voice. "Enjoy yourselves and thank you."

The applause didn't end even after Evelyn had left the stage. People didn't stop clapping until Malone swept her into his arms for a dance.

The night spun into a fund-raiser and celebration at which Evelyn could only marvel. Halfway through the night, DeDee approached and pulled Malone aside. When they regarded Evelyn with concerned eyes, Evelyn moved between them.

"What's going on?"

"Your mother is here," Malone said.

"Why?"

Marguerite had never defied her husband, so Evelyn couldn't understand her presence.

DeDee reached for her hand. "She gave me this."

Evelyn took the folded piece of paper and opened it. A check for twenty-nine thousand dollars.

"I can't believe it. It's for—" She handed it to Malone, who showed DeDee. "Where is she?"

"On the back deck."

Evelyn drifted there, knowing Malone wasn't far behind.

Evelyn stopped when she saw her. Her fair skin was smooth and tight over excellent bone structure. She was trim and attractive, but lonely in the space she dominated.

"Mother."

Evelyn was surprised when her mother did not speak, but approached her slowly. She enveloped her daughter in a hug and called her baby. "I'm so sorry. Please forgive me."

There was so much Evelyn wanted to say but couldn't. She finally let her mother go and held her arms. "I forgive you."

Her mother smiled through her tears. "Bless you." She gathered her wrap. "May I call you sometime?"

"I'd like that very much."

Evelyn took Malone's hand and walked inside where she met Cash. He gave her a check.

"Cash—"

"I know. You'd be crazy to stay. The TV job came through for you, if you're interested."

She caressed his cheek. "Thank you for understanding."

"No problem." He looked at Malone. "I suppose you have something better to do with your time too."

"I might," he said.

"The show is being revamped. Don't worry about it. *Atlanta Live* is still a good concept, we just need some interesting players. Good luck to both of you."

Relieved and happy as she was, Evelyn's feet didn't touch the ground until the last family stood at the door with her. Lindsey looked happy but tired. "Evelyn, I haven't danced this long ever."

Lindsey's mom sat down and rubbed the back of her daughter's hand. "This is going to be your last night out for a little while."

"I know, Mom." Lindsey smiled and rubbed her belly. "I'm looking forward to not being pregnant anymore and holding my baby."

Evelyn couldn't help but envy the young woman. She remembered how it felt to carry her son, how it felt when he moved inside her. She'd felt glorious. "Will you come back to Safe Haven?"

"When you offered that day, that's the one thing I had to hold on to. I prayed you meant it. I'd be honored to work here."

"Besides, I should hope my daughter's godmother and godfather would want her mother around."

Evelyn noticed Malone's jaw tighten with emotion. She and Lindsey hugged. "We'd be honored."

"Good, because we're both ready for bed." Lindsey rose and her father and mother hovered like two caring parents would. "Evelyn, we'd like to put our money where our mouth is and donate fifty thousand dollars to Safe Haven."

Evelyn started to cry again. Once during the evening, DeDee had told her they were close to having raised one million dollars. She'd seen DeDee and Mother Hunt talking to guests, and accepting donations, so Evelyn had made it her mission to thank each person that had come.

Malone put his arm on her shoulder. "Once she gets started, she won't stop."

Everyone laughed and DeDee came from the back, extinguishing all the lights on her path. "Tonight was a great beginning." She gave Evelyn a secured bank bag. "Take this. We'll meet sometime tomorrow to plan our year."

"You're a godsend."

"I believe that," DeDee said, her eyes bright. "Are we ready?"

"We are."

After everyone departed, Evelyn pulled the door closed on Safe Haven, a smile on her face.

Thirty-eight

Malone shut off the engine and lowered the garage door. Evelyn had been excited when they'd left the center, talking and laughing, happy like he'd never seen her before. Now she'd fallen into a quiet introspection, like the Evelyn of old.

"What are you thinking about?" he asked, almost afraid to know.

"You and me. We've been through a lot."

He chuckled. "Sure have. Tonight was something, wasn't it?"

"More than I ever imagined."

"How do you think your father will react to the press of Safe Haven?"

"He'll stick by his beliefs. But my mother"—her mouth worked—"surprised me. I'm pretty sure I'm homeless, though." She giggled, and Malone laughed at her.

"You're the happiest homeless person I've ever seen. Don't walk away from your home, Evelyn. You owe it to yourself."

"I have to break away from them."

"If you've paid the mortgage and taxes and the house is in your name, it's yours. I wouldn't give up that real estate for anybody."

"I'll think about it."

"You're welcome to stay here as long as you like."

"You're so good to me."

In his heart Malone believed she'd turn him down. Tonight's support of Safe Haven had empowered Evelyn to do or be anything she wanted. They walked inside, the house dark and quiet. The air conditioner stirred the sheer curtains creating a billow of silk.

She made herself at home as she left her purse on the counter, her gauzy shoulder wrap on the chair. He stood in the living room as she walked through his space.

"Tired?" she asked him.

"Yeah. I think I'll turn in right now. You hungry, thirsty?"

"Malone, you don't have to wait on me hand and foot anymore."

"I didn't mind. I don't."

With deliberation, he took her hand and kissed it.

She withdrew it and looked up at him.

"Can we try that somewhere else?"

Unable to stop himself, he drew his fingers down her cheek in a soft caress. "What are you saying?"

"I'm a grown woman and I want our friendship to go to that next level. I know how I feel about you."

"How can you be clear about anything after all you've been through?"

"Carvel and I were always unequally yoked. That's not love."

Malone smiled through what he thought might be a heartbreak. "What does that mean?"

"He didn't love me for me. I wanted to emulate my parents' relationship because I thought that devotion was real love. And I wanted their approval. Now I want what's going to make me happy."

"What's that?"

He saw her hesitate and that was enough.

"I want to be with you," she said.

"Don't play with me like that."

"I wouldn't. This is too serious."

Malone couldn't trust what was happening. He'd hoed around

for years. Before and after his marriage, and now he wanted only one woman. But he wasn't certain she could ever really be his.

"Would it make you feel better if we talked about the morning after right now? I'm still going to be here, not in the guest room either." She gathered her dress in her hands and started back toward him. "In your room. With you."

Malone took her into his arms. This was what he wanted. He looked into her eyes. "I intend to love you until the day I die."

"Good, because I feel the same way about you, Alonzo Malone."

Malone kissed her with all the love in his heart. He meant every word he'd said. She was his and he was hers forever.

Evelyn took his hand. Guiding him, she led him toward his bedroom and a new beginning.

Thirty-nine

The phone jolted Malone awake, just as he'd fallen asleep. Last night had been one of the most enjoyable nights of his life. Evelyn lay nude beside him, fast asleep, having temporarily drained him. He moved across her and got a thrill as he snatched up the phone. "Hello?"

"Malone, how quickly can you be in my office?"

It took a moment for him to recognize Ethan's voice, but Malone's brain shot into gear. "Ethan. What's wrong?"

"Get here. Call me once you're in your car, and I'll explain everything."

Evelyn was already up, searching his closet for a robe. "Where are we going?"

Love hit him square in the chest again. "You don't have to go. I don't know what he wants, but he said get there now."

"We'll shower together and save time." She gave him a look that shook his heart. "We're in this together."

"We're getting married today."

Her sexy smile melted him. "Okay."

Forty minutes later, Malone sat alone in Ethan's office, Evelyn in a private office down the hall. Mohala and her attorney had just arrived and were in a conference room.

Ethan couldn't hide his excitement. "All I know is that Mrs. Malone requested this meeting and wants to talk a settlement."

"Why the change of heart?"

"I don't know, but let's go see what they have to say."

Malone followed Ethan. He saw Mohala at the table, her attorney by her side.

He nodded to the man, but said nothing to his ex.

"Mr. Malone," her attorney started, "my client is prepared to make an offer that can be beneficial to all parties involved."

"What do you want? How much money?"

"A half million dollars."

Malone started to rise, but Ethan stopped him.

"My client can barely make his mortgage payments because of the child support increase. He's not eligible for his NFL pension for another thirty years, so he's a working stiff that leaves his home every day to go to his job. Unlike Mrs. Malone, who has done nothing to find gainful employment in the three years since the divorce. So if your client thinks she can siphon a half million dollars from Mr. Malone, she'd better think again."

"He owns two homes, a late-model truck, and has many other financial interests," her attorney argued.

"Nothing that can be liquidated. I have reports here to the condition of the residence of Mrs. Malone. It would take months as well as money to get that place up to sellable condition. Mr. Malone has drained his savings to pay for his attorney fees, living expenses, and child support. I won't let my client go bankrupt for trying to feed Mrs. Malone's greedy nature. If there's nothing else, we'll wait for a ruling from Judge Baker."

Mohala's confidence fled. "You can have custody of Lonzo."

Nobody in the room moved.

"For what?" Malone said.

"For five hundred thousand dollars."

"That's extortion!" Ethan hissed.

Then Malone saw the ring.

Four karats of diamonds sat on Mohala's ring finger and he knew what had happened.

"I don't have five hundred thousand dollars, Mohala. But I could get fifty thousand."

"I stringently disagree to you making—" Ethan interrupted, but Malone stopped him.

"When?" she asked.

"How soon are you leaving?"

Both attorneys looked at Mohala. "Who said she was leaving?" her attorney asked.

"The four-karat ring on her finger," Malone answered.

Mohala gave her attorney a sheepish smile. "The end of the week."

Malone nodded. She was leaving. After all the hell she'd caused and all the commotion, she was leaving with her new man.

He only cared that she wouldn't come back and take Lonzo. "Full custody," he said.

"I do love him," she said, her eyes shining with tears.

"I know you do, but you've got something good going for you. I'll talk to Lonzo, he'll understand."

"Can I see him sometime?"

"You're his mother. We'll make arrangements that are good for everyone."

"No more cursing."

He nodded. "Agreed."

Her jaw worked and she nodded. "Deal."

Malone stood and extended his hand toward his ex-wife. At one time in their lives, he'd worshipped the ground she'd walked on. Now she'd given him a precious gift. He shook her hand and then turned it over to look at the ring.

"Is he nice?"

She smiled. "Yes. A little younger than me. He doesn't want children yet."

Malone didn't care the reasons, he was just grateful. "Good luck."

"When can I get—"

"A half hour. Ethan, can we talk in your office?"

Behind the closed office door, Malone made two phone calls. One to Josh to accept the new job, and then to Cash to formally resign. The company also agreed to give him a fifty-thousand-dollar signing bonus.

He had Ethan write out a check. "I'll get this back to you tomorrow."

"I know you're good for it. You sure know how to work this business," his attorney said.

Malone fingered the check. "Will all this be fine with the judge?"

Ethan nodded. "Had we kept fighting, we'd have won. Your ex-wife just left a drug rehabilitation program. Your son has been staying with Mrs. Chow, who sent over a very interesting videotape of the events of that fateful evening."

Malone made a mental note to send Mrs. Chow some flowers. "Why didn't you stop me in there?"

"Because I thought, fifty thousand to her or fifty thousand to me in fees? You got the better end of the deal, trust me. One day you'll have good relations with your ex and now you have full custody of your son. And," Ethan said, pulling on his suit coat again, "a very pretty lady waiting down the hall. Shall we wrap this up?"

Malone finally felt complete. "Let's go get my son."

Forty

Jasmine rode the bus most of the way to Malone's and walked the last mile.

He was the only family that might feel empathy for her.

She had no more money, no home, no car, and no job. She just hoped he didn't hate her enough not to help her at all.

Jasmine walked up the driveway and heard laughter before she could see through the break in the curtains, Malone and Lonzo on the floor, tickling Evelyn.

They were having fun. A family. Something she'd never learned to appreciate. She did now that it was all gone, but Jasmine knew people were as she had been: slow to forgive.

The three collapsed in front of the TV, Malone kissing Evelyn's neck like a true newlywed.

She'd never seen them this way. Never known them to express such love and affection. She'd been too busy trying to undermine them. Too busy wreaking havoc, she hadn't seen them fall in love.

Suddenly Malone looked up and rose to his feet. Evelyn and Lonzo stayed on the floor, and Malone promised to come right back. He came outside and faced her.

"Hi," she said.

"Hi. What do you want?"

"I know I don't have the right to ask you for anything."

"You're right about that."

He was making it hard. Had a right to make it really hard. "I've done you wrong, Malone. But I have nothing."

He sat down on the front steps and she stood on the sidewalk. "You got your life. That's a start. How did that happen, Jasmine? How did you spin so far out of control? Was it drugs? What? Because I can't explain it, not to myself or Evelyn. Not to my son. You robbed her. You betrayed me and her. Why the—" Malone cut the word and she wondered why. He'd never had a problem cursing her out. She almost wished it upon herself. "Why?" he said again.

"Not drugs, just too much wanting. Too much greed. It's a sickness like everything else, I guess."

"You guess?"

"I know." She looked down the street and saw an endless road. "I was greedy."

"You were mean. Cruel. And now you're a fugitive."

"Can you ever forgive me?"

"You're my cousin. I'll always love you, but you'll never be allowed around here. You tried to destroy us, the only family that ever loved your dusty butt. I can't fool with you, Jasmine. I won't do it."

"Malone, please, I have nothing. Nothing. Just one night, please. Can I stay here? For old times' sake? I promise to be gone by sunrise."

Malone shook his head. "I can't help you that way. I paid your COBRA benefits for three months, and that will extend your medical benefits through the radio station. Seek help from the counseling program and figure out how you got yourself where you are. Get treatment, maybe then Evelyn will drop the charges against you."

Jasmine nodded, tears streaming down her face. Evelyn suddenly appeared and took her husband's hand. "What are you doing here, Jasmine?"

"I came to apologize. I was wrong for everything. I tried to hurt you—"

"You did hurt me."

"I know. I'm sorry. Please forgive me. I know you probably can't, but I'm asking."

Evelyn stayed quiet and then nodded. "Forgiven."

"Thank you. Congratulations on the TV show."

Evelyn refused to be drawn in.

Jasmine understood she could never regain their love and friendship. "I'll go now."

Jasmine started down the street hoping one of them would call her. Four houses away, she looked back and the porch was empty. She turned around, crying as she walked. A part of her raged at them for not extending help to a begging woman, but she saw the woman she'd been and understood.

Malone had given her a lease on life. She decided to take it.

ATLANTA LIVE

Carmen Green

The following questions are designed to enhance your group's reading of ATLANTA LIVE by Carmen Green. We hope the book provided an enjoyable read for all your members.

Bookclub Guide:

Can anyone identify with Jasmine?

Why?

What went wrong with her life that made her go so bad?

Why didn't Evelyn confront her parents sooner?

Why was Malone's character so attractive to women?

Will Malone's and Evelyn's marriage last?

Will Mohala come back for Lonzo?

What would it take for Jasmine and Lee to get together?

Will Jasmine ever work in radio again?